jessica's
promise

ALSO BY JILL CHILDS

Gracie's Secret

jessica's promise

JILL CHILDS

FOREVER

NEW YORK   BOSTON

Grand Central Publishing
Hachette Book Group
1290 Avenue of the Americas, New York, NY 10104
grandcentralpublishing.com
twitter.com/grandcentralpub

First published in 2018 by Bookouture, an imprint of StoryFire Ltd.

First Grand Central Publishing Edition: December 2019

Grand Central Publishing is a division of Hachette Book Group, Inc. The Grand Central Publishing name and logo is a trademark of Hachette Book Group, Inc.

The publisher is not responsible for websites (or their content) that are not owned by the publisher.

The Hachette Speakers Bureau provides a wide range of authors for speaking events. To find out more, go to www.hachettespeakersbureau.com or call (866) 376-6591.

Library of Congress Control Number: 2019931173

ISBNs: 978-1-5387-3291-5 (trade pbk.)

Printed in the United States of America

LSC-C

10 9 8 7 6 5 4 3 2 1

For my wonderful mum

jessica's
promise

The light looks yellow and sickly as the day fades. Shadows reach across the scrubby, open ground and the wind across the common is sharp on my face. The rain falls quietly, as it has all day.

I pick my way around the puddles and the soft wet mud in the ruts. I've been out in the open all afternoon, doing my bit, helping with the search. The toes of my boots are stained with dark, watery half-moons. My nose runs in the cold and I reach in my pocket for a tissue.

My hood makes a warm cave for my head and the fabric down the sides rustles against my ears. Everyone keeps talking about her, about little Jessica. Sharing memories, shyly, trying to stay positive as the police told us, but anxious, too. I can almost hear her giggling. If she were really here, she'd have her wellies on, the bright pink ones, and she'd run ahead, then back, a fireball of energy, nosing out puddles and runnels and patches of standing water where she could jump up and down, flat-footed, laughing, sending dirty arrows of wetness flying in all directions. And despite the waterproof trousers, the wellies, she'd have sodden socks in a heartbeat.

I stop and stare across the wiry grass and bushes, fingered now by wispy fog. The noise in my ears recedes until all I can hear is the thump of my own blood. A heartbeat.

A car passes on the top road, slowing as the driver looks at the fluttering tape stretched between stubby poles. The sharp sound of a whistle breaks through the stillness. An instruction. Someone may have found something. A possible lead.

I twist back to look at the ragged line of volunteers, some cheery and determined, others silent and somber. They're distant now. Police officers, marked out by their hi-vis vests, are peppered between *the locals as they all process slowly forward. They stir the grass with metal rods, endlessly searching.*

I pull my coat closer around my body, stick my hands deep in my pockets, and set off again, taking the path down toward the river. I quicken my pace. I need a break from it all. I need to get away, to walk off some tension. I'm jittery and I'm frightened of behaving oddly, of letting something slip. Of being noticed. They treat me carefully and with kindness. They think it's grief, warping me. But it isn't. It's guilt.

I never thought this would happen. Never in my life. All I wanted was to teach her a lesson. She deserved it. It just went too far, that's all. I just started something I couldn't stop.

CHAPTER ONE

ANGIE

August has been a scorcher. I'm teaching Harry how to fold up the paddling pool, taking turns to lie on the plastic and roll back and forth, trying to make ourselves broad and heavy to squeeze out the last gasps of air, Harry's small feet bare and muddy from the churn of spilled water, when the new patio doors on the other side of the fence squeak open and voices tumble out into the garden there.

"Look, Jessica. Isn't it lovely?" A woman's voice, gushing and rather too quick. "See? Our own garden."

Harry and I look at each other. Since Mrs. Matthews died, no one's lived next door. Just months of builders, banging and drilling and throwing up dust. We'd made a game of imagining who might move in. Trolls or witches, or maybe a hero with superpowers.

In a flash Harry is on his feet. He runs to climb up onto the edge of the rockery wall and stick his head up over the fence to look.

"Hello." A man's voice. "What's your name?"

Harry ducks down, startled. He's young enough to think he can stare at someone without being seen.

I force myself to climb up beside him. "Hello. Sorry. We heard voices."

There are three of them in the garden. The man is about

forty, strong shoulders and neatly pressed clothes that look expensive. He smiles but his eyes are cool as they look me over.

The woman beside him is a little younger, mid-thirties perhaps, but also carefully dressed in tailored slacks and a crisp blouse, unbuttoned low enough to show cleavage. She's attractive, with a sharp haircut, but she'd be prettier, to my mind, with less makeup. Her mouth is bright red and her eyebrows plucked almost to extinction. A cardigan hangs around her shoulders, the sleeves loosely tied at her neck. She wears sandals, and even through the roughly cut grass her toenails shine the same bright red as her mouth. *No better than she ought to be*, as my mum would say.

They don't respond at first. They seem to be deciding what to make of me and I feel embarrassed, as they hesitate, about my mop of curly hair that needs a cut, and my face, bare of makeup and lined by so many years in the open air. The truth is, I'm a bit awkward with people. Not with kiddies—just grown-ups.

The man collects himself and steps forward, reaches up to the top of the fence, and tries to shake my hand over the top panel.

"Craig," he says. "Craig Fox." He nods to the woman. "And this is Teresa."

"Angela Dodd." The words sound odd in my mouth. I've never been one for formalities. "But everyone calls me Angie."

The third person in the garden, who's been running circuits through most of this, exploring the pocket-handkerchief garden with its mud patch waiting to be planted, and poorly tended square of lawn, finally stops and looks up.

"And that's Jessica," says the woman.

Jessica's a sweetheart, I see that at once. Dark brown hair, cut in a bob, big brown eyes, and a solemn, thoughtful expression. Just like my Susie at that age. Bright as a button and gorgeous with it.

Harry, who's popped up next to me again, jiggling around on our bit of shared wall, says: "I'm Harry. I'm four and a half. I'm going to start big school. How old are you?"

Jessica considers him in silence.

"You're three, aren't you, Jess?" The woman steps closer to the child and messes her hair until she ducks away from her hand. I don't blame her. Children hate that; they're not dogs. The woman must catch something in my expression. She looks embarrassed and turns away, back toward the house. "And that's Fran."

I follow her gaze. They've built out, adding an extension with smart wall-to-ceiling glass doors and fancy lights. I can't see far inside—the closed panels reflect the sunny garden back to itself—but what I can glimpse is bright and modern. Very different from Mrs. Matthews' dingy old kitchen and peeling back door.

Something low stirs and catches my eye and I look more closely. There's a seated, slightly hunched mound of person there in the open doorway. She's in dark, baggy clothes with outsized headphones covering her ears. Her expression is dreamy, as if she's far away in a world of her own music.

The woman's voice is shiny with tension. "She'll be starting at really big school soon, won't you, Fran?"

No response. Harry, bored, jumps down and goes back to the collapsed paddling pool.

"Big job." I nod toward the house.

The woman looks away. She strikes me as a bit stuck-up.

He smiles and says: "Bigger than we thought. But it always is, isn't it, once the builders get going?"

I bet. That house hadn't been touched since the ark. I went round there with my mother when I was a girl. The Matthews boys never bothered with me—they were that bit older—but Mrs. Matthews and my mum liked a chat and she'd always give me a biscuit.

But that was a long time ago. And in recent years, after Mrs.

Matthews had the stroke, it became a real health hazard. I had to get a man out last year about the rats. Revolting. I used to hear them at night, gnawing and scuttling about in the dark cavities under the roof, hidden from sight on her side of the dividing wall. He found a few droppings in the attic and put down poison. But without getting at her side, there wasn't much more he could do. She'd stopped answering the door by then.

Anyway, all through June and July, the builders filled and re-filled their truck outside. The skin and bones of that house, of her long life there, were torn out piece by piece and sent to the dump. Faded old carpets, stained plasterboard, rolls of lino from that old kitchen, and the smashed-up units where she'd stashed her tins and packets, most of them rusted and out of date. Sad, but it needed sorting. And now, finally, the new people are here.

"Well, good luck getting settled." I'd love to find out more, even have a nosy inside and see what they've done with the place, but now's not the time. "Bye for now." I nod at the man, then add to little Jessica: "Come over and play sometime if your mummy doesn't mind. I've lots of toys."

She puts her head on one side like a bird and watches me as I climb down and disappear from sight.

The following two weeks are my last with Harry and we stay out a lot, having adventures while we can.

In the evenings, I sit at the back door, feet bare and tingling, feeling the final warmth of summer on my face and drinking white wine. I keep a permanent stock of those big boxes of white. It's good enough quality, not too dear and the supermarket delivers.

Next door, they clatter and bang until late and I imagine the work unpacking all those crates and boxes and getting straight in their shiny new house.

They keep the windows open, getting rid of the smell of new paint, I expect, and I hear more than I ought to. Craig's voice, booming and jolly, calling them to meals or rounding them up to play some game, or get ready to go out.

Her voice is sharper. When she gets cross, her tone becomes hysterical, a martyring wail, as if the children are torturing her with their naughtiness. Most of it is aimed at the little one.

"Why, Jessica? Why? What's the matter with you? Just stop it. Why can't you listen?"

No way to speak to little ones.

Once in a while, little Jessica screams back. Childish stuff, calling her mum stupid, saying she hates her, she won't do whatever it is she's asked. They all have tantrums at that age but, even so, it makes me sad, hearing them at it.

My head slackens and grows fuzzy as I sit there, drinking and listening and drinking a bit more and instead of feeling peaceful, I end up quite melancholy, thinking about families and all the shouting that goes on behind closed doors, all the children who grow up feeling they're nothing more than a nuisance.

September comes and the weather turns colder and Harry moves on, starting school, and I put the heating on and that's the end of sitting at the back door. Next door's noises become muffled by closed windows and the walls between us, reduced to the echo of a banging door once in a while. I keep an eye out during the day but there isn't much to watch.

Craig leaves early and comes home late. He has a silver car, a posh hatchback. Sometimes I glimpse Fran, hunched in a duffel coat, earphones on, heading off to her new school and, on occasion during the day, Jessica, buttoned up in a pretty red coat tripping along at her mummy's side, holding her hand. I assume they've put the little mite in nursery. Shame. I'm looking for work, now that Harry's gone, and I had thought she might be just the ticket.

CHAPTER TWO

It's about nine thirty, and I'm pottering in the kitchen doing the breakfast dishes, when the doorbell rings. I think it might be the postman although I'm not expecting anything. I open the door in my slippers.

Her perfume hits me first. Spicy. Then her smile, all teeth. Teresa looks glossy, even more so than usual.

"I'm so sorry. Am I intruding?"

I think: *Why did you ring on the doorbell if you don't want to intrude?* But I manage to shake my head, waiting to see what comes next. She's all made up, her hair glamourous, wearing a skirt and a neat raincoat, one of those short Audrey Hepburn ones, belted around a thin waist. She has style, if you like that sort of thing. Her own front door, on the other side of the low railing that marks the boundary between the two sides of the path, stands open.

"I know it's a lot to ask"—she hesitates, eyes on my face, reading me, as if she expects me to respond before I know what she's on about—"but is there any chance you could mind Jessica for a bit? They've just rescheduled my meeting, you see, and I can't say no, but Craig can't get back in time."

"OK." I wonder what sort of meetings she has. I didn't know she worked. "Now?"

Her face sags with relief. "Would you? I'd be so grateful." She looks past me into the hall. "Harry won't mind?"

"Harry's at school. I'm not his mum. I'm a childminder. Yes, send Jessica over. No problem."

She looks so pleased she might have hugged me if she were the type. Instead she just beams, nods, calls back across the path and, a moment later, Jessica appears. She's clearly been hovering in the hall, already buttoned into her coat, a lumpy, stuffed bunny under her arm. She hesitates on the threshold, even as her mother tries to urge her forward toward me. Her eyes are wary.

"Hello, Jessica." I crouch down to her level and smile. "I'm Angie. Who's this?"

"Rabbit."

"Well, Rabbit, I wonder if you'd like to come and play. And you can bring Jessica, too, if you like. Do you like biscuits?"

Teresa gives her a quick peck on the top of the head. "See you later, Jessica. Be a good girl."

She disappears in a click of heels down the path, leaving Jessica looking mournfully after her. I wonder if she's used to being dumped on strangers. I'd never have done that with my Susie, never. You wouldn't hand your wallet to someone you hardly know, would you? Or your house keys? So why your little girl, the most precious thing you have?

I reach out a finger and stroke Rabbit's head, gently, between its ears. The fur is worn.

"I think we're going to be friends," I tell Rabbit. Its glassy eyes are as sad as Jessica's. "Come on in."

I lead her through to the sitting room and open up the big toy cupboard. I've never yet met a child who can resist it. All my own toys are in here and a lot more besides, picked up over the years in jumble sales and charity shops. Bright colors and lots of variety. Plastic boxes of trains and cars. A small doll's house. Stuffed toys. Crayons and stamps. Boxes of games. Tubs full of building bricks. Her eyes widen.

"Now then, what sort of thing does he like?"

She hugs Rabbit closer. "She's a girl."

"Of course she is." I smile to myself. "How about building her a house, then?" I pull out some multicolored bricks. "Shall we have a go?"

I sit down on the floor beside her and we start to build. Within a few minutes, we're at peace together, working quietly, side by side. No grown-up questions. No demands. Just leave them alone to be themselves, that's my way of doing it. Keep it calm and friendly and a bit of respect and the world would be a happier place. What's the rush anyway? She'll take off her coat when she feels like it. Breakfast dishes can wait.

When Teresa comes back a few hours later, her mood is transformed. Perhaps it's the sight of the two of us, snuggled up together on my battered old settee, reading stories. Or perhaps it's just relief that her meeting went well. I make her a cup of tea and bring a tray through with a beaker of water for Jessica and a plate of plain biscuits.

"I can't thank you enough. Really."

Teresa perches on the edge of a chair, her raincoat unbuttoned but still on.

I don't know what to say so I just pour the tea and wait.

Finally, she asks: "How's she been?"

"Great." It's true, Jessica's no trouble—we understood each other from the start. Anyway, even if she were a handful, I never tell on a naughty child. That's not how it works. "We've had fun, haven't we, Jessica?"

Jessica takes a biscuit and goes back to the toys strewn across the floor.

Teresa prompts: "What do you say? Jessica? Thank you!"

We sit on for a minute or two. The clock on the mantelpiece has a loud tick and an old-fashioned mechanical purr when it hits half past—it was my mum's; she always said it would see her out—and it whirrs now and makes Teresa jump. Her nerves are terrible.

"I'm so grateful." Her words come out in a tumble. "I couldn't think who to ask."

I shrug. "It was good timing. Another half an hour and you might have missed me."

Her eyes move from the clock along the mantelpiece to the photos framed there.

"Is that your little girl?"

I nod. "Susie. Not so little now."

There are two pictures. My very favorites. One when she was two and a half, coming down a slide, hair flying, eyes shining. Full of joy. The other was taken on her fifth birthday. We had a proper do. A party in the church hall and an entertainer. She's dressed up in a sparkly dress with broad, stiff skirts. Usually my mum made Susie's dresses but I got that one at a department store and it cost a fortune. I just couldn't resist it and I'm glad I didn't. Her hair was long in those days and tied up in ribbons. Pretty as a picture.

"She's a gynecologist. Out in Australia."

"You must miss her."

Stupid question. Of course I miss her, every hour of every day. I just shrug. "That's what it's all about, isn't it? Love 'em and let 'em go."

"Have you been out there?"

"Australia?" I smile. "She keeps on at me to go but I'm not one for traveling. It's too far." And too expensive.

"Does she have children?"

"Not yet." I pause, trying to imagine being a grandma. A little girl like Jessica. Even better, two or three. "Career comes first with Susie. You know how it is."

She isn't really listening, I can tell. She's just making conversation while she checks out the room. Her eyes are sharp, prying, moving over the chaos of toys on the floor, the brick house built round Rabbit, the train track.

"You're certainly well set up."

"It's my job. Looking after little ones." All I ever wanted to do, since I left school.

I know what she's thinking; well, I can guess. It's a shabby sitting room in an old house. A dodgy gas-fire in the hearth. Stained carpet. I'm not blind. It isn't modern and shiny as hers must be now. But it's comfy. It's lived in. That's what kiddies like. No need to be afraid here if you knock over your juice or get chocolate on the carpet. Never mind, it'll wipe.

"So difficult." She sighs to herself. "Isn't it? Juggling work and children."

I sense where she's going and don't answer. I don't want to mess up.

"I don't suppose..." She looks down at Jessica, who's absorbed in catching the wooden fish in the fishing game, dangling the magnet to see how many can stick. The best reference for any minder is the sight of a happy child. "I mean, are you free at the moment? Would you be interested at all?" She nods at Jessica.

I try to act nonchalant, as if I need to think it over. "Full-time?"

"Well, yes. Ideally. I'm taking on a salon, you see. I'm in beauty. That's what the meeting was about. And, well, it's all moving rather quickly. They want me to start on Monday. The salon's been without a manager for more than a month. You can imagine what a state it's in. It'll be a lot of hours. And the odd evening, too."

I look down at Jessica, thinking. "What about your other daughter?"

"Fran? Oh, she's not mine." She speaks abruptly, then seems to realize how it sounds and flushes. "She's Craig's daughter. I am Jessica's mum, you see, but Craig's not her dad—he's Fran's. And I'm Fran's stepmother. The wicked stepmother." She laughs and looks embarrassed. "It's complicated."

I just nod. "How old is she? Eleven?"

"She's just starting at secondary. She can walk there and back herself, it's not far." She considers. "There might be after-school clubs. But I can't see myself being back until at least six thirty. Later, some days."

I narrow my eyes, getting the measure of her. "I'm a good cook. I'd do lunch for Jessica and tea for both of them. Healthy plain food. Cottage pie, Bolognese, that sort of thing." I look down at my hands, twisting the wedding ring. It looks too small. My fingers aren't as slim as they used to be. "I like to keep things simple. You know, cash in hand." I pause, waiting to see how she reacts.

"Of course." She gets it at once. No tax, no fuss, keep it between ourselves. "What sort of rate would you be looking for?"

"Well, for two of them. And there's the food." I hesitate. "Say, ten pounds an hour, all in?"

I can see the cogs turning as she does the calculations. She's no fool. But she won't find cheaper, not for two of them, sole charge. And she needs flexibility. What nursery will keep a little girl until seven o'clock at night? And literally next door.

She nods. "Let me have a chat with Craig, OK?" Already she's buttoning her coat, rearranging her legs to leave. She's got what she came for. "Come on, Jessica. Home time."

For a moment, after they've left and the house falls silent again, I feel a pang of regret. She agreed too easily. Maybe I could have pushed it to ten-fifty. Even eleven.

But then I walk back into the sitting room and see the floor alive with toys, the broken brick house so recently abandoned by Rabbit, and the trains scattered across the rug and the fishing game too and the biscuit crumbs on the carpet and I think: *No need to be greedy, Angie, my girl. It's more than enough and, anyway, it's only money.*

Because I sense already how right it is for both of us that Jessica, that dear little girl, has come walking into my house, as if she belongs here. As if she belongs to me. I know I'll love her, as I love all my little ones, and she'll love me, in a lightning strike of feeling, as children do. Each time I love a new kiddie—a little girl, especially—memories of my Susie at that age come flooding back. And with it comes a fresh wave of my own fierce, overpowering love for her, too, the most gorgeous girl of them all.

CHAPTER THREE

I set to work the next day, getting ready for Jessica. Harry was an outdoors sort of kiddie and I only minded him for a matter of weeks, over the summer holidays, until he started school. He was never one for make-believe. But Jessica's different. I can feel the magic in her. And I'm excited as I work, imagining how she'll react.

The big toys—the doll's pram and cot and the ride-on sheep and the old puppet theater—are stashed in the attic. I don't like to clear things out and the attic is solid with old things of mine and plenty of Mum's old boxes, moldering now. It takes me a while to dig out the toys and get them down the ladder and clean them off. It's a wonder they haven't been nibbled by those evil rats.

It's a ramshackle old house, I'm the first to admit. It needs a bit of "tender loving care," as my mum would say. She inherited it from Auntie Margaret years ago, when I was little, long before the area started to smarten up. I never thought I'd end up back here but I was glad to save on rent once Mum passed. I had all sorts of plans at first about improving it, but I've never had the cash.

I don't see that it matters, really. Children don't see the world like grown-ups do, and when you think about making them happy, it's not a question of fresh wallpaper and new carpets: it's all about pretend. With the right sort of kiddie, the magic's inside them already, if you catch them early enough, before school interferes and chases it away. It's just a question of drawing it out.

The sacks of material are musty and I have to do three washes and hang them all around the house to dry. I clear some of Mum's small furniture out of the back bedroom and stack it in the front room where I can and, by the next day, I'm ready to get started.

It's amazing what you can do with a pile of wafty curtains and a load of colored lights. Fairy lights around the windows and around the large mirrors. Battery candles on shelves and along the mantelpiece. I set up the puppet theater in one corner and pin a black cloth across the bottom half, to hide the person crouching behind. I gather up all the old cushions that dozens of children, over the years, have sat on, jumped on—peed on, too, if I'm honest. They all go in the washing machine.

On Monday morning, Teresa appears on the doorstep at eight thirty, dressed to the nines. Her hair's freshly cut and shining. I suppose you have to make a fuss about your hair if you run a salon; you're a walking example of the merchandise. Jessica hangs at her side, clutching her hand, Rabbit pressed to her side, shy again, as if she's forgotten me since last time.

"Here we are, then." False smile, tense lips. Nervous, maybe, about her first day in the new job. Most mothers would also be stressed about leaving their child all day with a new minder but she seems more worried about herself than about the children. She hasn't even followed up the references I'd given, which, in the circumstances, is just as well. It never ceases to amaze me that people will spend weeks researching a new car or a new oven but hand over their child to a minder on nothing more than a few endorsements that I've written myself.

"See you later."

She passes Jessica's hand to me as if it's a dog's lead, kisses the top of her head, whispers something in her ear, and is gone, clip-clopping down the path to the gate on her heels. I make a show of waving goodbye, for Jessica's benefit, then bring her inside and shut the door. We stand there, looking at each other in the dim light of the hall.

"Now," I say. "First thing we do, you and I, we have a snack and then we work out some rules together. Right? So what's it to be? Snakes' eye grapes or rats' tails carrot sticks?"

Her eyes widen. I lead her through to the kitchen and set her to work, showing her how to set out plates, find a beaker and fill it with water. Never do anything for a small child that they can learn to do themselves. Makes everyone's lives easier.

She sits on a chair, legs dangling, still in her coat, and sucks on a twirly straw. I wash some grapes and cut them in half, pop them in a bowl. Then, as she eats them, I stick up a large sheet of paper on the wall and write "Rules" at the top. She isn't reading yet but she soon will be.

"The first rule at Angie's," I say, "is that anything can happen."

I write up: *Anything*.

She stuffs a grape in her mouth and chomps on it.

"And do you know what the second rule is? Can you guess?"

She doesn't answer.

"Everything that happens here is a secret. Right? Secret from Mummy and Daddy, and everyone else in the whole wide world. Agreed?"

She nods, still cautious. When she's finished eating, I prompt again, pointing at the paper.

"So, Jessica, what are the rules at Angie's?"

"Don't know."

I point to the sheet. "Anything can happen. Everything is secret. Remember?"

"What else?"

"That's it. No other rules."

She frowns, considers this. "What about eating?"

"No rules about eating."

Pause. "What about hitting?"

"What do you think?"

She shakes her head. "No hitting."

I nod. "OK. Shall we make that a rule?" I write up: *No hitting*.

She reaches for another grape. "What about running in the house? And jumping on the settee?"

"What do you think?"

She gives me a cautious look, testing. "I like it."

"Me, too."

"Silly." She smiles, relaxing at last. "Grown-ups don't do that."

"Don't they?"

I turn and run a few laps around the kitchen as fast as I can, then rush through the doors to the sitting room, climb on the settee, and jump up and down until my face is flushed and my breathing comes in pants. She watches openmouthed, then finally, just as I'm slowing down, my poor old heart pounding, she jumps down from her chair and races through from the kitchen to join me, bouncing on the tired cushions at my side, just as I did when I was a child and then Susie and plenty of other kids since.

Later, when she's had a play with the sitting room toys, I ask her if she wants to come upstairs and see something special.

She considers. "Can Rabbit come?"

I put Rabbit in her arms and tie a scarf round her eyes as a blindfold.

"OK?"

She nods.

I lead her carefully up the stairs, hand in hand, and bring her to a halt outside the door of the spare bedroom.

"Do you know where we are?"

She shakes her head, her lips apart as she breathes heavily with excitement.

I bend down and whisper. "This is a make-believe room. You know what that is? Inside here, you can be anyone you like."

Her hand shoots to her face, fingers splayed by her cheek.

"Do you want to come in? It's not scary."

She trembles. I leave her there for a moment while I nip inside. The blackout blind is already taped shut. I feel my way around, switching on the fairy lights and rows of small battery candles and the endlessly turning mirrored ball that throws colored beams across the ceiling.

She's standing on the landing, waiting, Rabbit clutched to her chest. She looks as if she hasn't moved a muscle, her hand to her face, her eyes covered.

"Ready?"

She nods. I take her hand and lead her slowly inside, shut the door behind us.

When I pull off the blindfold, she stands still and just stares, letting her eyes adjust to the gloom, trying to make sense of it all.

After a minute, she breathes: "A *cave*."

The room is hung throughout with lengths of sparkly material and chiffon scarves and long tails of sequined cotton in as many colors as I could find. They glow in the low light and shimmer as they're stirred by the slightest movement. I got the idea from a Santa's grotto years ago. I took a little boy to visit it and when he asked: *Why can't we have one all year round?* I couldn't think of a good reason.

I let the silence stretch as she gazes. Her face, eerie and bathed in colored light, is tense.

"A fairy cave." She murmurs to herself as she reaches a hand to touch the nearest falling fabric. It swings from her, sways back into place, dances. She tilts her face to mine to be sure of me. Her eyes shine. "I can be anyone? Like an alien? Or a mermaid?"

"Anything you like, petal."

She takes her courage in both hands and creeps forward with Rabbit in the half-light. As she makes her way through the forest of hangings and scarves, she finds surprises. Hidden toys, gleaming in the gloom. Pockets of scattered cushions. The doll's pram with a baby tucked inside. I follow behind at a distance, watching, smiling despite myself, hearing her little murmurs of surprise, her words of reassurances to Rabbit not to be scared.

After some time, she finds the battered old puppet theater set up in the far corner.

"What's this?"

She crawls around to the back, pops up, her head poking above the stage.

"What is it?"

"It's a theater. We can do shows, if you like. With puppets."

She doesn't answer but the light catches the gleam of her teeth as she beams.

"How?"

I open the musty basket at the side and bring out a couple of the hand puppets to show her. The wolf from *Little Red Riding Hood*. There's a Grandma somewhere—I made her myself, years ago. A squirrel. An oversized mouse whose tail fell off.

She sticks her hand inside the wolf and makes it dance along the lip of the box.

"What do we do?"

"Shall we tell a story?"

She nods, all excitement.

"Well, then." I shuffle forward to sit beside her at the back of the theater, hidden behind the black cloth. She puts Rabbit on the floor between us and I help her to put squirrel on her other hand. I put a hand inside the large mouse and poke it up, to show her how it can walk across the open gap of the stage.

"So, what story shall we tell?"

She bounces on her heels and gives little gasps. I can barely see her in our dark corner.

"One about the wolf," she says.

"Isn't that a bit scary?"

"Not a scary wolf. A kind wolf." The low light catches one of the wolf's glass eyes as she jiggles it about. It doesn't look kind to me. "Go on. Tell the story."

So I do. Afterward, when we agree it's time to leave the room and go downstairs for a snack, we work together to pack away the puppets. They're looking a bit tatty now, truth be told, and although I've given them a good wipe, the basket smells musty. It makes me think of all the other stuff stacked in the attic and crammed into the front bedroom, all the moldy boxes and baskets, the broken lamps and dusty ornaments—precious remnants from my old life with Mum.

I lean in close to her and whisper: "You remember Angie's rules?"

She considers. "Don't tell any grown-ups?"

"Right." I bend down to her until our eyes are level and repeat: "Anything can happen. Everything is secret."

She frowns and whispers: "What if Mummy asks what we did?"

"She probably won't." I consider. Her face is tense again, with worry, and I wonder why she seems afraid of her mum and what goes on between them. All the more reason for keeping things quiet from her. "What could you say if she does?"

"We played. Just that."

I nod. "That's good. Grown-ups don't listen much anyway."

"Mummy's very busy."

"I expect she is." I think about Teresa's clicking heels and her eagerness to peck her daughter goodbye and be off without a backward glance. I've seen parents like that before, over the years. Always rushing. Always impatient. No use telling them that little ones need time. "Grown-ups are always busy."

I reach around and give her a hug as we get ready to go downstairs.

"Rabbit!"

A moment's panic as we feel around at our feet, find her, put her back in Jessica's arms.

"Did Rabbit have fun?"

She nods. "She loved it."

CHAPTER FOUR

Fran's a different kind of child, thoughtful and quiet. Generally speaking, I prefer the littler ones. They're so much easier because they still believe that anything's possible. The magic takes them by force and they give it the power to carry them away. Fran is eleven and the magic in her has already died.

That first day, she comes round to me after school. I don't see her straightaway when I open the door. She's leaning against the wall, shoulders hunched, looking out at the street. Her ears are covered with the same giant headphones she wore in the garden. They emit a low boom, boom, boom that I can make out even at this distance. Heaven knows what she's doing to her hearing.

So I just open the front door, then turn and go back inside, leaving it ajar. Jessica and I are making handprints on giant sheets of paper on the kitchen floor. Paint is splodging everywhere, including on Jessica's nose and cheeks. When she realizes Fran's come, she runs out to the hall and waves her daubed hands at her, giggling.

Fran goes to give her a high five, then pulls away her hand at the last moment—"Too slow!"—and they both grin. When Jessica runs back to me again, Fran comes quietly inside, shuts the front door, and settles in a corner of the settee, her coat collar up, locked in her own world of loud music.

Jessica and I carry on painting.

After a while, I go through to the sitting room and say: "What're you listening to?"

She considers me. "Why?"

I shrug. "Just wondered. I like Eric Clapton myself but only the early stuff, with Cream. And The Clash and The Jam. And The Doors. And Bob Marley, obviously, but who doesn't? It's almost a cliché."

She turns away but I can tell, by the shift in her shoulders, that she's interested. Just a bit.

"Jessica and I were figuring out the rules for being here. You want to see?"

She gives a theatrical sigh. "I don't need rules."

I smile. "There aren't many."

Jessica runs in to join us and starts bouncing on the settee. "It's allowed," she says. "She does it, too."

Fran looks skeptical.

"Can you remember them, Jessica?" I bring out our giant sheet of paper from the morning.

"There's nothing about headphones," Jessica shouts in triumph. "Is there?"

"Nope."

"Fran, you're allowed!" Jessica turns back to me. "Mummy makes her take them off downstairs. So she can hear herself think." She turns back to Fran. "No hitting." Jessica looks pleased with herself. "That one's mine."

I point to the list, still only three rules long. "Any you'd like to add?"

Fran shifts her headphones. "I can keep them on, then? Even to do my homework?"

I pretend to consider it. "OK." I write up on the list: *Fran may wear headphones when she likes.* "Tea's in the kitchen at half past five. And if you want to join in before that, you're very welcome."

For the rest of her time in the house that afternoon, Fran sits huddled in her corner, her feet on the coffee table, her head bent, listening to whatever's playing on her headphones. After a while, she gets out schoolbooks and bends over her homework. How she can concentrate with the music blaring, I don't know, but each to her own.

She leaves us alone when Jessica and I play hide-and-seek in the sitting room and kitchen, taking it in turns to go under the kitchen table, behind a curtain, or by the settee. When we sit together in the armchair for stories, the reading is undercut by the dull thump from Fran's ears.

I serve up chicken pie for tea—one of my better dishes—and Fran joins us at the table, headphones still on. She wolfs it down, but asks to be excused when it comes to fruit and the promise of a treat afterward.

"I'm a bit old for that," she says, when she sees the chocolate animals. I see her point.

Jessica reminds me so much of Susie, it makes my heart ache. Just the feel of her, all warm skin and bird bones, pressed into the fleshy curve of my side as we look at the pictures in a book. The smell of her hair. Her thoughtful frown when she tries to figure something out, and the endless stream of questions that come from nowhere. Good questions: *How do babies breathe when they're in their mummy's tummy? Why do we have to wear pajamas, why can't we sleep in our clothes and save time dressing? Why do people have to die?*

It's almost six thirty when Teresa comes for them. She looks tired and tense, standing there on the doorstep, work bag in hand. She doesn't want to chat, at least not to me.

She asks how they've been.

"Delightful." I beam and start to marshal the girls to get them ready to go.

Teresa looks unconvinced. She's finally stepped into my hall but reluctantly. I can tell she wants to be somewhere else. "*Delightful?* Really?"

"Really." I make it clear from my tone that this is all I have to say on the matter and turn away from her, trying to calm down the children and get them ready for home.

Rule number two. *Everything is secret.* I never tell on my friends.

CHAPTER FIVE

TERESA

I should be grateful, I get that. Cheap, flexible childcare right next door. She's had them for a week already and the girls seem fine with it. So far, so good, at least on that front.

It's been a different story in the salon, though. This first week at work has been intense and it has left me frazzled.

So I stand here, washed up, wrecked, ragged, and hungry, on the shore of her doorstep, looking at the peeling paint and the cheesy door knocker and trying to put an excited expression on my face, pretending to be thrilled to have the girls again and the prospect of the weekend ahead when all I'm really thinking is: *Come on, come on, hurry up, it's cold out here, I haven't got all night.*

She opens up and, once again, the smell of the house hits me. A mustiness that comes from a lack of proper heating and old wood and peeling lino, underpinning the smell of greasy cooking. No one else cooks like her anymore; well, no one I know. She cooks like someone in the 1950s; pies and lashings of meaty gravy and thick sauces. Just the smell is overwhelming. She says the girls love it. They won't love heart disease by twenty.

She peers out at me like Mother Hubbard, brushing stray hair from her face with a floury hand and leaving a white smear.

She smiles, showing those crooked teeth. "That time already?"

She knows full well how late it is. It's part of her old-fashioned manners. I bet she never swears beyond "Oh, sugar."

"Coming in?"

I step reluctantly into the dingy hall. The house reminds me of the wreck we bought next door, before we spent sixty grand making it habitable. Too late for this one now. They'll have to carry her out.

"How've they been?"

"Delightful!"

She lies well, I'll give her that. I suppose that's what I'm paying her for.

She turns her back on me and makes a big deal out of getting the girls downstairs.

She shouts: "Girls! Mummy's here!" into the dimness.

Jessica comes hurtling out from the kitchen at the back, a tea towel wound around her head. Her eyes are shining, crazy. I feel a pang at the sight of her. She looks happy, here in someone else's house, in someone else's care, and I wonder for the thousandth time what goes wrong between the two of us, why I can't get it right. My shoulders tighten.

"Mummy!" She throws herself at my legs and almost knocks me over. She's a heavy child. Not stout, just clumsy. If anyone is going to crash into a table or catch a vase or crack you in the shins, it's Jessica. I tell her ten times a day to be more careful but she won't listen.

I hold her by the shoulders now, trying to calm her down, and she wriggles.

"Coat on, Jessica. We're late."

"They've been such good girls."

I don't want to hear it. I should be pleased, I know. It's better than a whingeing childminder, I suppose. But it hurts, all of it.

I shout: "Fran! Time to go."

Angie tuts. "She gets such a lot of homework. Far more than I ever did."

I bite my lip. Fran lives in a world of her own, and it has a different time zone, too. Slower. I don't have time for this.

"One." I count loudly, ominously. This is my warning. "Two."

Jessica tenses and scrambles to find her coat. Angie bundles her into it. I don't bother zipping it up, she's only going next door. Fran—finally—drags herself into the hall, trailing her schoolbag.

"THREE!"

I reach behind me and open the front door, push them both over the threshold, even as they protest and whine, and lift my hand as we leave in a quick farewell to Angie.

Jessica starts wailing. "I didn't say goodbye! It's not fair. It's not fair!"

I wait until our front door closes behind us, then wag my finger in her face.

"Stop it!"

My head is splitting. Fran hangs back, watching the two of us already at war.

Jessica falls to the floor in the hall, screaming now, drumming her heels.

"For god's sake!" My voice wobbles. Why is she always like this? Is it me? "What's the matter with you?"

We've been together all of two minutes and already we're at each other's throats. My hands ball into fists at my side and I have to breathe carefully to calm myself down. I'm exhausted and stressed and in danger of letting rip if I don't watch it.

I manage to step over Jessica's small, writhing body without standing on her fingers and stomp upstairs to the bathroom to run her bath. The mirror clouds with steam. I pour in bubble bath and bubbles rise in billowing mountains where the water churns.

When I go downstairs, Fran is helping Jessica out of her coat, wiping Jessica's blotchy, wet face with her sleeve. The sight of the two of them together infuriates me. Fran has a way of making me feel worse. Always.

"I'll do that."

I get Jessica on her feet, pull off her coat, and push her up the stairs to the bathroom.

Later, as she sits in the bath, laboriously washing herself with her smiley sponge, she says: "You're the best mummy in the whole world."

That hurts. It's so far from the truth that it feels almost sarcastic. "No, I'm not."

She looks punctured. "Yes, you are."

"I'm a terrible mummy. Always have been."

Her face puckers and she looks about to cry and I lean over the side and take her sponge, squeezing warm bubbly water over her chest to distract her.

Soon, she's cozy in pajamas and snuggling down with that old rabbit, and I'm not there yet but I can see my way at least toward dinner and a glass of wine and I wonder for the hundredth time why this happens, with the two of us, and why we can't just get along like other families. I want to, I really do. And I wonder if she's old enough now to remember all this when she's an adult; if, someday, she'll remind me that I was always shouting at her and scolding her. Or if I still have a chance to set things right.

"I love you, Jessica."

I bend low to kiss her good night. She looks so peaceful as she settles to sleep and I tuck the duvet round her.

"I'm sorry I was cross. I just need you to be a good girl sometimes, you know? Mummy gets tired, too."

She closes her eyes, cheek on Rabbit, and doesn't answer.

Downstairs, there's no sign of Fran. I've been mainlining

coffee all day and, on top of my aching head, my heart's racing. I pour myself a glass of fresh orange juice and sit alone at the kitchen table in the stillness. I kick off my heels and the tiles are cold on my sore feet. My shoulders are somewhere up around my ears and I try to let go, to ease them down.

Chaos in the salon today. For the third time, and it's only been a week. It's tiny, only six chairs and three of us cutting. That's part of the plan, to increase the chairs by the spring and take on another junior stylist as soon as possible. I close my eyes, massage my temples, hear the throbbing in my head.

Lottie, the salon junior, messed up the bookings. Two customers arrived at the wrong time, when we didn't have capacity. One stormed out after a twenty-minute wait. The other stayed but complained so much when she paid that I ended up giving her a big discount to calm her down. I sigh, thinking about it. Margins are tight. We can't afford to screw up.

I told Lottie off afterward. She's a thin girl, hooped earrings and long, straight hair. Dark with honey highlights. Messy. I think she does it herself. She didn't say much, just looked anguished and pinched and bit down on her lip. Later, she came out of the toilets with red eyes and I felt bad but she has to learn. We're not a charity. I've got a lot riding on this job.

Helena, the senior stylist, is smart. Good cutter. Good with color. I told her, in my first meeting with her last week: "You've got the makings of a salon manager. Play your cards right and work hard and we'll see." She just smiled. I like Helena. She's older than the others, nearly thirty, and dresses well. Tough cookie.

My phone buzzes. I open my eyes, heave myself to my feet, and go to look.

Sorry. Working late. You go ahead and eat. C x

I stand there in the stillness and look at the screen until it fades to black again. He's done this a lot lately. It's tough getting a new business off the ground, I get that. And he's branched out into a new industry now, selling these funeral plans. But if he's behind with the paperwork, why can't he do it at home? I shrug, disappointed, and shake myself back into motion. There's soup in the fridge. Maybe I'll heat that.

I've just microwaved the soup when there's a scream of "Mummy!" from the child monitor.

Damn. I thought she was asleep. I sigh, lift my spoon, and take a mouthful of Thai spices and vegetables and try to ignore her.

"Muuu-mmy!" She's wailing now, upset.

I drop the spoon and scrape back my chair, angry as I cross the kitchen to the hall, head up the stairs.

"What is it?" My voice is curt as I stand there in the doorway, looking into the shadows.

Jessica hesitates, reading my mood.

I say: "I was just about to have my tea. What's the matter?"

She's wary now. "I need the toilet."

God help me. I hold the door open as she trails past, Rabbit in her arms. A small, forlorn figure in her pajamas, blinking in the landing light.

"Well, go on then. Hurry up."

Later, I have a quick shower. They're both asleep, finally. In the old days, before Jessica, before all of this, I used to light a candle and soak in the bath for ages, often with the radio and a glass of wine. Me time. Nowadays, I just wash.

I lie awake in bed, waiting for Craig to come home. Ten o'clock comes and goes. I think about Kate, his ex, and the nights she must have lain in bed, watching the clock, wondering where Craig was, when he was with me. I think of her more now, and with more sympathy. She feels more real. Perhaps it's just that, since Craig finally left her and we all moved in together, I'm suddenly afraid of becoming her . . .

I wake with a jolt. The room is dark and silent. The clock says ten past one. I turn and reach across the bed, feeling emptiness. I pull on a dressing gown and creep downstairs. The light from the streetlamps streaks across the hall.

The sitting room door creaks as I push it open and see a figure slumped forward in the shadows.

"Craig?"

He shudders and lifts his head from the web of his hands. His eyes gleam.

"You all right?"

"Fine." He doesn't sound it. His voice is thick. "Dozed off."

He gets heavily to his feet and sways.

I want to ask: *Where've you been? Why are you out drinking, night after night? I miss you. And don't tell me it's work—who'd buy a funeral plan in a bar?* But I just sigh and say: "Come up to bed. It's late."

I wonder if Kate did the same.

CHAPTER SIX

I was at a low ebb when Craig walked into my life. Jessica was eighteen months, a clingy, fussy baby developing into a screaming toddler. I'm ashamed to admit it but there were days when—maybe even most days—I wished I'd gone ahead with the appointment at the clinic and never had her in the first place. It would have drawn a line through that disastrous one-night stand. Her father still doesn't know she exists. He was on the plane back to Canada, no strings attached, before I knew I was pregnant. It was my decision to keep her, nothing to do with him. Life's complicated enough.

I was a terrible mother from the start. As my stomach swelled and my legs and back ached, I began to think: *My god, what have I done?* People talked such nonsense. Lies. *You'll be besotted! Don't worry! As soon as you hold her*, they said, eyes all misty, thinking back to their own newborns, *you'll fall head over heels.*

Nope. She didn't like me right from the start. I felt it the moment I set eyes on her. She looked up at me and screamed and I think the guilt started right then. I knew, and she knew, that it was all a big mistake and our job, for the next eighteen years, was to keep that misery secret from the rest of the world.

She took everything from me. My freedom. My sleep. My figure. My self-worth. I was the only mum in the world who cried from sheer frustration when her baby finally fell asleep as I dreaded the thought of her waking up again.

I was so glad to get back to work. All that nonsense about the pain of separation. I only hung on through those miserable, gray, endless nights for the thought of eight thirty in the morning when I could finally drop her off at nursery and be done with her for the day. Work wasn't always easy but at least no one screamed in my face. I worked as a senior stylist at a medium-sized salon in those days and just about made enough, with tips and overtime, to pay the childcare and cover the bills. Just about.

And then Craig walked in. He used to come whistling and singing into the salon on Wednesdays with a trolley full of product for delivery to the salon. I looked back later and tried to put my finger on what it was about him that attracted me so much. He's no looker. But something set him apart. An easy-going confidence. A certain style. And a big grin. He always cracked a few corny jokes as I checked over the order and signed the docket. He learned my name from it: "Teresa Law. Now, is that Miss or Mrs., I wonder?"

After a while, I found myself making an effort to wear a slinky dress or a sexy top on Wednesdays and broke off from hair-cutting to look up every time the door jangled. My insides fluttered. I smiled more than usual with customers when he was in the salon and sucked in my stomach, just in case he was watching. Often, he was. It started to feel inevitable that something would happen.

He was there, waiting outside the salon, one evening at closing time.

"Good evening, Miss Law. A libation?"

He had on a panama hat and doffed it. His expression, playful but also tense, made me want to say yes. It had been a long time since I'd had a drink with anyone.

"I'd love to but…" I paused. I couldn't say yes. There was no way around it. I took a deep breath. "But I've got to collect my daughter. Sorry."

I thought that would be that. What man wants to get

involved with a single woman with a toddler? But he just hesitated, his eyes thoughtful, then said: "Lunch, then? Tomorrow?"

And so it began. We found a dingy café a few streets away, the nearest London still had to a greasy spoon, and it became our regular. Beans on toast or eggs and bacon or frittata. For an hour, we huddled over the table together with mugs of tea and never stopped talking.

He'd set up the salon supply business himself, just a year earlier. A one-man band, buying, delivering. Minimal overheads. He was testing the waters, he said, his eyes shining, planning to expand rapidly, if the market was there, and take on staff.

It wasn't his first venture. There'd been door-to-door window-cleaning with a mate. Too labor intensive. Then an online job recruitment site. I felt sluggish, listening to him. I'd worked in the same salon for several years and was beginning to think maybe he was right: that you never got rich working for someone else, and you had to take risks to win.

He made me feel anything was possible. That's what made me love him, in those early days. It wasn't a physical attraction straightaway, not on my side. I was trapped inside a dark mass of darkness and depression and he hacked his way in to find me, let in a chink of light. Before long, I was drunk on him, thinking of little else but our meetings. He said the same as he reached for my hand across the Formica tabletop, gritty with spilled sugar, or reached under it, his fingers warm on my leg.

I can't remember who suggested it—him, I suppose—but, in the end, we agreed to have lunch at my place instead. It was empty, after all. We made the excuse to each other that it would save money. But of course that wasn't it. We lunched on each other, and an hour was never enough.

He was so passionate and such good fun. I don't think there was a room in the flat where we didn't make love, one way or another. He couldn't get enough of me. He even made me put a

wash on, one lunchtime, so we could try on top of the machine.
All those vibrations, he said, raising his eyebrows.

It seems incredible now, looking back, but in all that time, I
knew nothing about Kate.

I remember the day I found out.

We'd made love on the sitting room floor and were sharing a
packet of crisps before heading back to work. I was always late
back, in those days. His phone rang.

"Well, go on. Answer it."

He didn't move, chomped down on his crisp.

I was nearest his jacket so, without thinking, I thrust my
hand in his pocket and felt for his phone.

"It might be the call of a lifetime," I said, messing about.
"Richard Branson. Her Majesty the—"

His phone was in my hand by that stage and I saw the name.
My heart stopped.

"Kate?"

He didn't look at me, studied the carpet. My stomach
chilled. He might have got away with it if he'd brazened it out.
Told me it was his sister or some other lie. But he didn't. And his
face was leaden with guilt.

The ringing stopped. I threw the phone at him.

"Who the hell's Kate?"

He shrugged but his shoulders were tight.

"I've been meaning to tell you." He sounded so quiet. So
lame.

"Tell me what?"

"The thing is—" He swallowed, still couldn't look at me.
"It's not what you think."

I drew up my legs and laced my hands around my knees,
waiting.

"I'll leave her. It's been messed up for a long time." He hung his head, studying his white, stubby toes. "There's Fran, too. She's nine. She's the only reason I've stayed. She needs me."

"Fran?" I pulled back. "You've got a daughter? How could you not have told me?"

"Tess, I know I should have told you, but I was frightened. I love you." He reached for my hand and pawed at it like a child. His face was stricken, his eyes brimming. "You've got to believe me. What we've got..."

He saw my expression and trailed off. I pulled my hand away. He sank his face in his hands and hunched over. His shoulders shivered.

I could have thrown him out. I could have walked away right then and everything would have been different.

But I didn't. I couldn't. I reached out and drew him to me and he clung to me, his arms wrapped around my body, his face pressed into my shoulder, shaking.

"Please." His voice was muffled and wet. "Please, Tess. We're good together. I adore you. I'll leave her, I will, and we'll be together. Jessica, too. I'll make a good life for us. Just stay with me. Give me time."

CHAPTER SEVEN

ANGIE

Jessica and I settle into an easy pattern. The weather's crisp and dry in September and we spend a lot of time in the local park. We tend to go at lunchtime and I make a big event out of the fact we can pack a picnic. A few cream-cheese sandwiches, a few cold sausages, a bit of fruit, and a treat and she's a happy girl.

The real reason we go at midday is because it's quiet then. Most families are there in the morning and then head home for lunch, so there are no queues and no nosy nannies asking questions. They're such a chatty, gossipy bunch, nannies, especially the young ones who sit on the benches, with their lattes and mobile phones, instead of doing what they're paid for and playing with the children. They give us all a bad name.

Then Jessica starts fussing about going to one of the bigger parks, in the center of town. Her mum must have taken her there, I suppose.

"The one with the pirate ship," she says. "And sand."

I know exactly which one she means, I'm just trying to fob her off.

In the end, when I see how much it means to her, I agree but reluctantly. I pack up a picnic and we head off on the bus. It's a bright, sunny day and she's jittery with excitement. We sit right at the front on the top deck so we can pretend we're driving and she keeps up a stream of chatter about the world below.

"Look, Angie! A doggie and it's wearing a coat. Look! There's a lady with blue hair. Why's it blue? Did she eat too many blueberries? Why've we stopped? But why, why's there so much traffic? Are they all going to the park? Will there be enough swings?"

When we finally get there, she races through the park to the children's play area. Jangly music comes from a carousel just outside the gates and she jumps up and down and begs me for a ride. I won't let her ride a horse—too big for her, she'd slip off—but we join the queue and finally climb into a carriage together—two pounds a pop—and off it goes, whirling, the horses rising and falling, older children riding ahead and behind us, clinging to the twisted poles and beaming, the figures of parents and grandparents and nannies with waving hands and raised phones swirling around again and again as we whoosh past. I'm giddy by the time it stops.

And then it happens, just as we're climbing out, ready to cross to the main gates.

"Hey! You!"

A strident woman's voice coming from the queue for the carousel. Aggressive.

"I know you."

My stomach chills and my chest heaves. I know at once. Panic floods me as the memories surge back. I keep my head down, afraid to look around, and put my hand firmly on Jessica's back to hurry her.

The voice shouts after us. "You got a little girl there? She has. You see? My god!"

Jessica stops, tries to see where the noise is coming from. "Why's that lady shouting?"

I push her forward. "Keep walking."

"Do they know about you?" The voice pursues us. "Do they?"

I give a hasty glance back as we leave the carousel and strike out across the grass.

The woman, stout and middle-aged, with a dowdy green coat, leans right out of the queue, staring after us and pointing. Her hands are on the hood of a double buggy and her face is red with anger. Another woman at her side, with a single buggy, hand in hand with a toddler, says something to her, then shakes her head and they both look across at me in disgust. Others in the queue turn to stare too, curious and disapproving.

I reach down and grab Jessica's hand, drag her as I hurry.

"Ow. You're hurting."

The voice screams after us: "You should be locked up!"

I pull Jessica away from the park, from the carousel, from the entrance gates to the play-zone.

Jessica twists and struggles. "Don't. Stop it!"

"Please, Jessica." I hiss at her and tug. "Come on."

"But I want to go to the park." She digs in her heels and starts to wail. "It's not fair."

In the end, I loop my arm around her waist, lift her into the air, and carry her off as fast as I can, her legs kicking and hands clawing at my face. My arms sweat and my ears pound with blood as I struggle along under the weight.

The woman's cries, drifting across the grass through the autumn air, grow fainter with distance, merging now with the tinny music of the carousel, turning again already, whirling another set of children in never-ending circles.

Once I'm sure we're out of sight and that the woman isn't coming after us, I set Jessica down. She lies on the cold grass, screaming and writhing and pounding the earth. I sit nearby, letting her vent her fury, waiting for her to calm herself, wondering what bribe I can offer in return for the spoiled day: there'll be no going to the pirate ship now, not with that woman so near.

My chest is tight and my breathing labored, not just from the exertion of carrying her. My body trembles. It's shock, the shock of the sudden onslaught and the shock of the memory of the past, a wave that crashes and breaks over me, drenching me in misery and shame.

I take Jessica to soft play in the end, an expensive treat, and let her run off her disappointment there, buy her pizza and pop for lunch to say sorry.

Fran, when she joins us at home later, doesn't seem to notice anything's up. She settles in the corner of the settee as usual, plugged into her music, shoulders hunched, and gets on with her homework. I leave her to it.

They both eat a good tea and Jessica chatters away to me as usual, sulk over.

"Our secret, remember?" I remind Jessica when we head up to the back bedroom, into the world of make-believe, of lights and drapes, for a final play. We dig out the few old hand puppets and I put on a show for her, keeping the lighting so low that it's impossible to see the rips and mends in them, or the peeling paint on the wood of the theater.

When she leaves for home, I whisper to her as I button up her coat: "Don't spoil the magic, Jessica. Just between us. Don't tell."

That night, after they've gone, I sit up late. I can't face bed. The wine is cloying and after a glass or two, I move on to Scotch. My mum's favorite tipple, when she could afford it. The hard stuff.

The sitting room is silent and full of shadows. My mum speaks to me every half an hour in the chime and whirr of the clock, and Susie's there too, smiling out at me from the mantelpiece. My gorgeous girl, so far away.

The whiskey smells of bars late at night and stale breath and of my mum, too, when I was little. She rarely drank through the year but she always bought a bottle of whiskey at Christmas and drank it up through January, her mood melancholy as she sat late in front of the television—right here, where I'm sitting now. I lay upstairs and listened, heard her sighing, long after I'd been packed off to bed.

I think of her now, as I sip my Scotch. I thought I was safe here. I even dared to be contented just now, with Jessica. Such a happy little thing, filling my arms. I wonder if she'll talk to her mother or to Fran, tell them about the scene at the park, what that woman said.

The clock chimes midnight. I count off the beats as I always do, hearing my mum's voice telling me: *Midnight, Angela, stir your stumps, for heaven's sake.* I drain my glass and prize myself out of my chair, struggling to get wobbly legs to take my weight.

I'm at the top of the stairs when I hear it. A kiddie's cry. I freeze, listen. A sobbing, so muffled it's barely audible. My arms judder on the banisters.

"No!" A shriek, full of anger. "No! Stop it!"

For a moment, it's Susie's voice, calling out in the night. I tremble, feeling it all coming back to me. The feel of her, beside me in our shared double bed. The warmth of that sharp little body against mine. Her smell.

I shudder and force myself onward, up the stairs and into my bedroom. I shut the door.

By the time I ease myself into bed, the whiskey gently rocking the shadows across the ceiling overhead, the night is silent. It may just have been a bad dream. Little Jessica has a vivid imagination, I know that. But I feel sick to the stomach and it's not only because of the drink. Something is wrong in that house, next door. Something is wrong in that family. I can't explain it, but I feel it. And, whatever it is, I'm going to shield little Jessica and keep her safe.

The next day, Jessica and I sit together at the kitchen table. I've traced some pictures of butterflies and she is busy coloring the swirls and patterns. Rabbit, never far away, sits on a chair at her side.

"Is there a bear in the make-believe room?"

"There might be." I consider. I'm coloring my own butterfly red, yellow, and orange but the red felt-pen is starting to run out. I might try a few drops of water down the shaft if I can get the end off. "What sort of bear?"

She's clearly been thinking about this. "A big strong one with brown fur."

"Friendly or scary?"

She doesn't look up as she talks. Her hand colors furiously, pink at the moment, making a wild scribble outside the lines. "Friendly."

"Good. What's his name?"

"Her name." She frowns. "Lily."

"Lily the bear?"

She nods, pushes the lid back on the pink, and rummages in the box for another color. Already her fingers are rainbow stained.

"She sounds like a magic bear. The sort of bear who could take you on adventures."

She perks up. "What sort of adventures?"

I make a show of thinking it through. "I think I might have met Lily. Or maybe a bear just like her. She's got a broad, strong back and warm, cozy fur and if you climb onto her shoulders and put your arms around her neck, nice and tight, she can fly you away, anywhere you like. Is that her?"

She nods, pleased. A few lines and she can already see this bear, feel it. It's as real to her as I am.

"Hmm. So where'd you like to go?"

Jessica was subdued when she arrived that morning. I'd wondered if she was sickening for something, but now her shoulders are relaxed and her eyes become animated as we imagine where Lily might take us. I wonder why she needs this magic so much this morning. Why she needs to feel she can escape.

"Bearland." She pauses in her coloring and thinks about it. "Where Lily was born. Where her mummy and daddy live, and her uncle and auntie bears."

"Mmm. What do you think it's like there?"

"Great." Her eyes turn back to her coloring but a slight smile sneaks out. "Tell me about Bearland, Angie."

I do my best, watching her face as I tell a story about happy bears. Her hair's tied back in a ponytail but shorter strands at the front spill down over her face, hanging down toward the paper. I reach out, as I do a hundred times a day, and hook them back behind her ear, only for them to fall forward again a moment later. Her eyes are clear and full as she works.

I try to keep my voice calm and gentle as I ask: "Jessica, did you have a bad dream last night?"

She doesn't answer.

I carry on: "Everyone has bad dreams sometimes. And some nights, you wake up and you know it was a dream but they take a while to go away, don't they? That can be scary."

Silence.

"Does that ever happen to you?"

Her mood has changed, I see it in the set of her jaw. Her eyes are fixed on the paper but less happily now, as if she's determined not to look at me.

"I thought I heard you cry out, that was all. Very late in the night."

Silence.

"Maybe I was wrong."

She drops her pen, doesn't bother replacing the top, pushes her chair away from the table, and, grabbing Rabbit, jumps down and runs into the sitting room to search through the toy cupboard. I know better than to ask her about it again, but her reaction worries me. If there's one thing I know, it's children, and there's something about all this that doesn't feel right.

She seems preoccupied as she plays. I keep an eye on her through the open door as I potter in the kitchen. She isn't really absorbed in what she's doing, she's just going through the motions. After a few minutes, she comes wandering back. I've finished clearing away the pictures and felt-tip pens and am thinking about getting on with lunch.

"Angie." She stands close to me, her hands tense. Rabbit's under her arm. "Can we go upstairs?"

I know exactly what she means. She wants the make-believe room.

"OK." I put away the felt-tip pens and go to get the blind-fold. Rituals are very important to little ones. They like to feel secure. "Are we going to look for Lily the bear?"

She nods.

"Do you want her to fly you away somewhere? Where shall we go?"

"Bearland."

Her eyes have their shine back. She needs an adventure, somewhere far away.

CHAPTER EIGHT

Fran and I slowly get to know each other. I'm careful with her. She's a thoughtful girl, lost in her own world, away with her music. The kind who doesn't answer when a grown-up asks a question. Some adults would find that annoying but I don't mind. Mostly, she probably didn't even hear.

I can see, just from our short handovers, how much she riles Teresa. Her stepmum hasn't got the patience for it. She rolls her eyes behind Fran's back as her voice gets louder, as she starts to count out an ultimatum. She has a temper, that woman. I hear her sometimes when she thinks I'm not listening, if I'm busy in the hall getting Jessica into her shoes and coat and Teresa is hurrying Fran at the kitchen table.

"Don't be rude. I won't have it. You're old enough now. Switch off that noise and answer me properly."

She'd never talk to an adult like that. And there's no call for it with children either, not in my book. They deserve respect, too. Fran is a tall girl but she's still only eleven and still a kiddie, just a bigger one than Jessica.

Each day, Fran appears on the doorstep at half past four, leaning a shoulder against the wall as if she hasn't the strength to keep herself upright, ears deaf beyond her music. She never smells of drink or cigarettes or dope. She seems clean in her habits and her health's good, even if her movement's a little languid. I don't hear any alarm bells.

So, each day, I simply open the door and let her come in

when she's good and ready and settle herself in whichever chair she likes, and do what she wants, pretty much. Homework, usually. She never discusses it. She never talks much at all. Her choice. I get it. Rule number five: *Leave Fran alone.*

She isn't any bother. She eats in silence when tea's ready and later, when her stepmother finally appears, whatever time that is, she potters off home behind her. Her slapping shoes and sloppy, oversized coat make a stark contrast with her step-mother's trim silhouette and heels.

Sometimes Teresa asks me about her, usually in a whisper, as if we're conspirators just because we're both adults. I always smile and say she's a sweet girl, no problem at all, always a pleasure, and she doesn't contradict me but she grimaces as if she thinks I'm lying.

I see other things, too. The way Teresa narrows her eyes when she looks at the children. As Fran stirs herself slowly from a chair and trails into the hall or Jessica comes flying, hair in disarray, from the kitchen, Teresa shoots them hard little glances of disapproval. I catch them and I'm sure the girls do, too.

In the evenings now, the noises continue. I hear it all. Slammed doors, raised voices, scolding, shouting. No way to treat children. Not to my way of thinking.

Jessica climbs like a monkey. I never fuss her in the playground: what is the point of standing by a kid—who is doing what a child should do and swinging and balancing and testing her limits—and giving a constant anxious litany of, "Be careful, don't fall, watch out!" Best not to be there at all if that's your attitude. It just makes everyone nervous.

So I make it a habit to stand close, in case I need to catch her, and coach her as if she's training to be a professional. Left hand up a bit. Right foot forward, there's a bar right there if you reach. Now swing forward.

Sometimes we add an adventure.

On this particular lunchtime, as usual, the playground's deserted. It's chilly and the local mums and nannies have already headed home for lunch and nap time. It's rained overnight and the ground is a mulch of wet leaves. The metal bars are slippery but we don't mind a challenge. Jessica and I are being mountaineers, trying to climb Everest.

"Throw a rope round that rock, Captain, and climb forward."

She does some imaginary hurling of rope and I cheer as she encircles an imaginary boulder.

"That's it! Well done! Now, heave!"

She pulls herself up a few more rungs with great drama, then reaches a hand down to me and we make a performance of heaving me up.

"Look out, Captain, there's an avalanche!"

She looks blank.

"A load of snow coming down the mountain. Quick! Duck!"

She crouches low against the bars as the imaginary snowfall shoots past us, and settles. We climb on.

After a while, we're both hungry, and I spread my waterproof on the bench and we huddle there, crouched under a raincoat, eating our sandwiches.

"Well done finding this cave, Captain! Maybe we could spend the night here."

"No! We've gotta climb to the top."

"The summit. OK. Eat up first."

She presses in close to me as we eat our picnic. Cream-cheese sandwiches, then a banana, then a chocolate biscuit. Even mountaineers need treats.

A park worker chugs past on a leaf blower and Jessica clamps her hands on her ears, her face contorted, until he passes. She hates loud noises, that kiddie. Susie was just the same. If we were out and about, I had to go into the toilets before her and tell people not to flush until she finished her business and we could run out. Heaven knows how Jessica copes next door with all the slammed doors and shouting.

A low drizzle starts up, pattering on the raincoat over our heads.

"Captain, there's a storm coming in. We may have to go home for emergency supplies."

Jessica whines. "No." She twists and makes to hit me, then sees my face and manages to stop herself. "Please can we get to the top? Please."

I pack away the picnic bags, pull out her wooly hat, and push it firmly on her head, and then I put on the rucksack. "Five minutes. OK, Captain? Can we reach the summit in that time? The top?"

"Yes, we can!"

She jumps down and runs across through the lightly falling rain to the climbing frame. She's halfway up before I reach her, jumping and grasping at the bars in a hurry toward the top.

"Steady, Captain. Look out for polar bears."

She manages to drag herself up to the wooden platform on the turret, then lifts a leg to climb to the arch above it.

"Mind that loose snow." I position myself underneath her and reach up to guide her feet. The soles of her sneakers are wet. "Weather warning. We need to come down now."

"Not yet!"

She hoists herself upright and lunges for the top of the arch. As she propels herself upward, her foot skids on the metal and she slips and falls sideways. Her small hand, fingers open, grasps at empty air. Her body seems suspended against the gray sky, twisting and flailing as she falls, banging off the frame. I stick out my arms to catch her but she falls off to one side and the climbing ladder is in the way, leaving me reaching through, helplessly, toward her.

She hits the ground with a bang.

Silence. I feel sick. Her arm's twisted under her. She lies motionless.

I run to her. "Jessica!"

Her eyes are closed. Her face is still, horribly still. Rain gathers on her cheek, drops sitting in perfect spheres on her eyelashes, along the rim of her hair where her hood's fallen back. I kneel beside her, trying to remember my first aid training. It was a long time ago.

Her pulse is strong. Her chest rises and falls and her breath comes in short, smoky puffs in the cold air.

"Jessica. Can you hear me?"

My god. My hands shake as I reach for her, gather her up in my arms, bury my face in her warm neck. My poor, sweet girl. Pictures flash in my head of policemen and the blue light of an ambulance, of doctors and the starch white of a hospital bed.

"Jessica. Please." I'm weeping now, holding her close, pinning her to me as if the sheer act of hugging her can make her well.

"Stop it." Her voice is low but she's with me again, conscious. She squirms in my arms. "You're hurting me."

She suddenly opens her mouth and lets out a high-pitched scream.

"Jessica, listen to me. Is anywhere sore?"

I lift her into my lap and stagger backward to sit again on the bench where only recently we were picnicking in a cave. Her cheeks are pale but her eyes are open, struggling to focus on me. She's sobbing now, her face turning red.

"Calm down, Jessica. You need to be a really brave girl and tell me. Is anything really, really hurting?"

"I feel sick."

"OK. Do you think you might be sick?"

"Don't know."

I sit her upright on my knee, run my hands lightly down her arms, her legs, feeling for the sticky wetness that might be blood, or a misshapen bone. Nothing. *Thank god.* She stops crying and gradually quietens on my lap. She makes no effort to scramble down.

The rain's heavier now, soaking her hair. Rivulets run down the sides of her face. She starts to shiver.

"Come on. Let's get you home."

She doesn't move.

"Everything all right?" A man's voice, loud across the deserted playground.

I look up. The park worker, a spade in his hand. His mechanical leaf blower is parked farther down, by the edge of the path.

I pull her hood over her head.

"Fine." I hunch my shoulders, wave. "Just a tumble. All fine, thanks."

He opens the gate to the playground and comes across the tarmac toward us. "That was quite a drop. Did she hit her head?"

"She's fine." My tone is cross now. "Really." *Mind your own business.*

He stops and stands a few meters away, less certain.

"Come on, Jessica." I lift her onto her feet. She's wobbly, still dazed from the fall, and sways, leans in against my legs

"Even so." The man's still watching us. "Did she black out?"

I ignore him, roll up the waterproof, and bundle it into the rucksack, then take Jessica's hand and start to lead her away through the rain. She walks with slow, unsteady steps.

"You should take her to A&E. Better safe than sorry."

"Thanks." Abrupt tone. "Bye now." I turn my back on him, shielding Jess. "Come on, soldier."

She does her best, bless her, but she struggles. She seems stunned. All I can think is: *Please god, let her be all right. Please god.*

At home, I strip off her wet clothes and cuddle her up on the settee in a soft blanket. I sit next to her and stroke her cheek. I wonder about giving her aspirin. Arnica, maybe, for the shock.

"Shall I read you a story?"

She shakes her head. She's listless. That's not like Jessica.

"Does anything hurt?"

She doesn't answer. After a while, her eyes fall closed and she seems to sleep. I stay close beside her and keep watch. Her eyelashes flutter as she sleeps, such a tiny and fragile little thing. Her cheeks are pale. Her hair falls in damp strands on the cushion. I tuck the blanket closely around her shoulders and kiss her on the tip of her nose.

I wait until I'm in the bathroom before I let myself sob. I sit on the closed lid and sink my face in my hands and weep in big, noisy gulps. My body shakes. I start to rock myself, back and forth, losing all sense of where I am as memories flood in and drown me. Words tumble through my head: *I'm sorry, I'm so sorry, I wouldn't hurt you for the world. I love you, I do. I'd never harm you. I'd give my life to keep you safe.* I bite down on the towel to stop myself from howling.

Later, when I'm spent, I wash my face in the corner hand basin. My cheeks are blotchy and my eyes puffed up as if I've been in a fight. I take a deep breath and go out to check on Jessica.

I know that stupid man was right. She blacked out, just for a little while. She ought to go to A&E and get checked out. I bite my lip, kneel beside her, and bury my face in the blankets at her side, feeling her warmth and the soft lift and fall of her little rib cage.

I can't take her. I just can't. They'd ask too many questions: not just about her, but about me.

By the time Fran appears on the doorstep, Jessica's sitting up on the settee, tucked all around in the big blanket, eating breadsticks and cream cheese. She's subdued and still pale. Her clothes, strewn across the kitchen radiators, steam as they dry. The house smells of wet wool.

Fran stops dead in the sitting room and stares.

"What happened?"

I take a deep breath. "She had a fall in the playground. Fell off the climbing frame. That's all."

She pulls off her headphones at once. Loud throbbing leaks from them at her neck. "Jessica. Are you OK?"

Jessica nods, sticks the end of a breadstick in the cheese, and bites it off. Her quietness tells its own story.

"She banged her head." I speak very quietly, very carefully, my eyes on Fran's face. "I need you to do something for me. Will you? You need to keep an eye on her this evening and even during the night, if you can. Will you do that?"

She doesn't respond, just frowns, looking at her stepsister. After a moment, she crosses to sit on the edge of the blanket, close to Jessica. She reaches out and strokes her hair. It's one of the few times I've seen her touch Jessica. The gentleness in her hand and the worry in her face make me bite my lip to stop from crying again.

"What happened, Jessica?" She keeps her voice low. "*Are you OK?*"

Jessica shrugs. "What she said. I nearly reached the top of Egg-rest." She looks to me.

"Everest," I put in.

"Everest. But the rain came and I fell off."

"Did you hurt yourself?"

Jessica reaches a cautious hand to the back of her skull. "Is there a bump?"

Fran examines her head, parting her sister's hair, looking for something to see.

"Not really."

Jessica says: "It wasn't my fault."

"Of course it wasn't." *My fault*, I scream inside. *My fault*. "It was no one's fault. It was an accident."

Fran nods and considers us both. "I'll read you a story, if you like."

Jessica beams. She pushes the blanket aside and scrambles to her feet, trots across the sitting room to the row of children's books along the skirting board, and starts to search through them.

Fran switches off her music and sets her headphones on the table, within reach.

I look down at the mess of breadstick crumbs on the carpet. We are both feeling our way.

Finally, Fran says: "What did you mean, keep an eye on her? What's going to happen?"

"Well, nothing, hopefully." I take a step toward her and bend down to whisper. Jessica, busy with her books, hums to herself, oblivious. "Just look for any changes. She might be sick. Or say she can't see properly. Or that she's got a headache. I doubt anything will happen. She seems fine. But just in case."

She nods. I've never seen her look so serious, so grown-up.

"She's only three."

"I know." I take a deep breath. "So, here's the thing. If she seems OK, can we keep this a secret, just between us—? Please? If her mummy finds out, I'll be in big trouble. Do you see?"

She sees at once, of course. She considers me. It's a long, careful look. This is a parting of the ways and we both know it. Is her loyalty where it should be, next door with her father and his new partner? Or here, with a woman she hardly knows and isn't yet sure she likes?

"What if she isn't OK?"

"Then she needs a doctor and you have to tell them everything. Blame it on me. But if she's OK, you don't need to say a word. And if Jess tells them anything, just shrug it off. You know. Say it was something and nothing. Assure them she's fine."

Jessica comes trotting back with a picture book in her hand. Fran moves the blanket so the two of them can snuggle together to read. In the middle of everything, that sight at least makes me glad. Fran cares then, about her new little sister. She cares about her and she knows how to be loving. Fran opens the book and Jessica moves in close under her arm. Before she starts reading, however, she hesitates and looks up at me as if she's reached a decision. Her face is solemn.

"OK," she says. "I'll do it."

CHAPTER NINE

TERESA

Bookings are down by nearly 30 percent.

Just this morning, two customers whose appointments were messed up say they won't come back. I offered a free treatment to the third, out of desperation. I spent an hour before lunch going over the accounts. Not good.

After lunch, in the dead zone between two and five, Helena asks to talk to me and leads me into the back room for a chat. We perch on the fold-up chairs, surrounded by boxes of conditioner and dye, both squashed sideways so our knees don't touch.

"I don't know if it's OK to say this..." Helena looks amazing. She's got a great figure—big boobs, tight tummy, never eats anything but nuts and carrot sticks—and it's encased today in a tight red sheath dress. Her stilettos are the same shade of red. Gorgeous, but hard on the feet.

"I'm worried about Lottie." She wrinkles her nose and I see from her eyes how concerned she is. "I shouldn't really tell you, but she's not coping." I wonder what she means and how much to ask. "Maybe that's why, well..."—she looks embarrassed—"it's not just the mess with the appointments. That's bad enough. But the order was all wrong this morning."

She reaches out and touches the stack of cardboard boxes.

"I don't know if you realized."

I don't answer. With so much else going on, I haven't had the chance yet to go through the paperwork and check the delivery.

She starts to reel off mistakes, counting on her fingers. "Two hundred bottles of setting lotion, instead of twenty. There's nowhere to store them. Three bottles of in-house shampoo, instead of thirteen. If we're busy at the weekend, we'll run out."

"Can we send them back?"

She shrugs. "You can. But they charge us."

I bite my lip. The margins are so tight. "You know Lottie better than I do. What do you think I should do?"

She strains forward and her perfume, sweet and expensive, washes over me. *That's what customers smell*, I think, *when she's cutting.*

"Honestly? Put her on warning. One more screw-up and that's it."

Business picks up in the early evening. We end with four chairs and a walk-in all at once, and I leave the accounts and pitch in too, taking on a half-head and cut. The salon is warm with steam and dryers and suffused with the rich, heady smell of ammonia and coffee.

My client's face in the mirror is relaxed and I feel her watching my hands as I flash the scissors with skill; plucking the hair, section by section, between my fingers and snipping with perfection, sending clouds of fine hair drifting toward the floor.

Helena, working the next chair, keeps up a stream of chatter about the weather, about holidays. The red dress stretches and pulls as her arms move. She's an accomplished cutter and Sophie, the junior stylist, has potential too, and, for a while, as I cut and sculpt, my mood lightens and I think: *I'm good at this. This can work.*

All that confidence is punctured later, just before we close. I call Lottie into the back room. She's eighteen and she's been here nearly a year. It's her first job. She stands back against the wall of boxes, anxious.

I take a deep breath and put her on warning. It's a formal reprimand. I'll need to talk to head office about sorting out the paperwork.

Her eyes fill but as well as looking distraught, she seems defiant, too.

"I didn't do anything." She said the same thing last week, when I tackled her about the messed-up bookings. "About the order, I can't understand—"

I frown. I'd far rather she just took it from me and promised to improve.

"Lottie, I'm sorry but—"

"It's not my fault. All I did was—"

"Don't make excuses. I don't want to hear it."

We both stop. She fishes in her sleeve for a tissue.

"Let's draw a line, OK?" I'm trying to sound calm and resolute. I hate scenes. "What's done is done."

She blows her nose, her jaw set, and keeps her eyes on the floor when I reach past her for the door.

CHAPTER TEN

By the time I sort out the delivery mess and check over stock, it's after seven. I stand for a moment in the silence of the deserted salon, looking at the chairs, neatly tucked under the counters; the two washbasins, rinsed round and clean; the stack of dog-eared magazines on the coffee table. *Must get some more.*

Lines of light run across the floor and flash through the mirrors as cars pass on the road outside. It's calm in here, hidden away from the world, and, despite everything, I feel another surge of well-being: excited about my new job, about the success I want the salon to become. I shake myself back into motion, put on the alarm, and lock up.

Angie is her usual bovine self, shabby and large on the doorstep.

"Busy day?" Those bad teeth again.

I want to snap: *Yes, I'm late again. Why not come right out and say it?* But I just say: "Everything OK?"

She nods and calls back over her shoulder to Jessica and Fran to hurry up now, girls, Mummy's here.

They couldn't be less bothered. I had so many ideas about being a mum when I was carrying Jessica. A fantasy of cuddles and games and having fun with an adorable girl who idolized me and wanted nothing better than to be with me, to be just like me. I've tried. Heavens knows, I've tried. Tickle time and stories and buying her pretty clothes. We just don't get on,

Jessica and I. It's our terrible secret. How can I ever tell Craig or anyone else that my own daughter doesn't like me?

Jessica comes slouching along the hall wall, as if every step toward me is an effort.

"She's tired," Angie says, making excuses.

Later, as I bathe her, I try to get her to talk to me. We've barely seen each other all week.

"So," I say, "what did you do today?"

Silence. She squeezes a squirter pup against the side of the bath, sending out a stream of soapy water.

"Did you go to the park?"

She shakes her head.

"Did you do any coloring? Baking?"

She hesitates, as if deciding whether to tell me. "Went on an adventure. With Lily."

"Lily?" I frown. "Who's she?"

"A bear. A big, flying bear. We flew over the mountains and a waterfall and into a forest to find her cave."

I tut, exasperated. "Come on, Jessica. You're not a baby."

She fills up her squirter pup again and squirts so hard it fountains over the side, soaking the mat.

"Stop it!" I pull back, wiping off damp knees. "How many times have I told you—?"

And we're off, another bath time fight, leading to another bedtime argument when she bounces on the bed and refuses to stop. I ask nicely several times, then end up grabbing hold of her to pull her off and slapping her when she kicks me in the ribs.

"Right. That's it. No story."

She screams. "It's not fair!"

"You're not like this with her, are you? With Angie?" I scream back. "So why are you like this with me?"

She glares at me, furious, and hunches under the duvet with her rabbit.

At the door, as I turn off the light, I add: "What's the matter with you, Jessica? Why can't you behave yourself?"

Silence.

"I'm disappointed. Really. You're a very naughty girl."

I sit downstairs, cross and miserable, listening to her screaming on the monitor, frightened of going back up in case I shout again and make things worse.

I thought things would be better here, in a proper house, with a daddy, at last. Craig was so good with her when they first met. It seemed a fresh start for both of us. I wonder if perfect Angie next door is listening and whether she's judging me. No sign of Craig.

I go to check my phone. Nothing. I stick a TV dinner in the microwave and pour myself a glass of Chablis. Fran has disappeared upstairs, as usual. She's a sensible, independent girl and likes to stay in her room all evening and put herself to bed. I'll check on her in a bit.

I'm halfway through the TV dinner when the phone rings. I start. Craig and I use mobiles all the time and it's a surprise nowadays to hear the landline at all. I just make it.

When I say hello, there's a long pause. For a moment, I assume it's one of those automatic sales calls and move to hang up before the recorded voice kicks in.

Then a woman says: "Is Craig there, please?"

She speaks with care, as if she's braced for an argument with me, and her tone is carefully polite.

"He's not here at the moment. Can I take a message?"

"No, thank you. I'll call back."

Click. She rings off before I can ask anything else.

I stand, staring at the wall, then dial 1471 to get the number. Withheld.

I go back into the sitting room, bothered by the call, drink off a glass of wine, and pour a second. The TV dinner looks suddenly revolting and I put the rest in the bin. Something about that woman's voice bothers me. It didn't sound natural. As if she were acting, putting it on.

I tidy up the sitting room, then the kitchen counters, fill the washing-up bowl with hot, soapy water, and do the breakfast dishes, then the few I used this evening. I'm just making coffee when I stop, coffee pot in my hand, and feel my stomach go cold.

Was it *her*? That careful, calculating voice. Was it Kate? I stand there in the kitchen, in this newly sculptured home, stunned. I strain to remember what her voice sounded like, the one time I heard it.

It could be. It could fit.

I take a step toward the sink, the coffee pot leaden in my hand. I feel suddenly sick, remembering. If it is her, why would she even do that? She can call his mobile if she wants to reach him.

I set down the coffee pot without filling it and look at the tired, strained face reflected back at me in the kitchen window. Something about that call wasn't right. If it was Kate, what the hell is she up to?

CHAPTER ELEVEN

For months, Craig kept saying he'd talk to her and tell her about me. Tell her that this was the real deal, that he wanted to leave her. Several times, he promised me that he was ready, determined. I saw the strain in his neck.

But, every time, there was some excuse. For a while, Fran was ill with a nasty flu bug and Kate was exhausted from looking after her, from being up night after night. Then she became ill herself. Weeks passed. He had to choose his moment, he said. They'd been married a long time. He had to be fair.

Then her mother was diagnosed with cancer. She was in pieces. He grasped my hand, looked stricken as he tried to explain.

"They're so close, she and her mum. Always were." Tears in his eyes. "She's in such a state." He stroked my hand, clung to me as if he were drowning. "How can I, just now?"

I didn't know what to believe. My friends, the few who knew about him, said I was a fool. I could see it in their eyes. *He'll never leave her. Move on. Find someone who's free.*

But I loved him and, most of the time, we were happy together. I saw the way he tried to make it up to me. The romantic surprises—flowers and treats and lunch in expensive restaurants. He was ravaged by guilt, by need for me, by fear that I'd lose patience and leave him.

When we parted, he held me so tightly I could barely breathe.

"My angel," he whispered. "I don't deserve you."

I did wonder how she could fail to know. We met so often. *She must be stupid*, I thought. Or too busy having an affair of her own. I liked to imagine that. It made me feel less afraid of her.

I was in the salon one day when a new client came in. A smart woman in her late thirties with a long bob. Mrs. MacGregor, the booking system said. A re-style.

I settled her in a chair and ran my hands through her hair, feeling it with care. Seeing how it fell, how it needed to be cut. Full, strong hair. Healthy and clean.

"So, Mrs. MacGregor." The face in the mirror was neatly made up. The eyes were on mine, impassive. "What can I do for you today?"

"I'm not sure." She gave a tight smile. *Nervous*, I thought. "I'm thinking of a change."

Again I lifted handfuls of hair and watched it fall, judging the weight. "Really?" Highlights, perhaps. The first hint of gray was starting to appear. Copper highlights, perhaps, to blend with her natural brown.

"It's my husband."

I was only half listening, thinking about color. A mix might work. "What does he think?"

"He's thinking of leaving me. For another woman."

I nodded, trying not to react. Women did sometimes need to talk. Some came to us for a new look, to cheer them up or mark a new start. There's a streak of therapy in hairdressing.

"Are you thinking of a new style?"

She nodded. "Oh, yes. Very much. Something dynamic. Something that makes a statement." She paused, choosing her words with care. "A statement like 'Good riddance.'"

I smiled. She struck me as a tough woman. Direct. Good for her.

Her eyes were on my face, watching me in the mirror. "He's never been able to keep his trousers on. You know what men are like. All talk. But what amazes me is that they can always find women dumb enough to listen. To spread their legs. Even when they know he's married. Why do they do that?"

I focused on the hair. "We could take it to the chin." I showed a new length with my fingers. "Quite sharp."

"When it's silly young girls, I can just about understand. Naïve—you know. Don't know any better." Her voice was hard and every time I glanced at her in the mirror, her eyes were on mine. "But this one's old. Almost as old as I am. With a child of her own."

She swung round in her chair, faced me directly. Her lips, bright with lipstick, were tight.

For a moment, I couldn't speak. Finally, I stuttered. "It's you, isn't it?"

She gave a sarcastic grimace. "You think?"

She got to her feet in a single movement and leaned toward me. As she pressed into me, the feel of her warm, muscular body against mine made me shiver. The same body that caressed his, that lay under his weight, that bore his daughter.

"You think you're so clever, don't you? Causing so much pain. For what? For *him*?"

Her venom was hot in my ear. I was transfixed.

"He's pathetic. A fool. You'll get what's coming to you. Oh, yes, I promise you that."

I finally managed to take a step backward. My hands dropped to my sides and tightened to fists. The salon was busy, scented with shampoo and spray, noisy with the throb of hairdryers and chat and the low drone of background music. No one around us seemed aware of what was happening.

She tore off her nylon salon cape and dropped it on the floor at my feet, picked up her bag, and started to push past me.

"I'm glad. You know that? Should have left long ago. I only stayed because of Fran. You've done me a favor, love. And now that I've seen you, seen what you are...frankly, it's you I'm sorry for."

She strode out of the salon, banging the door behind her.

I stared after her.

The receptionist, alerted, I suppose, by the jangling door, called across: "All right, Tess?"

I tried to turn round to shrug her off but found myself sway and struggle to move. My body flushed hot, then icy cold. After a little while, I managed to get myself out of the main salon, out of sight, into the staff restroom. I sank my head in my hands, cheeks sweaty, hair prickling, and sat there, hunched over, shaking as much as if she'd struck me, fighting nausea. When I closed my eyes, I saw her cold eyes, the tightness of the sarcastic grin. *You'll get what's coming to you*, she'd said. I felt tainted, cursed.

Craig came around that evening with a hastily packed bag and a bottle of bubbly from the corner supermarket. His eyes were red and his face drawn. He opened the champagne in the kitchen and came through with two glasses held high.

"I did it. Last night."

We chinked glasses and drank down the cheap, warm fizz, but it was a hollow celebration.

He was needy and I tried to ask the right questions, to show concern.

"How was she? How are you feeling?" I asked. But I didn't want to hear.

Later, he wrapped his arms around me and buried his face in my chest, his lips too wet, his hands too heavy. I wasn't passionate. I couldn't be. I just wanted to be alone.

That night, he sprawled across the bed and snored and I lay awake, looking at the ceiling and thinking about her face, her threat. All these long months, I'd just wanted more of what I was getting. More romance, more affection, more love. Until that moment, I never thought of myself as the new wife. I never imagined trudging to the supermarket to get the shopping in or cleaning the toilet after he'd used it or lying, squashed, listening to him snore, without the luxury of retreating afterward to my own space. What if she was right? What if some other woman, a younger, more glamourous one perhaps, did the same to me as I had to her?

I never told him that she had come to see me that day in the salon. I told myself that I was sparing him any more pain. He had enough to deal with. He was struggling with enough hurt. But it wasn't really that. I was too ashamed.

CHAPTER TWELVE

ANGIE

Fran still arrives every day with her ears full of music and spends most of the time hunched on the settee, either doing her homework or staring into space. But there are days now when Jessica begs her to play with her or to read to her and she gives in, closes her books, and gets down on her hands and knees to make a shed out of blocks, or figure out a new way of dressing up Rabbit, or just cuddle together and read her a story or two.

I always keep my distance, disappearing to the kitchen and pretending not to notice—Fran doesn't want me to intrude on the two of them, I sense that—but I leave the sitting room door open so I can keep an eye. I love seeing them together. Fran's a different person with her stepsister, all gentle and sweet, and Jessica adores her.

I see Teresa every morning when she drops Jessica off. Her manner's curt and I worry for a while that she's cross with me, that she knows about Jessica's fall. But she never mentions it and, as the days pass and it's clear Jessica's suffered no ill effects, I'm gradually reassured that Fran really did keep our secret.

Teresa just seems keen to push Jessica through the door as soon as I open it and be off. She isn't much different in the evenings. I ask her once how the new job's going and she shrugs.

Maybe she's one of those mothers who think minders are beneath them, just the paid help. I've met plenty like that and it's never the really posh ones who are snooty; it's the middle-class ones who aren't used to help and don't know how to treat us.

I had a job years ago, before Susie came along, where the family made me eat separately. I don't mean in the nursery with the kids. That I could understand. But at a separate table in their dining room. There was barely space. She and her husband sat at either end of the polished table and I had a folding one squeezed into a corner. I wouldn't mind but I wasn't in danger of interrupting anything. They barely talked to each other—they just sat there and chewed in silence. It was embarrassing. I didn't stay with them long.

And Teresa has no reason for airs and graces. She might think a lot of herself, but when it comes down to it, she's a hairdresser and even childminders get their hair done, same as everyone else. I've a good mind to go into her salon and ask for a cut and see how she acts then, when I'm a paying customer.

Some days she doesn't look well. Heavy, black circles under her eyes, despite all that makeup. Her cheeks sort of pinched.

I don't see much of the husband, Craig. He comes and goes at all hours. He drives a sports car with one of those unnecessarily loud engines and parks it in the street right outside the house so I can hardly miss hearing when he comes home. Now that autumn's here, I mostly sit in the sitting room with a glass of wine in the evening and maybe a bit of television, if there's anything on. They've had a special offer on an Australian red in the supermarket. Very nice. Leaves me with a pretty clear head in the morning, all things considered. And a very reasonable price.

Once or twice, I have a peep around the curtain when I hear the rev of the engine and see him climbing out. He dresses well, I'll give him that. And he isn't bad looking, if you like that sort of thing. A bit flashy, like the car. Once I linger a bit too long and he catches me looking and gives me a cheeky wave as he opens the front gate. I'm more careful after that.

But I hear things. Quite often. The slammed doors and shouts. Mostly they're high-pitched, either Teresa's voice or even Jessica's, sometimes. But sometimes a low boom. Then I know the car is parked outside and he's in there, too.

I don't worry too much about him and Teresa. They've made their bed, however crumpled and messed up it may be now. But I worry about the girls: Jessica, of course, but Fran, too. They deserve better.

There are days when I hear crying and screeching and feel like marching next door and picking Jessica up, wrapping her in a blanket, and carrying her home with me. To keep her safe and calm in my house, where anything's possible and she can be whoever she wants to be. To keep her for my own.

The salon stays open until eight on Thursdays, and Teresa starts asking if I can keep the girls until eight thirty, even nine. Their dad's rarely home, not so regularly you could rely on him, anyway.

I agree, of course. What else can I do? I don't mind giving them their tea and a bit of television or a story afterward. And the money adds up, that's good. But I don't like it. It's too late for a little one. I buy a toothbrush for Jessica and clean her teeth after her milk and she ends up falling asleep on my settee, her cheek resting on Rabbit, both of them cuddled around with blankets. Even so, Teresa then has to carry the poor mite home and start all the business of bathing her and getting her into pajamas and then into a cold bed. It's late even for Fran.

So I make a suggestion. How about I have my own key on Thursdays and take them home after tea so Fran can get on with her homework or do whatever she wants while I bath Jessica, put her into pajamas, and tuck her into bed with Rabbit, all nice and cozy?

Teresa fobs me off with the usual answer at first: "Oh, I'll have to ask Craig." But he can't mind, because finally she comes round, all sweetness and light, and hands me a key on a fob with a pink tassel and says she'd be sooo grateful, I'm an angel and all that because the very next Thursday, she has to stay until at least nine because they're so short-staffed, there's no one to cash up and restock product as well as cut, and Craig has a dinner.

Thursday comes and when Fran appears, home from school, we all head next door.

Something between Fran and me has shifted since Jessica's fall. I think it's the fact I asked for her help and she deigned to give it—and to cover for me with her parents, just as I never tell tales on her. But I'm on probation, I understand, and I take care.

So I let Fran take the lead in showing me in. She wants to make it clear that this is her home, she's the grown-up around here. She switches off the alarm and hangs up Jessica's coat in the hall, puts her shoes underneath.

I'm pleased to be inside at last and free to have a good look around. I can see as soon as we walk in that it's barely recognizable from the same house where Mrs. Matthews and her boys once lived. I wondered what Mrs. Matthews makes of it, if she's peering down at us now. It all looks so different. I have to concentrate to remember the old layout.

The small, poky rooms are all knocked through to make one giant open-plan downstairs, leading seamlessly from the front windows—all new sashes, that alone must have cost a bomb—through the old sitting and dining rooms and out to a broad, open kitchen at the back.

The faded carpets have gone. Now there are varnished wooden floors with splashes of rugs here and there, and the settees and armchairs are white leather. There's a glass-and-metal coffee table on one rug and a wood-burning stove—the kind that looks like an old engine boiler—in the fireplace where Mrs. Matthews had a three-bar gas fire that was as old as mine and never threw out much heat. No sign that children live here. No toys. No piles of books. No stuffed animals. That strikes me as rather sad.

Fran, acutely aware of the fact I'm looking the place over and still acting the hostess, draws me through to the giant kitchen. It's in the same style: monochrome surfaces—the counter tops are gray slate; they must be a nightmare to keep clean—with occasional splashes of color. A framed painting that is a daub of red and yellow stripes. A startling green cozy. *Tea cozy*, I think at first, but it's the wrong shape. No, *cafetière* cozy. Did you ever.

"Can we go in the garden?" Jessica, running around us, heads for the sweep of glass doors that marks the end of the extension.

"It's almost dark." Fran shakes her head. "I'll put the floods on, though."

She crosses the kitchen and presses a button and beams thin fingers of colored light into the blackness. Lasers. They strike the stone flags, a marble birdbath, and the dark, empty space where, I imagine, they will set out a garden table and chairs in the summer.

"Well," I say. It isn't my taste but I like to be polite. "You could land an aircraft with those lights."

Jessica giggles. "Silly!"

Fran, unsure whether to laugh too, switches them off again. "Anyway," she says. "I'm going to my room."

That's clearly one part of the house that's off-limits to visitors. Probably even to her parents.

I have to call her down again when it's time to cook tea to

show me how to work their fancy oven and I think Fran likes
that, acting the adult and being in charge. She doesn't even
make a fuss when I start to read them one of Jessica's stories
while they eat. As soon as Fran's eaten, she scrapes back her
chair and heads back upstairs.

I don't mind. Jessica and I enjoy being together. It's as simple
as that. Strip everyone else away and leave us to it and we're fine.
She brings out another book and I read to her for a bit, then we
play a simple board game—a bus going around the board, picking up all sorts of crazy passengers and running into roadworks
and traffic lights. The things they think of nowadays. When I
was a girl, it was dominos or ludo or snakes and ladders and that
was it.

When she starts to mess about, I warm up some milk for her
and find a couple of plain biscuits in a tin and we go up for her
bath. She takes charge, showing me where things are kept, intro-
ducing me to the sets of squirty ducks and puppies that are her
bath toys. I run a deep bath with plenty of bubbles and we play
until the water cools. She has a row of pots along the side of the
bath and fills them all with water, gives her plastic toys their own
baths in the bubbles, and hoses them down, chatting to them.

"Come on, little doggy. Up you go. No! Naughty! Not like
that."

She's a tyrannical mother to them and I wonder who speaks
to her like that: her mother or stepfather.

"Listen to me! Right, I'm giving you one last chance. Kitty-
cat, don't you know how to behave?"

The poor toys never get a chance.

"Right. That's it. Out you go. Sit there until you say sorry."

She turns back to me, all smiles. "Can I choose the story,
Angie? Pleeeease?"

She has her own towel with a picture of a unicorn, her name
embroidered across the top. Soft, and warm from the radiator.

I wrap it around her and carry her up the final flight of stairs to the top of the house where the girls have their bedrooms. That smell. There is nothing in this world as wonderful as the clean, soapy smell of a small child. And the feel of her, that warm, damp weight in my arms, strands of wet hair falling clear, body snuggled against mine. Susie, my love, my own sweet girl. I could close my eyes and it would be you, all those years ago, just as gorgeous, just as precious, pressing yourself into my curves and soft fleshy chest. My life.

Jessica pulls on her own pajamas—"Clever girl!"—and settles on my lap while we read a story. Then into bed, no nonsense, no trouble, and cuddles up with Rabbit at once. I don't much care for her bedroom. Not that it's small. That's quite cozy. Just that it's too contrived. All pink fairies and princesses and everything matching as if it were ordered as a job lot by someone with no idea about what a little girl wants. Someone who doesn't really know her. The framed pictures around the walls are part of a fake Victorian set: pastel watercolors of fairies and elves sitting on toadstools, that sort of nonsense. Her small wardrobe, chest of drawers, and bookcase are all brand-new, painted the same clean white. One shelf on the bookcase has stories that are far too old for her. Beneath them, plastic dolls, dressed in stiff clothing, sit along the lower shelf. Too hard and new to love. Only Rabbit, stained and misshapen where Jessica cuddles her, is in her bed.

"Good night, Rabbit." I bend over her and kiss the top of her head. "Good night, little Jessica." Her forehead is smooth, her cheeks flushed after the bath. "Love you lots."

She doesn't answer, just closes her eyes and smiles into Rabbit. She looks tired and comfortable and ready for sleep.

"I'll be downstairs if you need me. OK?"

I tap on Fran's door before I head back down. "I'm making supper. Fancy a treat?"

No answer. I go down, put teacakes in the toaster, and make

myself a tray of tea. I don't expect her to join me. They only have
low-calorie spread in the fridge; no such thing as a butter dish. I
rummage around in a dairy compartment full of odds and ends
of fancy cheese but no sign of butter. They clearly don't cook.

I've just carried the tray through to the sitting room when
the door opens and Fran's standing there, her hair messed up,
her clothes disheveled as if she's been asleep. She looks different
without those earphones. Younger. Gentler.

She hesitates, looks at the tea tray with its milk jug and teapot, the cups and saucers, two side plates, and a pile of toasted
teacakes, oozing jam.

"Where'd you find all that?" She takes a step farther in,
points to the teapot. "That's for when Gran comes."

I'm not surprised. I've trawled through a cupboard of dusty
mixing bowls to find it. I put milk in two cups and lift the pot
to pour. "You like teacakes?"

She's awkward and perches on the arm of a chair, her legs
splayed, only half joining me.

"Done your homework? They do give you a lot."

She reaches for a teacake and allows herself to be drawn into
conversation whilst making the point that she finds small talk
absurd. That's OK. I think so, too.

"I hated school." I hand her a cup of tea and take my own.
"They thought I was stupid. I wasn't but that's what they
thought. Hated exams. Never did well in them."

She doesn't answer but she takes the tea. "It's pointless," she
says, finally. "What use are exams, anyway?"

I shrug. "Depends what you want to do. You just need them
for some jobs. You play the game, do what you have to, you get
what you want. That's how it works."

She bites into a teacake and sprays crumbs on the white
carpet. I don't say anything but hope she's more careful with
the jam.

"My mum's got a degree. All that studying. Look where it got her."

I wait for her to carry on. They sound like someone else's words, but I'm not sure if they're Teresa's or her real mother's.

"What did she study?"

"English. She's a teacher. Well, she was."

I nod. Her real mother then. "Not anymore?"

She stuffs the rest of the piece of teacake into her mouth, chews and swallows. Finally, she slips sideways into the chair. It's a slovenly movement but I understand. She's committing to joining me. I pass the plate and offer her another teacake.

"She's gone back to college. Law." She looks around the room with disgust. "That's why I'm here."

"You couldn't go with her?"

"Apparently not." She pulls a face. "She's in Chester for a year, doing a law course. She didn't want me in and out of school." Her forehead is tight and her expression sour. "You know what I think? She's punishing Dad. Getting back at him. Dumping the daughter on the love birds."

I look away and drink my tea. Her hard act doesn't fool me for a minute. I wish I could put my arms around her and give her a big, long hug. She'd cry if I did, I can sense it, but I also know she'd feel she'd let herself down.

We sit in silence for a while. I munch a teacake myself and think how quickly Jessica's gone down. Susie was the same. Asleep by the time I left the room, then up with the lark. You pay for it one way or the other.

"I'm never getting married. Not a chance."

I don't answer for a moment. "There's a lot of luck in it," I say at last. I mean it. "You think you know someone when you get married but you don't, not really." I hesitate and consider, doing her the courtesy of doing my best to get it right. "At least, you don't know who they'll turn into."

She shuffles about and tucks her feet under her. I wonder if that's allowed in this house with its expanses of white and cream. No skin off my nose.

"You were married, weren't you?"

I nod. We're talking at last, person to person. It's all she needs, I know that. To be treated properly. With kindness and a little respect. It's all any of us want, really. Whatever age.

"What happened? Did he leave you?"

"In a manner of speaking." I swallow. "He died, not long after we got married. It's a long story."

She looks embarrassed. "Sorry. I mean—"

"That's OK." I shrug. "Long time ago now. I do miss him, though."

"And that girl in the photo, she's your daughter?"

"Susie. She's grown up and gone now. Made her own life. But just because I can't see her every day, doesn't mean I don't miss her. Love her to bits. You do, if you're a mum. You can't help it. Goes with the territory."

She bites her lip. "Mum says it's her turn now."

I can imagine. "Do you still get to see her?"

She shrugs. "Not much. She's renting a room up there, with some old couple. I'm not allowed to stay." She pulls out her feet and straightens her legs, stretches, gets up. "Anyway, whatever. I'm off to bed."

"Good night."

She flounces out without replying.

I sit in the quietness for a while, following the sounds in the house as she uses the bathroom, climbs the top flight of stairs, and closes her bedroom door. I look at the freshly painted sitting room wall and imagine the shabby room on the other side, my room, with its cozy, exhausted furniture and small-screen TV. I want to melt through it and be back there, to have a drink or two, wash away the day.

I carry the tray through to the kitchen and try to work out how to switch on the taps and wash up. They don't even have washing-up liquid or a proper sponge. I open the cupboard under the sink and stick my head in, rummaging amongst the bottles of cleaning fluid.

"That's all right." A man's voice. I jump back and nearly crack my head on the rim. Didn't hear him come home. "All goes in the dishwasher."

He seems larger indoors. Imposing. He shrugs off his expensive coat and puts it over the back of a kitchen chair. "Thanks for helping out."

"Pleasure."

We both hesitate, awkward. I wonder if he's thinking about paying me but I don't like to say. In my experience, childcare is usually the mum's department.

"The girls are fine. Fran's just gone up."

He nods. He looks preoccupied. I walk past him to the hall and get my coat.

He follows me out there. "Angie, isn't it?"

I nod, noncommittal.

"Angie, can I ask you something? Ever thought about your funeral?"

I start. "My funeral?"

"They do all sorts nowadays. It's not all black and gloom and doom, you know. You could have a horse-drawn carriage to the church. A theme. Princess. Fantasy. *Star Wars*. Go out in style." He pauses, watching my reaction. "There's no avoiding it. We've all of us got to go someday."

I frown. "That's a bit morbid."

He grins. "Not morbid, just practical. You seem a practical person. I'm sure it's a long way off. Mine, too—well, I hope so, anyway."

His smile is strained. He's so close that I feel the heat rising from his skin and smell the spice in his aftershave. I think, not for the first time: *I don't like you. I don't trust you.* Men should smell clean, of soap. Perfume's for women.

"You've got a daughter, haven't you? In Australia. What's her name again?"

"Susie."

"Right. Susie. Imagine, Angie, imagine how upset she'd be if anything happened to you. What a blessing for her to know everything was arranged, everything paid for. All she had to do was say her goodbyes." He inches forward. "Have you ever thought about a funeral plan? It needn't cost much."

I reach behind me for the door and pull the catch. "I'm off now."

"I've got a brochure you can read. Wait just a minute."

He disappears back into the house and I seize my chance, open the door, and bolt down their path and back up my own. So that's what he does, he sells funerals to people who don't even need them. Well, not yet, anyway.

I'm just going in when he appears on his doorstep and reaches across the railings. He thrusts a glossy booklet at me.

"Just have a little look." That false smile again. "No pressure."

His voice follows me as I close the door.

"After all, we none of us know when we'll be called."

CHAPTER THIRTEEN

TERESA

Things in the salon go from bad to worse. I'm getting close to the end of my rope. Lord knows, I have good reason.

There's yet another screw-up with an appointment at lunch-time, just when we're busiest. A young woman comes in during her lunch hour for a cut and blow-dry and her appointment isn't in the system. We just don't have the capacity. In the end, she storms out.

Lottie, red-faced, shrinks behind the counter.

I'm too frantic all day to talk to her but I can't let it go without saying something. At five o'clock, when I see her reaching in the closet for her coat to leave, I dash over.

"Another mess-up today. Really, Lottie, I'm very cross."

I may come on a bit too fierce but I don't have long to talk. I'm partway through a cut, scissors in one hand, comb in the other.

"You're already on warning. I thought you understood that? You realize I'll have to take this further."

She can't look me in the face. She strains forward, buttoning up her coat.

I say: "You're not giving me much choice."

She doesn't answer, just turns away from me and makes to go.

I glare and say sharply: "Is that it? Not even an apology?"

When she finally lifts her eyes, they're thick with tears. She tries to open her mouth to say something but her lips twitch and she suddenly starts to cry, then turns and runs out of the shop. The door hangs open behind her. My customer, watching in the mirror as it all unfolds behind her, pulls her eyes from mine as I go back and stares fixedly at the pages of her magazine.

Once again, I stay after closing time to catch up on checking through stock and looking through deliveries.

I'm kneeling in the midst of the boxes in the small staff room when I become aware of someone hovering in the doorway, watching. I look up. Sophie, the junior stylist.

"It's not her." Sophie looks scared but defiant. She's got her coat on, ready to leave. Her hands are thrust deep in the pockets. "I know Lottie. She's good."

I sigh. They're good friends, those two. I've seen them chatting.

"I'm sorry she's upset—"

"It's just not her." Sophie's jaw is set. "You've got it wrong."

I think about Helena and the tip-off she gave me.

"I admire you for standing up for her but I'm afraid that's not what I've heard."

"Heard? Who from?"

I lift a weary hand. "Let's not get into who said what. The point is—"

"It's Helena, isn't it?" Her eyes are suddenly sharp. "She went for your job. You do know that, don't you? She threw a wobbly when she didn't get it. Said they owed her. She's been here five years. Waiting."

I stare. "Waiting?"

"For the manager's job."

An awkward silence. I shake my head and turn back to the boxes. I've got work to do. I'm a manager. I shouldn't listen to gossip.

Sophie shuffles her feet. "Look, I don't like Helena. None of us do. She'd do anything to get ahead. There was another stylist here—Josie. You should have seen what she did to her. She quit in the end. And she was a damn good cutter."

I shake my head. Salons can be hothouses: a bunch of temperamental types shut up together all day long. There are always rivalries and jealousies.

"I don't want to hear it."

"All right." She turns on her heel to leave, then hesitates and turns back. "I'm just saying. Lottie's good. If someone's screwing up, it's not her. That's all."

After Sophie has left, I potter about for a while on my own, rearranging the stock so we can access it more easily and creating more space for us to sit and have a coffee when we can. I switch off the main lights and am about to get my coat and leave when something stops me. I stand there, in the shadowy, empty salon, watching the headlights from the road streak across the mirrors and drinking in the rich, fuggy smell of ammonia and conditioning lotion.

In the midst of everything, despite my worry about the strange phone call last night and whether it might be Kate, my preoccupation with Craig being so absent and detached, and the tensions here in the salon, I feel a sudden surge of well-being.

I grab the nearest black leather chair by the back, pull it out, and sit in it, feeling the creak and give in the seat and arms. I spin myself around in it to look out at the salon, asleep in the stillness. The day's cuttings, the blond, brunette, and gray strands, are swept and cleaned from the floor. The hairdryers, hanging in their holsters, are quiet. It was a noisy, crazy day and tomorrow, early, another one just as hectic, will begin, but for now, for these few dark hours, there is peace.

I smile. I love this business. I look around at the clean outlines of the fixtures and fittings, at the fake cupboard fronts that
hide shelves of product, the mirrors that reflect us all to infinity.
This is my salon. I'm in charge here and it's up to me to make of
it what I can.

I sit for a while longer, thinking, then cross to the computer
on the receptionist's counter and switch it on. The light flickers
and brightens. I open up the appointments system and check
through the settings, working out how to create a password to
keep it locked.

From now on, everyone will still be able to view bookings
but only Lottie and I will be able to change them. It's not ideal
but we're a small salon and we can make it work, at least in the
short term. If Lottie is the problem, I'll soon have a proper case
to share with head office. And if she isn't? I shut down the computer and go for my coat, jingling the salon keys in my hand as
I put on the alarm and lock the glass door. If she isn't, the real
culprit should be blocked.

At home, Angie has put the children to bed. Even Fran is quiet,
already in her pajamas, reading a schoolbook, looking as if butter wouldn't melt.

Angie looks smug. "No problem," she says, when I ask how
the children have been. I hardly recognize the little darlings she
describes as my own monsters. "Good as gold."

Her phone chirps and she checks the screen, beams.

"My Susie." She looks absurdly proud. "Time for our weekly
call. Got to dash."

That's a relief. She grabs her coat and is gone in a flurry. I
stand in the hall and listen. Our gate clinks, then a moment
later her own ancient gate squeals. Footsteps. The rattle of her
key and the bang as her door closes. The hall is suddenly silent.

I check my phone. Nothing from Craig. No sign of him at home. I go wearily through to the kitchen and pour myself a drink, take a first gulp. I imagine Angie easing off her sensible lace-up shoes and plumping down by the phone to wait for her darling girl to call all the way from Australia.

Upstairs, Jessica's fast asleep, sprawled across her small bed. Her hair flies in all directions on the white sheet. Her duvet is kicked off to the floor and I lift it, straighten it, tuck it around her again. Her forehead is damp against my lips.

As I head downstairs, I realize I'm cross and it takes me a while longer to realize I'm actually jealous. Jealous of Angie, that lumpy stout creature, because the girls seem to love her more than me. Jealous that her daughter, although so far away, loves her enough to keep in regular touch. I can't see Jessica doing that. She'll be out the door and away from me as soon as she can, I can feel it. I'll never hear from her again.

I make myself a sandwich and switch on the TV but I can't settle. I give in and text Craig.

All OK?

My phone sits on the arm of the chair beside me as I wait for an answer. It takes an eternity to come. Finally, the screen beeps and flashes.

Fine. See u later.

I wonder who's with him—if some leggy young woman is teasing him as he texts back, and thinking to herself: *What a fool she must be, that little woman at home, minding the kids. How can she not know?*

I thought the same about Kate once. I remember thinking: *Well, she can't care much about him if she can't sense something's wrong.*

I didn't understand a thing. Do I sense something's wrong now, sitting on my own with a glass of wine and watching an inane program about dating, wondering who he's with? It's gnawing at me, this worry, this doubt. I can't help remembering what Kate said. That I wasn't the first. That he couldn't keep his trousers on. I thought, at the time, that she was just being vicious because she was jealous. But what if she was right?

I can't relax. In the end, I put the chain on the front door, just so I have some warning if he comes home unexpectedly, and then head upstairs.

His study is a poky room on the second floor, a back bedroom really, by the family bathroom. I draw the curtains and switch on the light, feeling like a burglar in my own home. His desk is piled with papers and I rummage quietly through them. Circulars and bills and sales brochures about funeral flowers and eco-friendly coffins. Some of them date back months.

I ease open the desk drawers. Tidy and dull. Scissors and an old hole puncher. A worn Perspex ruler. A pencil sharpener. A stack of headed writing paper for the funeral business. At the back, several boxes of business cards belonging to businesses long abandoned.

I recognize one and prize it out with my nails. A card from his hairdresser supply business. Happy Hair. I carried one of those in my purse for months, before the business went under. I was so proud of him, this entrepreneur who was sweeping me off my feet. Proud of his courage. I push it back and close the drawer.

There are box files stacked on the bottom shelves of the bookcase and I sit cross-legged on the carpet and go through them, one by one. My head's dizzy with wine and my hands shake as I riffle through receipts and paperwork from the past. All these different people he's been, in all these different businesses. My stomach tenses and chills. I've never pried like this before. There was no need and besides there was no opportunity, we were always together in the evenings. Now, as I reach and rummage, I feel I'm opening a door I won't ever be able to close again.

Underneath the files, stuck into a cardboard folder, are personal certificates and documents. His birth certificate. I scan through it, suddenly anxious. It's all just as he's always said. His date and place of birth. Craig Oliver Fox. The names he never liked. I fold it back into its envelope and go on.

In the next file, I find his divorce papers. The Decree Absolute. He showed me that the day it came. He had tears in his eyes.

"I'm pleased, really." He looked anything but happy. He kissed the top of my head, standing there in the tiny hallway of my flat, just home from work, the post freshly opened in his hand. He was still wearing his coat. It smelled of petrol fumes.

"It's just sad, isn't it?" He blinked, looked away from me. "It seems so final."

I slipped my arms around him and gave him a hug. "We're going to be very happy together. It's all right."

We'd already bought the house. He was constantly on the phone, supervising the builders.

Now I stuff it back out of sight. Finally, hidden at the bottom of the same file, under all the official envelopes, is a packet of loose photos. I lift them out and hold them to the light. Pictures from their wedding.

I go through them, one by one. He's never shown me these. It's a whole chapter of his life from which I'm excluded and always will be. An important part of him I can never share. No wonder he's never shared them. How could he?

Craig, so young, looking handsome and broad-shouldered in a dark suit. Kate at his side, her hand on his arm, beautiful and beaming. I tilt the picture and scrutinize her.

She's wearing a tight white dress with a mermaid's tail, showing off her curves. Elegant. The satin shines with sequins.

Her hair is pinned back with combs. It's professionally done, I see that at once. A veil flies away to the side, lifted by the breeze. I bite my lip. I know her face from that visit to the salon but it looks almost like a different woman, beaming there in the picture, because she looks young and so happy. So innocent of everything that was to come.

A creak. I freeze. A soft tread. I push the box back, hands trembling, and tiptoe to the door. I peer through the crack to see. I jump. A figure there, still and dark on the landing.

I pull open the door, spilling out light. Fran, looking at me, her eyes sleepy, blinks. Her hair's loose round her shoulders and her feet bare. With her pale skin, she looks timeless, a phantom from another age. We stare at each other, both too shocked to speak.

"What are you doing?" She looks past me to her father's study.

I move to close the door a little more, to narrow the gap and stop her from seeing the mess strewn across the floor behind me.

"What are you doing out of bed? It's late." My voice is sharpened by guilt and embarrassment.

She shrugs. "I needed the toilet."

She moves on past me to the bathroom. I hastily tidy away the photographs, the folders, the box files, wondering how much she's seen. If she has her own pictures of her parents' wedding day. If she'll tell Craig what I've done.

Downstairs, I pour another glass of wine and take the chain off the door again, ready for his return. I feel stupid and no more reassured than I was before. What did I expect to find anyway? Hotel and lunch receipts? If he is having an affair, he'd have more sense than to keep them.

Upstairs, Fran's bedroom door closes with a bang. I imagine myself through her eyes and feel hot with shame. I've no right to snoop on Craig, on her father. It's beneath me. Somehow, I need to find a way of trusting him and to stop torturing myself, or I'll go mad.

Craig finally walks in after nine, looking tired. I don't ask questions, just make him a cup of tea and a sandwich. He seems relieved. We sit for a while, side by side, on the settee, watching the news. *Nothing wrong with this*, I think. Every couple needs quiet time. It can't be champagne and roses all the way. That's not real. But when he heaves himself up, announces he needs an early night, no hint of romance in his eye, it hurts. I follow him up.

He's in our en suite bathroom when his phone flashes. I'm there in a second, while the screen is still bright. A stark message. No pleasantries. Two people who are clearly already in touch. Already seeing each other.

Call me. Soon. Lorraine.

I switch off my light, pull the bedcovers high to cover much of my face, and curl away from the center of the bed, on my side. I'm shaking. As soon as the bathroom door opens, I close my eyes and keep them closed, following his movements by sound. His heavy tread round the room, the opening and closing of the wardrobe door, of a drawer.

The bed rocks and bounces as he climbs in beside me.

He leans over me. His breath smells of gin, cut through with minty toothpaste.

"Work OK?"

I don't answer.

He switches off his light and settles beside me. I open my mouth to say: *You had a text.* Then close it again. Let her wait.

Within minutes, he's asleep. I lie awake beside him for a long time, listening to his thick breathing and the rumble of passing cars on the road outside, trying to imagine Lorraine.

CHAPTER FOURTEEN

ANGIE

The following week, the rain holds off and Jessica and I make the most of the weather, packing a picnic and going out onto the common.

I lead her down the steep path from the road and onto the open grass, picking my way toward the southern flank. The common has shrunk a bit since I was a girl but not much, and I know it like the back of my hand. I never met a child yet who didn't like roaming there, and I keep them safe. I know where the roads suddenly cross it, which rocks are good for climbing and which too steep.

The north end runs to marsh after rain. Filthy and treacherous. At the south end, a stream surfaces from under the earth and runs out into the open between the bushes for a while before disappearing into a culvert that takes it deep underground, heading for the housing estate on the edge of the common and, beyond it, to the river.

I'm being Jessica's pet today. She's desperate for a dog to train and I'm the next best thing. I don't mind. If you can't have a bit of fun with a little girl, what kind of person are you? She's happy, that's the important thing.

"Fetch, doggy. Go fetch."

She picked up a stick and keeps throwing it for me to scamper after and retrieve, shouting encouragement. Funny kid. I run after it, woofing and barking like a mad woman, my hands raised like front paws, and when I come back and drop the stick at her feet, she pats my head, strokes my imaginary floppy ears, and her eyes shine with pleasure.

"Good doggy! Good girl!"

Make-believe is so real to a child. I'm a stout woman who's nearly sixty, for heaven's sake. She knows I'm not a dog and yet, when she pats my hair and says: "Good doggy! Well done!" and I do my bit, pretending to nuzzle her and pant, she really sees a dog too, her own warm-coated, bright-eyed dog that she loves.

We play around like that all the way to the rocks. Then we scramble. The last time I was here was with Harry and it was hot and the grass was withered and the air buzzing with flies. Now the weather's turned cool and the grass is slippery underfoot. The heather blazes with purple flowers.

"Who are you now?" The game changes all the time: she likes variety.

She considers. "Baby bear."

I nod. "Is your mummy Lily the bear?"

She looks pleased. "Yes. She's a kind bear. She has magic powers. My name's Lulu."

"Come on, Lulu. Let's go into our cave."

We hold hands to steady ourselves as we climb across the rocks. There's a cleft on the far side and a boulder has fallen across the top and it makes a good hiding place. Harry and I played dens in there when the sun blazed. Now it's more about sheltering from the breeze and the first spit of rain.

I cover the earth floor with my waterproof trousers and we sit side by side in there, knees pulled up, wriggling around to get comfortable on the stony earth. There's a sour smell under the rocks as if an animal, a fox maybe, has been sheltering there too, but Jessica doesn't seem to notice. I tell her a story about Lily the bear and we play at being cubs for a while, then get out our sandwiches and have bear lunch.

Afterward, we have a game of hide-and-seek, centered mostly on hiding behind the same bush, time after time. Then we climb down to the stream and I show Jessica how to gather stones and build a small dam to stem the flow on one side and divert the river to the other. She takes it very seriously, her face tight with concentration and effort as she digs out rocks that she can barely lift and drops them with a crash in the water.

It's clouded over again. The wind picks up, whipping low and cool over the grass. I give her a five-minute warning to leave. It's partly my fault—I think the warning stresses her because she still has so much to do on the dam and tries to hurry, her hands busy with the rock she's carrying, and a moment later she slips and crashes into the water. It isn't deep, only a few inches, but cold, and because she hangs on to her stone, instead of putting out her hands to save herself, she pitches backward, flat onto her back.

She screams out at once. She isn't hurt, just shocked and suddenly soaked down the seat of her trousers, the back of her coat—even her vest is wet where the water splashed up. For a moment, neither of us moves. Then I jump forward and lift her up onto her feet. The back of her clothes are heavy and sodden.

"Oh, dear." I'm calm on the outside as I draw her to me in a hug. She's crying now and buries her face in my coat. Inside I'm already calculating what spare clothes I've brought with me, how long it'll take us to get back. "You're all right."

"I'm all wet." She tugs at her trousers. "Get them off."

The water's freezing and she starts to shiver as she presses against me. I lift her up and carry her back to our cave, strip off her shoes, wet socks, and trousers and rub her down.

She's trembling with cold and upset, saying: "I'm cold. I don't like it. I'm freezing."

I rummage in my rucksack for spare clothes and start to get her dressed. She's still crying but quietly now, starting to recover.

"It was an accident."

"Of course it was." I kiss the top of her head as I bundle her into her dry trousers. "You'll soon be nice and warm again."

A thought seems to strike her and she looks panicked. "Don't tell Mummy, will you?"

"Why not? She won't be too cross, will she?"

She paws at me, her face suddenly stricken. "Please. Promise me you won't tell."

I kiss the tip of her nose. She seems so anxious and it worries me. No child should be afraid of her mum. It was only an accident, after all.

"Of course not. It's all right, petal. I promise."

She's calmer now and starting to warm up again. I give her a biscuit to munch and feel under her coat to see if anything else is wet. Her vest and top are soaking along the bottom. I open my bag again and bring out dry ones.

"Here we go." I work quickly, trying to get wet clothes off before the poor kiddie freezes. "Arms up."

I stuff the wet clothes in a plastic bag and pull the dry ones over her head. I hold the material away from her body so she can find the sleeves and push her hands into them. Suddenly, I stop and stare.

"What?" She squirms, her flesh shrinking in the cold. "Come on!"

"Jessica!" Her side, at the back of her ribs, is black with bruising. A central mark about the size of a fist and several smaller ones above it. Deep, fresh bruises. "What happened?"

She hunches her shoulders and says in a small voice: "Nothing."

"Did you have a fall?"

"No. Stop it." She flails her arms, trying to get her hands into the sleeves and cover it up.

"Did someone hurt you, Jessica?"

"Stop asking. It's a secret."

"A secret?"

She feels my change in mood and twists round, puts out a hand, and pats my hair. "Good doggy. Good girl." A three-year-old's way of changing the subject.

I don't answer. I'm no longer in the mood to play, not just at that moment. I pull the vest and top down around her body and help her back on with her coat. She shivers and I lift her onto my knee, wrap the sides of my own coat around her, and cuddle her to get her warm. She puts her face into my neck and I feel her short, warm breaths on my skin, feel the tiny cage of bones expand and contract as her ribs heave.

"You know, Jessica, nobody has the right to hurt you. Nobody. Not ever. You know that, don't you?"

"Stop."

When I try to lift her head so I can look her in the eye, she fights back and keeps it pressed against me. I tighten my arms around her and rock her on my lap.

"You can always talk to me, Jessica." I whisper into her ear. "Whatever it is. You can trust me. You know that, don't you? I'm good at keeping secrets."

She won't answer. She lets me hold her a little longer, then pushes away, climbs down, and starts to run back along the path, leaving me to pack away the bag of wet clothes and chase after her, thinking—as I watch her bobbing head, her small fragile body—how much she reminds me of Susie and wondering what or who caused her to bruise so horribly.

The worry stays with me. I find myself thinking about her late into the night as I sit in my chair, soft with wine, watching the streaks of lights from car headlights stream across the side of the window, bouncing in from the road. I feel as if it's my mission to keep watch over her, to listen for suspicious cries leaking through the walls from next door.

Even more than before, I strain to read their comings and goings in their sounds. His car engine as he parks outside. The keys and slam of the front door. Later, an occasional bang of an inner door, the low rumble of television. Nothing out of the ordinary. No screams or cries. No slams and stamps. Just quietness.

They bother me, those bruises. Not just the sight of them, although that's bad enough. But the fact she won't talk about them, that she's so secretive.

No one has the right to hurt a kiddie. No one. It makes me angry just to think of it. It's bullying, pure and simple, a big strong adult touching a little kiddie. If anyone had laid a hand on my Susie, I can't think what I'd have done to them. I wouldn't have cared what they did to me afterward. Anything to keep her safe.

And if little Jessica needs someone to protect her, I'll do that, too. I'll do whatever it takes.

CHAPTER FIFTEEN

The following Thursday, Teresa warns me that I might be babysitting even later than usual. Craig's going out to some sales meeting and isn't expected back until late. She has some staff meeting on top of the usual stock take. Would I mind very much?

Jessica seems a bit under the weather that evening, as if she's worrying or sickening for something. I cook the girls sausages and beans and potato waffles—usually their favorite tea—but Jessica just plays about with it, sitting miserably on her chair. In the end, I dose her with kiddie paracetamol and take her up to bed.

I find myself looking her over in the bath. Those bruises are fading fast—they do when you're a kiddie—and there's no sign of fresh ones. I almost ask her again about how she got them but I manage to stop myself and we tell stories instead.

Once she's dry and cozy in her red fleecy pajamas, we follow our usual routine. I lie squashed beside her on her little bed and thread my arm around her and we read a few stories until she's ready to sleep. I'm happy then, lying in the warm, feeling her snuggled up to me, inhaling her soapy, clean smell. Knowing she's safe and warm and that she trusts me, that she's let me in and loves me completely as only a small child can.

She's a fool, that mother of hers, running after her job when she could be here, cuddling her little girl. She doesn't know how lucky she is. This is a day, an evening, she'll never get back again, and by the time she realizes, Jessica will be older and busier and ready to push her away. I've seen it a hundred times before. And then, when these self-important parents get old and retire and suddenly find themselves with long days to fill, they wonder why their busy children don't have time for them. *You reap what you sow*, that's what my mother always used to say, and she was right.

I spend time tucking in Rabbit beside her and sit there for a while after I've turned out the light. Rabbit doesn't like the dark so we agree to leave the landing light on and the door open for her, even though Jessica's mum likes it closed. She isn't here, is she? She'll never know.

Fran comes downstairs for tea and teacakes as soon as I call her. I've brought my own butter this time. She seems almost cheerful as she kicks off her slippers and tucks her feet up under her, reaches for a buttered teacake. She's nearly ready for bed and looks young again in dressing gown and slippers.

I pour the tea and sit quietly. I'm happy to respect our rules and leave Fran alone in this house too, if it helps.

She starts almost at once, as if she's been holding it in. "I'm going to have Christmas with Mum."

"Are you?" I try to keep my expression neutral. I know now what she's like. If I put a foot wrong, she'll clam up again.

"Well, I've asked Mum if I can. I don't see why not." Her tone is defensive. "I'm old enough to have a say, aren't I?"

"Right." I pass her a teacup and settle back with my own. She isn't really telling me: she's unsure of her ground and is fishing for my opinion. I sense the tension and I'm not sure how to respond.

"It's still a way off, isn't it?" I say.

It's only October but it's no wonder she's thinking about it. The shops are already full of Christmas trees and tinsel.

"The old couple, the ones who own the flat, they're going to their daughter's place in Edinburgh. My mum told me on the phone. She can't stay there all on her own, can she? She might as well come here."

I don't answer but just busy myself with biting into a teacake. "Have you talked to your dad about it?"

She frowns. "Not yet." She pauses and I sense her anxiety. "Why? Do you think he'd say no?"

I shrug. "It might be more complicated that you think, that's all. What about Jessica and her mum? Don't you think they might want Christmas all together, here?"

"Jessica's only three. She doesn't know." She blows out her cheeks. "Anyway, I'll make it up to her."

I don't say anything. Not a sound from upstairs. Jessica's gone down quickly again. My Susie to a T.

"It's not a lot to ask. To be with your own mum for Christmas. Is it?" The fierceness is back in her face.

I feel sad for her. "Your mum must really miss you, Fran. But it sounds as if she's got a lot on at the moment. She may have a lot of studying to do. Hasn't she got exams?"

"She can study with me. I don't mind." She shrugs. "I'll help out with the dishes and everything."

She slurps her tea. Her mood has shifted, from nervous excitement to hostility. I'm only trying to help, to smooth the way a bit, but I've annoyed her. Perhaps I should just have agreed and said it would be marvelous, Christmas all together. I just have a bad feeling about it.

She unfolds her legs and gets up abruptly. "I'll be in my room. You needn't come up. I don't need putting to bed."

I don't rise to the bait, just smile. She's pushing her feet back into her slippers when I say, "Fran, can I ask you something? Just between you and me?"

She stops and looks up.

"It's about Jessica."

Her eyes narrow.

"She's got some nasty bruises, down here." I run my hand

down my side. "They look really sore. You don't know how she got them, do you?"

She turns her attention back to her slippers. "She's always banging into things," she says. "Teresa says she bruises like a peach."

A moment later, she's gone.

I sit quietly in the empty room, looking across the pristine furniture with its swaths of white and chrome, and feel anxiety flutter in my stomach. I don't exactly understand it, I just feel it. It's about little Jessica and her parents and her life here. Fran's sudden blush, the one she tried to hide by bending forward over her feet, has only made it worse.

I wait there, following Fran's movements by sound. Up both flights of stairs. Into her bedroom. The distant bang of the door. I finish my tea and turn the pages of a hair magazine, one of those thick, glossy ones with ridiculous styles, the sort they hand you when you're under the dryer. At least there aren't any magazines about coffins.

Upstairs, Fran emerges from her room and goes down to the bathroom. Nine o'clock. The shower drums for a few minutes, then she goes back to her room. At nine thirty, I creep up to the top of the house. Silence. No light showing under Fran's door. I daren't risk knocking.

Next to it, the door to Jessica's little room is still open. I tiptoe in. She's lying on her side, her mouth slightly open, her hair spilling across the pillow. Rabbit's fallen out onto the floor and I pick her up and tuck her back in bed at Jessica's side. I bend down to kiss her hair and hover there for a second, breathing in her warm, sweet scent.

"Love you, sweetheart. Sleep tight."

I used to whisper the same to Susie, every night, when I went in to check on her. A long time ago now, but there are some things you never forget.

I close her door and start to head back downstairs when I

hear a noise. I stop, hand on the banister, and listen. It's coming from the main bedroom, at the front of the house, on the first floor. An intermittent banging, as if something loose is being buffeted by the wind.

I creep to the closed door, my heart beating hard. The layout of the house is similar to mine but they've clearly spent money up here too. I've only got two bedrooms, mine and the spare, on the second floor. The top of my house is just a bare-boarded attic, cold and drafty and full of all the old suitcases and oddments from my mother's day, and bits of junk. But they've extended into the roof to create the girls' bedrooms and done it properly, sealing it off from the eaves with wooden panels and proper insulation and putting in carpeted stairs, rather than my poky trapdoor and ladder.

I've already had a good look up there, putting Jessica to bed. But I am intrigued to see what they've done to the middle floor. I creep to the bedroom door and hesitate for a moment, stiff with embarrassment. My blood thuds in my ears. Silence. I wait a little longer and then turn the handle and creep in.

The door opens into a large bedroom, freshly painted in cream, with a spotless cream carpet. I slip off my shoes and my stockinged feet sink into deep pile. The room is dominated by a king-sized bed. The duvet, red with a cream stripe, is tousled and hangs off at one side. The pillows are scattered along the top, pillowcases a crisp cream cotton with matching red trim. I plump them up and straighten the covers. I wasn't brought up to walk past an unmade bed.

I stand for a moment and breathe raggedly as I stare around, tracing the architecture. Down the far wall there are built-in wardrobes and cupboards. On the other side, where their house joins mine, they've blocked off the alcove and turned it into a small adjoining room with its own glass-paneled door. I think of my own damp-stained bedroom on the other side of the wall, cold and bare, and feel a moment's self-pity and, rising behind it, jealousy. *Beware the green-eyed monster*, my mum used to say. I swallow it down.

It's all so clean and luxurious. Heaven knows what it all cost. I think again of Jessica's bedroom, where everything is brand-new and matches, as if someone just walked into a show bedroom in a big store, flashed a credit card, and said: *Yes, please, I'll take the lot.*

Bang. I jump. The wind blows again and the sudden hammering is close now. I pad across the carpet and follow it to the glass-paneled door. Inside, there's a shiny white-and-chrome bathroom with splashes of red in the tiling that pick up the color in the bedroom. Thick red towels. A red bathmat. A red wicker linen basket. They've installed one of those posh showers with no sides that must spray water everywhere. The toilet is hidden discreetly behind a glass half-wall. And there, at last, over the toilet, I find the banging window. I reach across and pull it properly shut, securing the latch.

I should go straight back out of their room and downstairs, of course. That's the polite thing to do. But I don't. I'm too stirred up. I'm thinking of my own bathroom with its cracked cork floor and dim lighting and the same worn towels I've had for years. *A sorry specimen.* That's what my mother used to say about the widow who lived down the road who had no one but a cat for company and smelled sour. Is that what people say about me?

I'm cross. That's part of it. Cross that they have so much and their lives look so easy when mine, right there on the other side of the wall, is sad and hard. And I'm cross too that they have little Jessica, such a precious little girl, and Fran too, and they've left me to look after them all evening when they should be here, acting like proper parents. I don't like them and I don't trust them. Something's wrong in this family. They're not taking proper care of those two girls.

I go back into the bedroom, feet disappearing in all that

marshmallow softness, and stand there, not touching anything, just looking.

They have matching bedside cabinets, shiny and new, each with a set of small drawers. It's clear from the hand cream and emery board and pink clock radio which side is hers. I steal forward and find my hand on the handle of the top drawer. I hesitate, listening. I know it's wrong, but I can't stop myself. I can't explain it, but I feel she owes me something. She's out and I'm the one in charge, taking care of the children. Somehow it seems fair game to pry a little. *Just a peep*, I think. That's all.

I slide open the top drawer and look at the clutter inside. A mess of pens, elastic bands, bookmarks, old receipts. I poke around with an extended finger. Toward the back, pushed slightly out of sight, is a black notebook with "No Peeking!" printed in shiny pink lettering on the cover.

I open it up, hands shaking. The first few pages are covered with lists of passwords and security numbers. A stupid place to keep them. If I've gone straight to it, so would any decent burglar. After that, the book's filled with cramped handwriting. I tip it toward the light, trying to read. It isn't exactly a diary, more a notebook where she seems to pour out thoughts every now and then. Poor spelling and punctuation. Most of it's a poorly coded account of her relationship with Craig—I make that out at once. It all starts about eighteen months ago.

Met C for lunch at Beckwith's. Such a gentleman. Made a point of being early so I wouldn't wait. Table at the back, hidden away in the corner. Lobster and Sauvignon—he remembered! Talked nonstop about everything: work, girls. My place afterward until 4. Ben looked cross when I walked in late but Anthea covered. C already emailing, begging for next meet. Insatiable! Told him I need sleep!

I flick through. The tone is smug. I purse my lips. All this schoolgirl excitement as she fancies herself in love. The confessions about her feelings, about their eagerness to be together. I think about Fran and her mum and wonder where they fit into all this. Judging by the snatched meetings, the secrecy surrounding it all, I get the sense they were very much still on the scene and didn't even know. In the spring, she writes pages about their first weekend together, in Paris. *He's told his wife he's at a sales conference*, she says. As if lying and deception were something to joke about.

I think about little Jessica. In the diary, Teresa seems obsessed with her new lover, with herself, and there's hardly a mention of her little girl. I shake my head.

I sit for a moment, the diary in my hands, thinking what fools people are. Sex is all very well—I had my moments, when I was young—but I never understood why mature adults ruin their lives because of it. It seems to do something funny to their brains. All those power games and lies. They start confusing a moment's physical pleasure with real happiness. I've seen it time and again. People messing up their lives for the sake of a roll in the hay. They never stop to think about the children.

I wonder sometimes if that's why I get on so well with little ones. Most of the time, they know the difference between right and wrong and they tell the truth. They say what they mean. That's what I find, anyway. Lying is something they learn later, from grown-ups, like tying shoelaces and telling the time, but far less useful.

I push the notebook back in its drawer and get up to leave. I've never warmed to that woman and nothing I've found here makes me feel any differently. My mother used to say that you can tell a great deal about a woman from the house she keeps. I look around now at the unmade bed, the messy drawers. She's more interested in taking care of herself than tending to her home. Or those kiddies.

I walk around the room, inspecting it more closely. I stoop to run my fingers along the skirting board and they come away black. There's a light deposit of dust on the dressing table—that surface hasn't seen a cloth for two or three weeks. My house might be shabby but at least I put a duster round. There's no need for it, for slovenliness. No woman is so busy she can't take care of her own home.

The corner of the carpet against the far wall is raised and lumpy and I bend down to fix it, to press it properly back into place. The corner comes up easily in my hand. The backing is loose. But when I try to force it down, to neaten off the line, it doesn't fit back as it should.

I lower myself to my knees to look more closely. These are new carpets. They should get the fitters back if they haven't done their job properly. No excuse for it.

The floorboards underneath look brand-new and recently sanded. Very different from my splintering floors next door. The surface of the wood feels smooth under my fingertips but the end of this one panel isn't flush with the others: it's slightly raised. That's what made the carpet corner so lumpy.

I feel for it, hoping to nudge it back into place, and my finger-tips slip into a natural groove at the far end. The wood lifts easily under my fingers, revealing a small hollow beneath. A hiding place.

I look around, heart thumping, imagining someone at the door. No one. The house is silent.

I lift the wood away and feel underneath. My fingers touch paper and I prize out a buff envelope. I sit down heavily on the carpet and open it.

The papers inside look freshly printed. A life insurance policy for Teresa and one for Craig, clipped together. They're dated just a month ago. And, tucked under them, another set of documents. I open them out and look them over, then start as I realize what I'm reading.

A family funeral plan. Just looking at it gives me the shivers. I'm not one for wordy documents but I'm no fool and I can read the names as clear as day. All four of them are listed: Craig, Teresa, Francesca, and little Jessica.

The papers tremble in my hands. What kind of parent plans their own child's funeral? Imagines the death of a sweet little girl who's only three? How could they? I can almost see her tiny body, lifeless and cold, packed inside a coffin. They'd have to screw down the lid and she'd hate that so much—she's scared of the dark, that kiddie. She'd need Rabbit in there too, tucked at her side. They'd never remember but I'd make sure of it.

For a moment, I can't breathe. It's sick, the whole idea of it, the very thought of lowering her into the clay. That kid's got her whole life ahead of her. Why are they thinking about such a thing, about her funeral? I put a hand to my face and wipe my eyes. And why've they hidden away the papers like this, like a big dirty secret?

I put everything back as carefully as I can, my fingers shaking.

Upstairs, the girls' landing creaks as I creep out of the bedroom. Fran's door opens. She must have been awake, listening. She leans over the banisters to see me.

"What're you doing?"

I say, stupidly, "Nothing." Then, after a pause: "Shouldn't you be asleep?"

She gives me a strange look. My heart pounds and my face feels flushed. I wonder if she can see, in the low light, that my eyes are bright and probably red too.

Fran says, "Were you in their bedroom?"

I say, "The window was banging." It sounds lame, even to me. "In their bathroom. I popped up to close it. That's all."

She doesn't reply but her face is strained with suspicion. She looks like a little waif, standing there in bare feet, her thin, childlike body in a voluminous cream nightshirt that reaches to her knees. A pink flamingo stands on one leg across her stomach. Her calves and feet look white and bony.

I gesture back toward her room.

"Don't catch cold. It's late. Your mum'll be home soon."

"She's not my mum."

"You know who I mean."

We hesitate. She wants to tell me something—I see it in her eyes, but she stops herself. Her forehead is tight and troubled. Then she says: "She can't stop me, anyway. It's not up to her."

I take a moment to catch up. She's still thinking about Christmas and being with her mum. That's what matters to her, not whether I was spying on Teresa. I mount the stairs and put my hand lightly on her shoulder. The bone feels sharp, protruding under her nightshirt.

"Talk to your mum about it. Tell her how much it means to you. I'm sure she'll sort it out with your dad if she can."

I bend forward and kiss the top of her spiky hair. She doesn't move a muscle.

"Now in you go, off to bed. Don't get me into trouble."

She disappears without another word.

Downstairs, I make a fresh pot of tea, just for something to do, and sit in front of the telly to wait for Teresa to come home.

There's a daft program on about a middle-aged couple looking for a move to France now their children have grown up and left. There's tension between them, you can tell that just by watching. They're being good sports for the cameras but she keeps telling him she wants a bit of garden and some modern comforts and all he wants is a drafty old barn with a garage for his vintage car. Maybe he's already meeting someone else for long lunches. Maybe that's why she wants them to leave the country.

It washes over me but I can't concentrate. I keep thinking about little Jessica, asleep upstairs. I'm frightened for her and I don't know what I can do to keep her safe.

CHAPTER SIXTEEN

TERESA

My head aches. I wake up in the morning and it's no better. I feel trapped. As if I'm drowning, kicking weakly against a tidal wave that is sweeping me along, dragging me under, into darkness.

It's one thing after another. This is the latest: I can't find my gold chain. One of my very favorites. It's a thick rope, eighteen carat and worth a lot, and, besides that, it means a lot to me. One of my first big presents from Craig, a surprise on my birthday.

He was trying to make it up to me at the time, I knew that, because I was having my birthday on my own with Jessica while he played happy families with Kate and Fran. It was before he told her. *It'll be the last time*, he promised me. He had fear in his eyes, scared I'd get fed up and walk.

Anyway, I love that chain and I turn the house upside down, looking for it. No one's seen it. Blank faces. Too blank. No one seems to remember what it even looked like.

At work, the atmosphere is poisonous. Everyone's tense.

It takes me a while to realize what's going on. I simply walk into the salon one morning and Helena, feisty in a low-cut top and pencil skirt, doesn't answer when I say good morning. She's with an early client and looks preoccupied, talking brightly to her as she cuts, so I don't make anything of it.

Later, I take a phone message for her, someone calling about her flatshare, and instead of saying thank you, she glares at me. Her anger is so venomous that I feel myself blush. I stutter and go through to the storeroom to avoid her, to calm down, thinking: *This is ridiculous, this is my salon. I can't hide from one of my employees.*

Later, I walk to the back of the salon, near the washbasins, to find Helena whispering in a corner with the new stylist, a thin girl sent by the agency, barely out of her teens. They break off abruptly as I approach.

At lunchtime, Helena plucks her coat off the rack and stalks out.

I buy a sandwich next door and eat it in the staff room with little appetite. Sophie gives me a sympathetic smile and I wonder what's being said behind my back, if everyone apart from me knows what's going on.

Lottie finds me. "Helena's one fifteen has arrived." She plucks at her fingertips as she talks, a nervous habit. "Are you OK to cover?"

I stare. "Cover?"

"I offered Sophie but she says she wants a senior. Cut and blow-dry."

I gesture to my half-eaten sandwich. "Where's Helena? Didn't she know she had a one-fifteen?"

Lottie looks embarrassed. "She's gone home sick." She shuffles. "Sorry. I thought you knew."

I push away my sandwich, cross. I spend the rest of the day picking up Helena's clients between my own. When Lottie tries to get Helena on the phone, there's no answer.

At closing time, I look over the appointments. No mistakes today. Helena has several clients booked in for tomorrow and I have no idea if she'll be here or not.

"Does anyone know what's the matter with Helena? Did she say?"

Sophie and Lottie don't look at me, suddenly absorbed in collecting their coats and getting ready to leave. Clearly, they know far more than they're letting on.

Helena sweeps in to work the next day with no apology. She ignores me again when I say good morning to her; just puts away her coat and sets up the chair for her first client with a stony face.

I stand beside her. "Are you feeling better?"

She doesn't answer.

"Helena?" I feel anger welling. "You went home sick yesterday. What's the matter?"

She faces me down, eyes hard and cold. "You have no business asking that," she says. "It's personal. I've got rights, you know."

I take a deep breath. I saw her as an ally, a friend. The hostile woman in front of me is another person entirely. Lottie stands silently behind us, setting up at reception, well within earshot.

"Of course you have rights. I understand that. I'd just appreciate it if you'd let me know if you're going home sick. That's all. I don't expect to find out from someone else."

She shoots back at once, eyes flashing: "And I'd appreciate it, actually, if you'd let me know before you lock the computer system. I'm the senior stylist here. And in case you've forgotten, I've been here for five years. I don't expect to find myself shut out when I try to add a booking."

We glare at each other. The tendons start out from her neck with strain and her lips, richly painted, are pursed with rage. I turn on my heel and walk off. I shut myself in the toilet for a few minutes until my hands have stopped shaking.

Later, Sophie brings me a cup of coffee and a cinnamon biscuit in the staff room. I'm auditing the new delivery but also hiding in there, trying to make sense of what's going on. She doesn't say a word, just puts the coffee on the box beside me and heads back to her work.

I sit quietly while I drink it. It's already five and in all the upset, I've missed the bank. I'm wary of leaving the day's takings in the empty salon overnight. I'll have to take the money home with me and go straight to the bank in the morning. I nibble on the biscuit. It's getting to me, all this. I'm usually so efficient. Now I'm starting to doubt myself.

I lick the crumbs from my fingers, drain the coffee cup. Only a few days have passed since I added the password protect and there hasn't been a single error since. Either Lottie knows she's being watched and is on best behavior... or Sophie was right and Helena was interfering, trying to sabotage me by going into the system and messing up appointments and pinning the blame on Lottie.

The door is half-open and noises drift in. Chat, hairdryers, the splash of running water from a basin, the low throb of constant music. I remember what Sophie said about Helena. That no one trusts her. That she was furious when they chose me as the new manager. And that she'd do anything to get ahead.

CHAPTER SEVENTEEN

That evening, I'm so pleased to see a friendly face, even if it is Angie's, that I let her drag me into her shabby house and agree to have a cup of tea. I politely remove my heels in the hallway, then become aware of stickiness underfoot and the rank smell of moldy carpeting and rather wish I hadn't.

I clear some room amongst an array of plastic toys and stuffed animals on the lumpy settee and sit to wait while Angie boils the kettle. It's chilly in the sitting room and I keep my coat on. The only source of heating in here is an ancient gas fire. It looks so antiquated I doubt it even works.

Fran is there in the kitchen, sitting in a sea of books at the table, doing her homework. She's wearing those ridiculous headphones—not allowed in our house; she can't possibly concentrate—and the thud of drums vibrates through the air.

Jessica sits beside her, her head bent forward. Her crayon squeaks as she colors. I have to admit, they look unusually peaceful together.

"Care for a biscuit?"

Angie sets down a tea tray, complete with teapot and cozy and a plate of misshapen chocolate biscuits. She nods at the plate as she pours into proper cups and saucers.

"Jessica made them this morning. She's a good little cook. Do try one."

I murmur a polite refusal and wonder how many Jessica has eaten. I don't keep sweets or biscuits in the house.

We sit together, teacup awkward in my hand. It's like visiting some eccentric elderly aunt. Late fifties, maybe. I run a professional eye over her hair. I'd love to get my hands on it. Bit of color, a proper cut.

"My Susie was always clever." Angie nods toward Fran and Jessica in the kitchen. "She could write her name at three. Knew all her numbers. I don't know where she gets it from. Her brains."

I didn't know how to answer that. Clearly not from her mother.

"What sort of work did your husband do?"

Angie looks away. "He was in the bank. You know, behind the scenes." Her eyes stray to the photograph of Susie as a child and her look is wistful. "They all worked in banks, his lot. His dad. His uncles. He was always trying to explain to me exactly what he did—something to do with currency—but I never did understand. I've not much of a head for figures."

"He sounds like Craig. He loves all that. If I get stuck with my accounts, I go to him." *When he's around to ask.*

Angie smiles and turns her head, bringing her attention back to me. "He tried to sell me a funeral."

"Oh." I shrink with embarrassment. "I'm so sorry. He does—"

"I didn't know where to put myself, to be honest. I felt like saying: I'm not done yet. Not quite."

She throws back her head and laughs and it's so unexpected and so warm that it catches me off-guard. Suddenly I have a vision of Craig, earnestly trying to flog floral tributes and eco-coffins and poor Angie, astonished and embarrassed, trying to escape him, and I start to laugh too and the sight of me laughing seems to allow her to let go and suddenly we're both at it. It's such a relief after the worry and tension of the last few days, and my teacup starts rattling in the saucer and Angie starts to hiccup and that sets me off again, like a schoolgirl, and a moment later, Jessica appears in front of us, looking from one laughing woman to the other, disgusted by us for not behaving ourselves, and the sight of her cross face makes it all even funnier.

"Oh, I haven't laughed like that—" Angie wipes her eyes with the back of her hand.

Then the hysteria disappears, as suddenly as it came, leaving us both exhausted and bewildered but better for it.

Jessica says: "What?"

Angie reaches out an arm to her but Jessica doesn't move. "Nothing, darling. Just Angie and Mummy being silly, that's all."

I drink off my tea and get up. "I should probably..."

"Yes, of course."

I leave them and go through to the kitchen to find Fran. It takes a while to persuade her to stop what she's doing and close her books and pack up. Behind me, Jessica tears up and down the hall, her coat flaps flying. I go back for my bag to find Angie sitting serenely in the sitting room, unaffected by the chaos exploding all around her, the mess of toys and games.

On the doorstep, I turn back and say: "Thank you, Angie. You are kind."

"It's not easy being a mum." She reaches out and pats me on the shoulder and it feels like a blessing. "They're great girls."

The fight starts as soon we're through the door. Fran heads upstairs to carry on with homework. Jessica sheds her coat on the hall floor, kicks off her shoes. One lands in the hall, the other in the doorway to the sitting room.

"Excuse me." I follow her into the sitting room, brandishing one of the discarded shoes. "What's this?"

No answer. She's got out a box of building blocks and tipped it upside down and is now rummaging through the pile of colored plastic spilling across the carpet. She's been home all of a minute and already my smart sitting room looks a mess.

"Hello?" I put the shoe right in front of her, where she's trying to play. "Put that in the hall, please. I'm not a maid."

She ignores me and carries on building.

"Jessica! Did you hear me?" My temper's rising. It's late and I'm tired and the longer she takes getting to bed, the longer it will be before I can do what I long to do: flop into a chair with a glass of cold juice, and eat something.

I take her by the shoulders and try to force her toward the hallway. She squirms.

"Bedtime. Now."

"Won't."

"I beg your pardon?" My voice is rising.

She mumbles.

"What did you say?"

A pause while she gathers her courage, then says: "You can't make me."

"We'll see about that." I fold my arms, take a deep breath, and shout at close range like a sergeant major: "One." My jaw is clenched. I'm really getting angry now, and she knows it. "Two." I count down each stroke with a chop from my arm. "Three."

She breaks down just as I reach the magic boundary of three, her face tight with fury, and pushes past me. I hear her rapid tread up the stairs as I call after her: "I'll be up in one minute and I want you undressed and in the bathroom."

I scoop up the bricks, clatter them back into the box, and shove the lid on top.

I run the bath in an empty bathroom. Steam rises, clouding the mirror. I shout up to her bedroom.

"Jessica! Now! If you're not here in two minutes, there'll be no bubbles."

Silence. In the end, I clomp up the stairs. Her bedroom's empty.

"Where are you?"

I look in the usual places: under the bed, behind the door. Sometimes she curls in a corner under a towel, as if it's a cloak of invisibility.

"Jessica. That's it." I'm *really* losing it now. Why is this so hard? My hands are shaking. "What's the matter with you?" I let go and my voice becomes a shout. It shocks me as much as it must her. "Come out *now*. I mean it." Nothing. Still. Nothing. "Right. That's it. *No* bubbles. *No* story."

The wardrobe door creaks open and she tumbles out. Her face is defiant. She makes to slip past me and run out again, as if all this is just a game. Something bursts inside me and I grab hold of her, start to yank off her clothes.

"Ow! You're hurting."

"It's your own fault." I'm beyond myself, worn ragged. My tone is defeated now, not angry. Just miserable. "What's the matter with you? Why can't you do what you're told for once?"

I lift her up, carry her down to the bathroom, and dump her in the water.

"No! It's too hot!"

"It is not." It's warm, no more. She's such a baby.

"It is. Stop it." She starts to scramble about in the water, making waves that slosh and slap at the sides. I hold her firmly and rub her down with the soapy sponge while she struggles and fights.

I've almost finished when she suddenly ducks her head and I feel a flare of pain. She's bitten my wrist.

"Ow!" I pull back my hand, shocked. A set of sharp, vixen teeth-marks in the flesh. "You little—" My hand flashes out and slaps her across the face before I know it.

The smack shatters the air in the bathroom, ricochets off shiny tiles and fittings. Afterward, a moment's silence, as if the air is as stunned as we are. I stare at her, unable to breathe.

Then she screams. "You hit me! You hit me!" She folds

forward into her knees and rocks there, a slight, shivering, naked child.

I reach down and pull out the plug, put my arms under her shoulders, trying to comfort her, then lift her out of the water onto the mat, wrap her in her towel, and carry her up to her room. She doesn't fight me, she just keeps screaming: "You hit me! You hit me!"

"Calm down." I feel a moment's panic. *How could I? I'm out of control. I'm a monster.* "You're all right."

Fran's door opens a crack as we pass and I sense her there, listening.

I shout over my shoulder: "Get on with your homework, Fran. She's fine."

My tone says: *Butt out and mind your own business.*

I shut Jessica's door behind us with my heel and collapse into the chair with her in my arms. She sobs into the towel. "You hurt me, Mummy. You did."

"I'm sorry. I am. I'm sorry." I try to hold her to me, to cuddle her and make it all right again, but she fights me, still furious.

"You shouldn't do that, Mummy. You're naughty!"

"Let me look." I prize away her hands to look at her cheek. She flails in a weak attempt to hit me but I hold her wrists. Her cheek is red but it's as much from the crying as the slap. I pull her closer and try to kiss it better. "You're fine."

"I am not."

I wrap the towel and my arms more tightly around her and rock her in my lap, back and forth.

"I'm sorry, Jess." My voice tumbles on, wretched. I'm so tired, so wrung out, I hardly know what I'm saying. "You bit me." I pause. "But I shouldn't have hit you. I know that. You're right."

She stays stiff in my arms, refusing to yield to me. I feel sick. I think of the way she sat at Angie's kitchen table, with her head bent quietly over her coloring, stray strands of hair falling forward as she worked. Peaceful. She must have loved making those lumpy chocolate biscuits today. Why doesn't she like being with me? Why does it always end in a fight? It's broken, this life we have together. It always has been. Maybe I'll never mend it.

"Why are you so naughty with me? Why?" I try to pull her round to look at me but she won't lift her head. Her eyes are red and puffy with crying. It breaks my heart. "You're not like this with her, are you? With Angie? Do you want to go and live with her, have her as a mummy? Is that what you want? Go if you like. If that's what you want."

"No, Mummy!" She shakes her head and sobs.

She softens against me at last and we cling miserably to each other, rocking, slowly coming down from our rage. I kiss her cheeks, her neck, smooth her hair.

"I love you so much, Jess. You know that, don't you?" I can hardly speak. "Beautiful girl."

Later, when we're both quiet again and she's in her pajamas, she turns to me before she gets into bed and hugs my legs.

"You're the best mummy in the world."

My breath catches in my throat. Why does she always say that? She must see it tears me apart. I turn away and say softly: "No, I'm not."

She looks stricken. "You are, Mummy! You are!"

"I'm a terrible mummy." I can't bear it, I can't just pretend everything's all right. I don't deserve that. I know I don't. I pull her to me and give her a fierce squeeze, then lift her into bed. "Off to sleep now, Jessica. It's late."

I tuck her up, kiss her on the forehead, and switch off the light as I leave.

Downstairs, my hand shakes as I pour myself a drink. Not juice after all, but white wine. I sink finally into a chair and gulp it down, feel the alcohol numb me. My shoulders sag. I lean forward, bury my face in my hands, and burst into tears.

CHAPTER EIGHTEEN

There's no sign of Craig and I eat without him. I'm just finishing when the landline rings. I sit and stare at it for a moment, hating it. When I finally answer, I don't speak at first, don't even say hello, just wait and listen, trying to unnerve the person at the other end.

A long pause. A woman says uncertainly: "Hello? Craig?"

It's the same careful voice as before. My stomach clenches. All I can think is that it must be Kate. Trying to cause trouble between us. To take revenge.

She says again: "Hello?"

"It's you, isn't it?"

Pause. "Is Craig there, please?"

I consider slamming the phone down but I want to know more. To keep her talking.

"What do you want?"

"It's personal."

"Why are you calling here? Try his mobile."

"I have. He isn't picking up." Her tone is firm but calm.

I hesitate, thrown, trying to find firm ground. There's a slight northern accent there, a trace. Not Kate's voice after all. And the steadiness. That doesn't sound like a vindictive ex-wife. I remember Craig's late-night text. "Is this ... Lorraine?"

She hesitates and I know I'm right. Finally, she says: "Please tell him to call me. He has my number."

I sit bolt upright. *How dare she?* "You keep away from him. You hear? Leave him alone."

The line goes dead and immediately I feel cheated, cross that she hung up on me when I wanted to be the one to be rude. I dial 1471 but, as before, the number is withheld.

I sit on my own, staring at the television, barely aware of the program, thinking about Craig and wondering who she is, this woman called Lorraine.

It's close to midnight by the time Craig comes home. This time I can't pretend to be asleep. I sit up in bed as soon as the front door slams, put the light on, and listen, wait. Clumsy footsteps clatter down the hall, into the kitchen. Silence. He must be in the downstairs toilet. Moments later, I catch the low hum of water vibrating through the pipes.

He comes heavily up the stairs. When he finally enters the bedroom, he starts as if he's forgotten that I live here too, as if he's surprised to find me in his bed.

His eyes are red and his cheeks are pale and flabby. The bed rocks as he sits on it, kicks off his shoes—they thud on the carpet. He lies down on top of the duvet, fully clothed, loosens his tie, and closes his eyes.

"What's going on?"

He doesn't answer. For a moment, he seems already asleep. I reach over, smell the stale fumes on his breath. Wine.

I pull at his shoulder and say something I swore I'd never say: "Where have you been?"

I've gone from sexy mistress to nagging wife in just a year. It hurts.

He sighs but doesn't answer.

"Lorraine called. Who is she? Don't say you don't know."

"Work." He sounds as if he's already sinking backward into sleep, out of my reach. "She's trying to flog me stuff. You know, urns or something."

I shake my head. "In the evening? At home? Come off it."

He rolls away from me onto his side and his breathing thickens.

I get up and go across the room to our bathroom. The tiles are cold. The face in the mirror is drawn and my eyes glassy. I feel dead with defeat and wretched, utterly wretched. I thought I knew Craig. I thought he really loved me. What if Kate was right all along and he's already cheating on me, the same way he cheated on her?

My mouth trembles and I bury my face in a towel and let the tears come, shaking as I sob. It had felt like a new chance. Meeting Craig. Starting again, in a new house. A chance to set things right. To be successful. To be happy. To be a real family. To show Jessica what a good mum I could be, if I really tried. To make her like me, before it was too late.

Later, I blow my nose, wipe off my blotchy face, and sink into the corner, my arms wrapped around my knees. I stay there until I'm stiff and shivering. I can't do this. I just can't. Work. Jessica. Craig.

What a mess I've made of everything. What a total bloody mess.

CHAPTER NINETEEN

It isn't the usual bank teller: it's a young lad, a new joiner. A supervisor stands at his shoulder, showing him what to do, answering queries. I'm already late for the salon and tired after a poor night's sleep. They should train staff in their own time, not ours.

He takes forever counting the takings.

"Six hundred and seventy-four pounds and fifty pence."

"It must be more than that." I tut. "It's always around a thousand."

Most people pay by card but we still get a percentage of cash customers, especially the walk-ins and those who come just for product. And most people who tip use cash.

The tops of the lad's ears turn red. The supervisor says something quietly to him and he turns over the pile and counts again, even more slowly this time. The supervisor's eyes are close on his hands as she silently tallies it up, too.

"Six hundred and seventy-four pounds and fifty pence."

He types it into the computer and starts to file away the notes in his drawer.

"Hang on." I strain forward to see through the glass. "You've missed some. Honestly."

The supervisor leans over him to speak through the holes in the glass. "That is the total." Her voice is firm, brooking no nonsense. "Perhaps there's more in your bag?"

I feel round the zipped pocket of my bag where I'd stashed

the money. Nothing. I pull open the main part and rummage there too, even though I'm sure that's pointless.

"We can always add it in," the supervisor says. "If you find more."

The lad, his whole face flushed now, sensing my anger, hands me the printed receipt.

"Anything else I can do for you today?"

He sounds like a bloody robot. I take the receipt with bad grace and walk out, frowning.

Back at the salon, I spend twenty minutes I can't spare looking over the previous day's appointments and totting up the accounts and card receipts. I'm right. We're about £300 short. I sit in silence in the storeroom, thinking. Rudeness and going off sick is one thing; surely no one here would steal from the till...would they?

It gnaws at me all morning. I can hardly look the staff in the eye. Every time Lottie takes cash from a client, I find my eyes straying to the till, to check it's all going in. When Sophie goes behind the counter to get a brush, I follow every movement. And Helena, when she finally arrives, barely speaks to me. The atmosphere is more strained than ever.

At lunchtime, I run home. I want to check through the pockets of the coat and jacket I wore the day before, just to satisfy myself that I hadn't, in some fit of craziness, bundled cash into them.

I'm in the bedroom when I hear rapid clicking footsteps and the clunk of the letter box, the light smack of something dropping onto the mat. The clicks hurry back down the path and away. The hair prickles along my scalp and I stop, trying to work out why it bothers me. It is odd. Too late for the postman. We get loads of flyers and adverts through the door but they're never delivered by a woman in heels who dashes away down the road afterward.

I run downstairs. A red envelope, handwritten. *Craig. Personal.* That's it.

I tear it open. There's a single sheet inside, handwritten in green ink.

My love, I miss you. I love you. I long for you. Call me. Soon. X

I stare at it. The scrawl is confident, sloping to the right. Bold. A flamboyant loop around each letter "l." A woman would have to be very sure of herself, of him, to write a love note like this and deliver it to his house. Doesn't she know he's living with someone? Did she want me to find it, to find out about them? I sniff the paper. A strange scent.

I fold the note in half and rip it across, then again. Almost at once, I'm cross with myself. I should think, be smart. This is evidence, I'm just not sure of what.

I gather together the pieces and take them up to our bedroom, shove them inside an ancient address book in my bedside table drawer. The bed is cold and crumpled. I sit for a moment on the sheet and pull the duvet around me, hugging it for comfort. It smells of him. Of his aftershave and skin and sweat. I used to think it the most intoxicating, sexy smell in the world. I scrunch up my eyes, bite my lip, and try to breathe.

I was so excited the first time Craig brought me to see this house. We christened it by making love in this room, rolling around on the floorboards, crazy with passion, feeding off each other. *Our love nest.* That's what he called this room. *Our hideaway.*

Later, I'm just locking up downstairs, heading back to the salon, when Angie opens the door on the other side of the railings and she and Jess step out, buttoned into their coats. Angie carries a shabby rucksack on her back.

"Hello, hello!" She's all smiles on the surface but there's awkwardness too. "Look, Jessica, Mummy! What a surprise!"

I can't answer. I find myself looking at the two of them, standing there hand in hand, and for an instant I feel I barely know Jessica, as if she belongs next door in a different family, instead of here with me. She seems to inhabit a world so distant that I barely qualify as a visitor there.

Jessica and I catch each other's eye. She looks away. My eyes stray to her cheek and I realize I'm checking, without even thinking about it, to see if the slap I gave her yesterday has left a mark. I wonder what she tells Angie about me, what she says about her life with me.

"Won't keep you." Angie has finished locking up now and turns to lead Jess down the path.

Jessica calls back over her shoulder, beaming. "We're going shopping, Mummy. Angie needs stuff. And I'm getting new toys!"

Angie shushes her at once and bundles her out through the gate and away, even as Jessica strains to turn back to wave.

I stand for a moment, watching as they disappear down the street. Angie scurries away, her head low, and Jessica, clasping her hand, skips and hops at her side.

For a moment, I can't breathe. I stand there, in sudden shock. The hairs prick on the back of my neck. I think of the shabby furnishings next door and the peeling paint. Of the ancient appliances and the chill, worsening now that the days are getting colder. I think of the paltry amount I give Angie for looking after the girls.

Why does she suddenly have money in her pocket to spend on herself, to buy toys?

It stays with me during the afternoon, that sense of unease. I stop and stare blindly at my client's face in the mirror, her hair pasted with color and shiny with strips of foil, and all I can see is Angie's embarrassment as she caught sight of me on the path and her rush to get away as fast as she could.

Why was she so awkward about bumping into me? What's both-ering her? I can't stop thinking about it. Even as I brush on color and tuck foil into pleats—brush and tuck, brush and tuck—in my head, it gnaws at me. *Was she the one who took the cash?* I start rushing ahead of myself, piecing together in my head what might have happened. She had an opportunity. She did. I left my bag, stoked with bundles of cash from the salon, unattended by my chair in Angie's sitting room last night while I pressed Fran to stop working and put away her books and please come home, it's late.

Angie didn't come to help me. She wasn't with Jessica, either. Jessica was running wild in the hall.

Angie was still sitting right there, all alone, within easy reach of my bag, when Fran finally packed up her homework and agreed to move.

I fix my eyes on the hair and my fingers work on, but my mind is elsewhere. Did she really think a handful of twenty-pound notes mightn't be missed? With a lurch, I think of my missing gold necklace. It was worth a lot. I blink, remember-ing. She was babysitting in the house just the day before it dis-appeared. There too, she had every opportunity to rifle through my jewelry, to help herself.

I finish off the foils and hand the client a stack of magazines, then go into the back room to be alone for a moment. My hands are shaking. I think of bovine Angie, so motherly, so cheery, so eager to take on the girls and it hits me, with a sick sense of dread, that really, I know nothing about her at all.

CHAPTER TWENTY

ANGIE

The next week, Jessica comes to me as usual during the day and Fran after school, but when Wednesday arrives, Teresa says she doesn't think it's really worked, the three of us going next door on Thursday evenings, and perhaps it would be better for the girls to stay here after all, at my place, if that's OK.

She has an odd look on her face and her gaze falls not on me but off to the right, somewhere on the door frame. I have to breathe carefully and think about snow to stop myself from blushing. Something's wrong. I see it in the tightness of her jaw. She knows. My legs tremble beneath me and I can't answer. I just turn away and hide my face as I organize the girls and shrug them into their coats and send them out to her. No question of her coming inside. I don't even ask. I close the door on them all and lean against it, catching my breath. My chest aches and I stop and force myself to wait it out, to focus. *Steady, old girl. Calm down. You'll do yourself a mischief.*

I don't bother eating that evening. I've no appetite either for food or telly. I just sit in silence in the kitchen, which is warmed still by spilled heat from the oven when I cooked for the girls. Slowly, with each glass of red, the panic that set my hands shaking and my heart racing starts to ease. I strain to listen for noises next door and the story they tell: the shudder in the pipes as she runs Jessica's bath. The low rumble of the radio as she potters in the kitchen.

I think about Teresa, moving to and fro in her new home, just a wall's width away. There was a time, that day we laughed together, when it felt as if all the nonsense choking both our lives relaxed its grip just for a little while and we were free of it. Two normal women, having a laugh. I'd thought then, for a moment, that maybe it was possible, that we might be friends. Silly.

But how does she know? I think of the stiffness in her tone, her averted eyes. And how much? Not enough to sack me, not yet, anyway. Or she would have. She isn't the kind to dilly-dally. I pour another glass and my spirits revive a little. No point assuming the worst, is there? Maybe she doesn't know as much as I fear. Maybe the game's not up.

Then I think, from nowhere: *The bed*. I could kick myself. *Of course*. I straightened up that messy duvet and the pillows without thinking. I should have left everything just as it was. That's it. That's all. She thinks I snooped in her room. Peeked in her diary. That's why I'm banned. I almost laugh out loud. Well, if that's all I've got to worry about...

I pour another glass and think: *Careless, Angie, my girl. Can't afford to be careless*. I pick at my fingernails until they're sore. *Only stupid people make stupid mistakes*, that's what my mum used to say. If I'm right, if that's it, I'm not done yet. But I do need to watch my step in the future.

After that, the mood between us stays awkward. No more coming in for tea when she picks up the girls. Just coats on and off they go. One week passes and then another, and I start to breathe a little more easily. Whatever thoughts she has about me she keeps to herself, and I do likewise. We might not like each other, but we need each other. She pays me, notes packed into an envelope, at the end of every week and I'm glad of the money. And besides, I can't tell a lie: it would be a real wrench if she took Jessica away from me now. I love that little girl. And someone needs to look out for her. When I see that woman's face, with all its lipstick and powder, all I can think is that she's a mum who doesn't love little Jessica the way she should. A strange sort of mum who plans for her own kiddies' deaths.

The weather's turning bitter now and Jessica and I rush out to the playground when we can, between the showers, and for the rest of the time, we play in the make-believe room and with the toys in the big toy cupboard.

We make up our own games. Hide-and-seek. Doggy and master. I'm Robin to her Batman, sitting cross-legged behind her on the rug while she pretends to steer the Batmobile. And we act out Red Riding Hood and the Wolf quite often. She loves that. Every kiddie has a favorite and that's hers.

One day, I'm down there on my hands and knees, playing at being a doggy while she grooms me with a hairbrush and teaches me tricks and feeds me pretend doggy biscuits as rewards, when she reaches her arm around my neck and clears away my hair and whispers low into my ear: "I love you very, very much."

I make light of it, just say something daft like: "Woof, woof, love you too, master!"

I never burden little ones with heavy stuff. They live lightly. I don't say what I long to say. *Don't be frightened, Jessica. I'll protect you. I'll keep you safe.*

But that really touches my heart, I can tell you. It stays with me. It's been a long time since anyone said they loved me. I've almost forgotten how it feels.

CHAPTER TWENTY-ONE

TERESA

I struggle to concentrate at work. I feel too sick, too anxious. It's all crowding in on me: Helena. Angie. Lorraine. The missing money. Craig and his strange disappearing act.

Helena barely shows up for work and when she does, she flounces around the salon, lips pursed, radiating hostility. I've stopped taking her on. I haven't the stomach for it. I just keep out of her way, miserably aware of the others as they watch the whole petty drama play out in front of them.

Things with Angie are almost as strained. I haven't mentioned the missing money. I don't know whom to blame—her or Helena or one of the other girls. They'd deny it, of course. I go over it again and again in my mind, late at night, as I lie restless in bed, staring at the clock.

What do I do if Angie is a thief? How can I trust her? The girls seem happy with her. Happier there than in their own home.

And, in a way, I don't want to find out. She's keeping me afloat. I know that. I'm barely coping with work and home and the children as it is and, without her, who else would take Jessica so cheaply all day and throw in Fran too, fitting around me at all hours?

And Craig... please god, I don't want to lose him. I think how happy we were when we moved in, full of plans. Only a matter of time, I thought, before he proposes. He hinted at it, right from the start. He's free of Kate now; in fact, it's been months since the divorce was finalized, and he hasn't said a word. When I think about it, the anxiety suffocates me. Why hasn't he brought it up again? Is he disappointed? Is he bored with me, now that we're living together? Has it all been a terrible mistake?

In the salon, my hands, usually so confident, shake as I cut. As I trim the short hairs under a tight bob, I nip the client's neck and she yelps. I stare in horror as a bead of blood appears.

"You all right?" Sophie gives me a queer look. "You need me to finish up?"

I leave her and flee to the toilets. The face in the mirror is pale and sweaty. I wash my hands in a stream of hot water and try to steady myself.

"Stop it," I whisper to the scared eyes. "Keep it together."

Craig's late again. He comes home smelling of beer. I don't even ask. I make him a cup of tea, kiss him on the top of his head, and go upstairs to bed.

I pretend to be asleep when he finally comes up to join me, the creak and bounce of the bed as he eases himself under the covers beside me.

When he's snoring, I slide my legs out, creep round to his side of the bed, and take his phone. He doesn't stir. I head downstairs and lock myself in the toilet there, my feet cold on the tiles. I sit on the closed seat, key in his passcode, and start a frantic search.

I don't know what I'm looking for, exactly, and I don't know what I hope to find. Nothing, perhaps. Or enough detail to make sense of the strange calls to the house, the childish love letter. My heart pounds as I read through his texts, his messages, his emails.

Most of the threads are boring. He works his patch, I'll give him that. He's a born hustler, that man, always chasing down leads about possible clients. A pal of his who works in a nursing home bungs him contact details for a few quid. Another friend of a friend in a hospital does the same. They seldom amount to much, from what I can tell, and it all seems dodgy, but he shrugged me off when I asked him about it. *All's fair in love and business*, he said. *You've got to be smart to get ahead.*

Kate. There are recent emails from Kate. My hands shake as I open them. He didn't tell me they were back in touch—why?

Her emails are brief. Carefully bland. My stomach clenches and I hunch over on the closed toilet lid, struggle to breathe. It's clear that they've been talking. She makes reference to it. What's going on? Why hasn't he told me? She drops a hint about meeting up. About Christmas plans.

She says in one: Have you talked to T?

He replies: Not yet. Give me a break.

I stare at the screen and shudder. They're talking about me, then, behind my back. What's that about? Is Kate the force behind all this? Is she trying to get him back?

Craig and I had exchanged similar emails about her, once upon a time, when she was the wife and I was the mistress. Now the two of them are plotting something and keeping me out.

I wander miserably into the kitchen and pull open the fridge door, mindlessly graze on the cheese and sliced chicken there. My eyes run over the bright, lit interior, the packets and cartons and jars, but my thoughts are far away, thinking about Craig. I'm frightened. I'm losing him. I think about Lorraine and the strange phone calls, which have stopped now as abruptly as they began. He's warned her, clearly. *Don't call home. She suspects something.*

I swallow down the cheese without tasting it. And Kate. She hates me. She has every reason to. They shared so much together, so much history. I see the wedding photograph and the shine in Kate's eyes. She looked so lovely, so happy, with her hand firm on her man's arm.

The house is dark and silent. I let the fridge door suck closed and, shivering now, go back to the downstairs toilet and the phone. I carry on searching, reading, snooping.

I scroll through texts. Then stop at one, go back and reread it. The tone catches me. It's intense.

Don't ignore me. I know where you live.

I pause for a moment, staring at the letters. My hands fumble on the keys.

I don't know the number. It's not Kate's. There's no name against it in his contacts. I search out other exchanges with the same person. There are several. The first pops up just two weeks ago. My stomach tightens. Lorraine again?

A simple but direct message, without pleasantries. This is a text chat between two people who know each other and know their business together.

We need to talk. Call me.

I keep reading. There are far more messages to him than replies. As if he's shrugging her off, hoping she'll go away and leave him alone.

The messages become more sinister.

Don't ignore me.

Call me. It's in your own interests.

And later: *Better for you that we talk.*

He sends a cross response: *Don't call my home again.*

I stare at the date and remember her voice on the line. Definitely Lorraine, then. But why? What's she got on him, that she won't give up?

Don't have much choice. When can we meet? Tonight?

No reply.

A day passes, then a message from her: *No more excuses. Thursday. 8pm. The Railway.*

Two hours later, a follow-up from the same number: *Last chance. Meet me there or . . .*

He replies a minute later: *OK.*

That's all.

Thursday. Tomorrow night.

I go back through the exchanges, trying to read between the words. The tone is insistent. That could be threatening, a sour business contact tracking him down. Or menacing. A jilted one-night stand refusing to let go? It could be sexy: a demanding lover insisting on seeing him again soon. Or else. Or she'll call his home again and tell me and force him to leave before he's had the chance to talk to me himself?

Upstairs, in bed, I lie beside him, this man I thought I knew, and listen to his deep, even breathing. The space between us is warmed by his body and smells faintly of his sweat, of his stale beery breath. I think of how much I've trusted him, how much I've invested in this house we bought together, and how much I want to be wrong about all this. I think about Jessica, tucked up in her own room upstairs, the princess bedroom paid for by her generous new dad.

After a while, I inch toward him and put my arm around his thick, soft waist, put my face against his side, and breathe him in, willing it to be all right.

CHAPTER TWENTY-TWO

The next day, I make an excuse to Angie about staying late to cash up and she agrees to keep the girls at her place for the evening. She'll put Jessica to sleep in her bed, she says. Fran will stay up. It's not great but neither seems to mind and it's the only solution I can find. I don't trust Angie in my house anymore.

I wait alone in the salon after closing time, grateful for its dark calm, its lingering chemical smells and neat order. I'm exhausted. Sophie and I have been flat-out all day, trying to cover for three. Helena is off sick again. My phone calls and messages go unanswered.

I log wearily into the computer and start composing an official note to HR at central headquarters to tell them about Helena's absences. I've been reluctant to go this far. She's a good stylist and smart, and I wanted so much to like her. It reflects badly on both of us to get HR involved. But this can't go on. The missed hours. The rudeness. Even if she didn't steal the money—and I'm still not sure—her hostility is poisoning the atmosphere. It shouldn't be like this.

I go back through the last few weeks and list all the days she's come late. Or gone home sick. Or just not shown up for work at all. She's careful, I can see that. She knows the rules and she's playing by them. Never more than three days off in a row. A day back in to reset the clock, then she's off again. I stare at the screen, feeling sick at the thought of the battle to come. I need to be as smart as she is and follow protocol to the letter. I take a deep breath, steady myself, and press SEND.

Afterward, I make myself a coffee and sit in one of the client chairs by the window, looking out at the street. Cars flash past, headlights streaming across the tarmac like searchlights. Gaggles of young people chatter past, giggling and messing about, on their way out. The girls are carefully groomed and I check out the hairstyles, long and short, pinned and loose, streaked and dyed.

A middle-aged woman pauses just by me and checks the back of her skirt in the darkened glass, straightens her coat. I'm invisible to her in the shadows and I watch her face, wonder who she is, where she's going, if she's happy this evening or as wretched and alone as I feel.

At quarter to eight, I put on the alarm and lock up, turn up my coat collar, and push my hands deep into my pockets. I set off down the high street, shrinking into myself in the middle of the steady flow of people along the pavement, afraid of what I may discover.

The Railway is at the bottom of the high street, an old Victorian pub that's been around for as long as I can remember. Probably since the railway came out here a hundred and fifty years ago, and shook this sleepy suburb into life. It was recently refurbished and turned from a grotty old-fashioned pub with jukebox and gaming machines into a family friendly gastro pub with decent food and a children's play area at the back. We had lunch here with the girls in the summer when we came to show them the half-renovated house.

I stop at a distance and try to think what to do. A few smokers stand outside, puffing in silence. It's still only ten to eight. I cross the road and stand in a poorly lit doorway there, feeling ridiculous. What am I doing here? It might not even be this pub. There must be dozens called The Railway.

The shop, closed and shuttered now, sells phones and gadgets. The doorway smells of urine and stale beer and it's sticky underfoot. I stand my ground, keeping in the shadows and fighting back the urge to give up and simply go home. The air is cool and I hug myself through my coat, cross my arms and rub them with my hands to keep warm. I feel frightened as I wait, and foolish and absurd. Maybe Craig and I will laugh about this someday, turn it into a funny story between us. *You did what? What were you thinking? Did you really think I'd—*

I stop. There he is on the far side of the road, hurrying out of a cul-de-sac—he must have left the car there—and turning toward the pub, his steps rapid, his bag loose in his hand. He looks so familiar and yet so apart from me—his face creased in a frown as he rushes along, illuminated in sudden bursts of light from shops and restaurants, from colored signs—that it makes my heart ache. He reaches the pub and disappears into the brightly lit interior, the door letting out a stream of noise, then slapping shut behind him.

For a moment, I don't move. The street seems unbearably still and quiet. I try to think. I want to go home but I can't leave yet—I need to see for myself what he's doing, who he's meeting, but it's a big pub on two floors and I don't know where they are, how to see without being seen.

Finally I creep out, cross the road to the pub, steel myself, and open the door.

It's crowded, thick with chat and music, and dense with tightly pressed bodies. I squeeze through the crowd, scanning the faces, ready to bolt. The main bar is jolly with drinkers. I walk through from one end to the other, embarrassed as I press through groups of joking, drinking men. No sign of Craig. I stop to consider. The second floor is quieter, more intimate, with dark corners and padded chairs. I take the stairs.

I see Craig as soon as I reach the top and I stand in the

shadows, concealed by a thick wooden post, and watch from across the lounge. He's sitting in a booth, opposite a smartly dressed woman. He has a pint in front of him and she has a colorless drink. Gin or vodka tonic, perhaps. Or even just water.

She's neatly made up, her hair well cut in a dark bob. Her clothes are tailored. A gray jacket and plain white top. She wears a simple silver chain. Her face is solemn and she sits with her hands folded lightly on the table. They both lean toward each other, their eyes intent on the other's face; even across the general hubbub from the upstairs bar and the undercurrent of background music, I sense that they're talking earnestly in low voices. As if they have something to hide.

Two hours later, I am waiting at home for him to come back. Upstairs, the girls are already silent. I've had the best part of a bottle of wine and my senses are befuddled as I listen to him parking the car, revving and reversing as he eases his way into the tight space on the road. I don't move.

Footsteps down the path. His key rattles in the lock. The door opens and he closes it carefully behind him, clinks on the chain. He pauses in the hall and I sense him listening, wondering perhaps where I am. In the bathroom? Already in bed? Finally, the sitting room door opens and he spills in, bringing the smell of the car and the pub. His look is innocent, genial at first as he sees me there, then it clouds as he feels the tension in the room, as he realizes I'm sitting in silence with my hands clutching each other in my lap.

"Where've you been?" I don't care anymore. I'm done with all this. The wine loosens the tension in me and spits it out.

"Nowhere." He shrugs, sets down his bag. "Work."

"Work?"

He sighs. "Don't, Tess. Not tonight."

"Then when?" I can't stop. I can't swallow it back and go up to sleep beside this man with so many secrets between us, so many lies. "I saw you."

He looks startled.

"With your lady friend in The Railway. Don't lie to me. That's Lorraine, isn't it? The one who called the house."

He sinks down into a chair on the other side of the room. His face is blank.

"Are you sleeping with her? Are you?"

He shakes his head. "No. I am not sleeping with her. OK?" He pauses. He looks weary. Beaten. Caught. "You spied on me?"

"What did you expect?" My voice rises now, letting out the fear and anger that's been building inside me for so many days. "You're out, night after night. Come home late. You barely talk to me. What am I supposed to think?"

He doesn't look at me but I see the anger in his face. We've quarreled before but over small things. Choosing a film. The chores. The children. This is different. We've crossed a line and we both know it. I don't trust him. Whether he's cheated or not, what we had before is spoiled and I'm not sure what remains. I plow on, unable now to stop.

"And what about Kate? She's back in touch, isn't she?" I'm on my feet now, my hands in fists at my sides, losing control. I could hit him, I feel it in me. I want to punish him for lying, for taking me for granted, for treating me in the same shabby way he once treated her. "Are you going back to her, is that it?"

"Tess." His voice is small and quiet. "It's nothing like that. Please. Listen to me. She wants to meet up, that's all. At Christmas. Fran's desperate to see her, to see the two of us together. I was trying to figure out what to do. I should have told you."

"Yes, you bloody should. Why didn't you?"

He spreads his hands, an appeasing gesture. It just makes me crosser.

"I haven't had a chance. You're right, we never see each other. You're always asleep when I get back."

"How dare you blame me, how dare you!" I cross to the wall and slap it with the flat of my hand, punching it until the fresh paint crumbles and flakes.

"Tess! Stop it! You'll hurt yourself."

He's on his feet, moves to grab my wrist, to hold me. I swing at him, catch his cheek with the back of my hand. A gash opens where my ring cuts the skin. Blood wells at once. He pulls back from me, wincing, and puts his hand to it, then looks at the red that comes away on his palm.

He twists away from me and I go after him. I'm shaking and frightened and I can't stop. I want him to shout too, to lash out at me if he needs to, to even the score. But he doesn't. He just walks away, to the kitchen, and opens the cupboard for the first aid box with one hand, the other pressed to his cheek to staunch the blood.

"You deserve it!" I scream at him as he dabs antiseptic on cotton wool and holds it against his cheek, as he searches for a plain plaster amid the brightly colored ones of princesses and Disney cartoons. The quieter he is, the more he ignores me, the wilder I feel. "You're cheating, aren't you? I know you are, you bastard. Why don't you just admit it? Tell me the truth."

I follow him back down the hall and watch him shrug on his coat again, unhook the chain, and open the front door. "Where are you going? You can't just walk away. Come back!"

I fly at him but he's too quick for me and too strong. He holds me off as he leaves.

I stand there, screaming into the darkness: "That's it. If you leave now, we're through. Finished."

He doesn't reply. As he closes the gate behind him, he turns and says softly: "Go to bed, Tess."

*　　*　　*

I sit in bed, drinking the rest of the bottle of wine and sobbing. The bed never felt so wide and so empty. My hand aches where I hit the wall. I think of the gash across his cheek and cry, hating myself, wondering what's wrong with me.

Outside, there's a space. He's gone. I wonder if he's with Lorraine, if I've driven him to her. If she's holding him, examining the cut, shaking her head. In the haze of alcohol and tiredness and sickness, I struggle to remember what he said. He did deny it, didn't he? That he was sleeping with her. But what else could he say? I think of the way they sat, with their heads leaning close together over their drinks, their eyes intent on each other's faces. And of the love note, slipped through the letter box in broad daylight. She must have known I would find it.

And Kate. What did he say... that she wanted to see him and Fran at Christmas? What was he thinking? They're divorced. Through. How could he even talk to her about it? And what about me? Am I supposed to have Christmas on my own, here, with Jessica? Is that what he wants?

CHAPTER TWENTY-THREE

I wake with a throbbing head. I'm irritable and cross with the girls as I get them ready. I manage to get coffee down but I can't eat. The smell of the girls' porridge makes my stomach heave.

I leave them having breakfast together while I go up to shower and stand for longer than usual under the hot water, trying not to cry. My body aches. I wonder where Craig is. When he'll come back.

When I go down, Fran has pushed breakfast into Jessica and is helping her to get dressed.

We're reaching for coats when I hear the key in the lock. I don't look up, I can't.

"Dad?" Fran runs out into the hall, puzzled.

His voice is a low murmur as he speaks to her and I wonder what he's saying. He's normally at work by the time she gets up, not coming home. I busy myself with Jessica, standing over her to button up her coat. She struggles free of me as he walks in.

"Ouchie!" She runs across to him and he bends to kiss her. Her hand goes to his cheek. "Was it a wolf?"

I glance up quickly, trying to look without him seeing. His cheek is a mess, a thick streak of deep red, not yet scabbing over. The skin around is puffy with bruising. A fresh wave of sickness takes me and I twist away and head toward the downstairs toilet.

"It was. A very bad wolf." He manages to sound playful. I wonder again where he's been all night.

"Did you teach it a lesson?"

The sound of running water as he fills the kettle and puts it on. "I did. I gave it a good telling off. And it's a kind wolf now, it promised."

"Come on, Jessica. Let's go." I come out of the toilet and sweep her along in front of me, my hands on her shoulders, even as she tries to resist, tries to twist to keep talking to Craig.

"But Mummy—"

"Come on, Jessica."

Fran waits quietly by the front door. She stands very still and her eyes are studying the mat. She doesn't speak to me or raise her eyes as I open the door and usher them both out. I try to imagine what she makes of her father's face, of what's going on between us.

I go to work with shaking hands. It isn't just the hangover. I don't know what's happened between us, between Craig and me. I'm frightened of going home at the end of the day, of checking the bathroom shelf to see if his toothbrush is still there and of opening the wardrobe doors to check for his clothes.

I arrive at the salon to find Lottie and Sophie poring over the appointments, trying to work out what to do. Helena's called in sick yet again. The new stylist, already being pushed to take on more than she should, hovers in the background, pinched and anxious. The phone is ringing but no one stops to answer it.

They look up as soon as I walk in, their eyes desperate, and both start talking at me.

I send the new stylist to make coffee and start trying to sort out the mess. I'll have to take on most of Helena's clients myself, there's no other way. Another day of working through breaks and cutting corners and staying late to catch up on paperwork. I set Lottie to work mixing color and ask Sophie to squeeze in an extra cut and blow-dry. They don't complain but no one's looking me in the eye, and the air is thick with resentment.

Maybe it's the hangover or the mess with Craig that tips me over the edge. Or just the fact that everything in my life, frankly, is so bloody messed up, it couldn't get much worse. But as soon as I get the chance, I march behind the counter and email HR again, logging Helena's absence today and asking advice about the formal dismissal process. I feel better as soon as I hit the SEND button. It needs doing and it needs doing carefully. One thing I really don't need is to end up facing her across a hostile employment tribunal. She's just the type.

Sophie and I fit in as many clients as we can, with just two of us cutting and the new stylist rushing between chairs to help with washing and blow-dries. When walk-ins arrive, we just have to turn them away.

I'm in the middle of a half-head and cut when Lottie beckons me across to the phone and whispers theatrically: "It's head office."

Finally. They do pick their time. I tell Lottie to give extra coffee and biscuits to the customer with a head bristling with silver foil and take the call.

The woman at the other end is officious. "You had a query about an employee?"

No apology for taking so long to get back to me. "Yes. Helena Wright. She's the senior stylist here. She's hardly been at work for the last few weeks."

"If she is absent for more than three consecutive working days, she must provide a doctor's note."

The woman reels off more rules about sick leave. I check again on the computer as she talks. Every fourth day, Helena miraculously reappears for a day or even a half day. Then falls sick again. Clearly she knows the company rules backward.

"But she's never off for more than three days at a time. That's the thing. She looks fine to me. And she won't tell me what's wrong. She just says I'm not allowed to ask."

The woman hesitates. "Well, technically, as her manager—"

"Look." My customer is glaring at me, cross about being abandoned. If I don't get on and finish her color, it won't be even. "It isn't only the absence. She's difficult. She's causing problems. I want her to go. OK? What do I need to do?"

The woman sounds curt. "It isn't that easy, getting rid of someone. There's a whole disciplinary process. It all needs to be documented and, frankly, it doesn't sound as if—"

"For God's sake, I'm trying to run a business here."

Long pause. "There's no need to be rude." Her voice is cold. "I can email you the relevant documents."

I take a deep breath. "Yes, please. Could you do that today? I've already waited—"

"I'll see what I can do. I'm very busy." The phone goes down.

Now the customer is grumpy, saying she has to be out of here soon or she'll be late for a meeting and my hands shake as I paint on the color with my brush and fold the foil. I hate the stupid, jumped-up woman in HR. I hate Helena. I hate Craig. I hate Angie. My palm is sore and bruised from smacking the wall and it hurts to bend my fingers. I avoid catching sight of myself in the mirror. My eyes are red and my cheeks look puffy. I look like a woman who's falling apart.

It's nearly closing time when HR calls again. It's a man this time. I sense I've been escalated.

His tone is unfriendly and he comes straight to the point: "You were making an inquiry about terminating Helena Wright's employment?"

"Yes. I know there's a formal—"

"It seems an odd time to formalize a complaint."

I hesitate, confused. "Well, I've only taken over the salon recently and obviously I hadn't met—"

He says: "I mean, just as she's being transferred."

"Transferred?"

"To the Ealing branch." He waits, and there's something in his manner that makes me feel as if a trap is opening up at my feet.

"That's the first I've heard about it. When did—"

He interrupts me. "I have the paperwork in front of me, Ms. Law. With your testimonial. And your approval."

A long pause. "Testimonial?"

"I have it here: 'Helena is an outstanding member of the team and an excellent stylist. She has great potential as a future manager. We'll be sorry to see her go.'"

"I didn't write that."

"It has your signature on the bottom. Teresa Law?"

"Yes. I mean, that is me." My cheeks are flushed. "But I didn't sign anything about a transfer."

He lets the silence stretch for a moment. "Fraud is a very serious allegation, Ms. Law. Please think carefully about where you want to take this. In the meantime, I can copy the documents and send them across to you. It might jog your memory."

Sophie emerges with her coat on after I put the phone down. I have the feeling she was listening. She doesn't ask, just stands there for a moment, taking it all in: the sight of me, leaning heavily against the counter, my face hot.

"Maybe it's for the best." She shrugs. "I mean, at least she'll be out of our hair." She attempts a weak smile. "No pun intended."

She and Lottie leave and the door jangles shut. They walk closely together as they set off down the street, long coats unbuttoned and fluid round their knees. I wonder how much they knew.

The girls sense my mood when I collect them from Angie's. I stay on the doorstep. Even Angie's smile fades when she sees my grim face and I say tightly: *No, thank you, no tea, I won't come in. Just tell the girls to get their things and not mess about.*

At home, Fran hangs her coat and goes straight upstairs without saying a word. Her bedroom door closes. I remember the look she gave me this morning when she saw her father's bruised face and absorbed the coldness between us.

I set Jessica up with some coloring and she sits silently at the table, the felt-tip pens swishing back and forth across the paper. The tip of her tongue protrudes between her teeth as she concentrates.

"What did you do today?" I sound too bright.

"Nothing." She shrugs. "Played."

She looks somehow older, sitting there, swinging her legs. A fast-growing child who's almost ready for school. I think how little time I spend with her nowadays. How far apart we've grown.

"Did you go to the park?"

She nods but doesn't speak.

Later, she goes to bed with so little fuss, it worries me. I read her a story and tuck her in. She lies impassively as I stroke her hair, kiss her on the cheek.

"You OK?"

She doesn't answer, just turns away from me, hunches herself around her rabbit, and burrows down into the bedclothes. Her hair splays across the pillow.

I make dinner for myself and sit in front of the television to eat. No sound from Jessica or Fran. I check my phone again, for the hundredth time. Nothing from Craig.

It takes me a long time to get to sleep but I must have dozed, because I'm startled by the sound of him stumbling up the stairs, banging against the banister. I lean over and check the clock when he goes into our bathroom. Twenty-five past one.

I lie still and try to keep my breathing even when he comes

back into the bedroom. Warm breath falls on my face, sour with beer. He's leaning close, right over me, and I almost open my eyes, then don't. I work on keeping my face slack, as if I'm really asleep. He draws away without kissing me and I wonder what to make of that, if it means anything, or if he's just trying not to wake me.

The wardrobe door creaks open and I strain to listen, imagining that he's looking through his clothes to decide which to pack. He doesn't. A few moments later, the bed sags and strains as he settles down heavily beside me, and his breathing thickens and clots in his throat as he falls quickly into sleep.

CHAPTER TWENTY-FOUR

Next morning, early, I sense him getting up. The mattress bounces and flattens beside me. He moves stealthily around the room, as he often does, gathering clean clothes. Later, the shower drums. I lie on, drifting in and out of sleep, until the front door slams.

Fran is quiet at breakfast. I have a coffee but I can't face food. I try to focus on the morning routine: packing Jessica's bag and checking the state of the fridge. Fran gets up and dumps her dishes in the dishwasher. I check the clock. Ten to eight. It's unlike Jessica to be so slow coming down. She's usually awake by the time I am.

"Any sign of Jessica?"

Fran shrugs and heads up the stairs to clean her teeth.

I call after her: "Tell her to hurry up, will you?"

I wipe over the table and pour Jessica's cereal into a bowl, finish my coffee, and stack the mug. It's nearly eight. I've got to get breakfast into her yet and then get her dressed. I wanted to get in early this morning and call HR about Helena. If she doesn't get a move on, I'll barely make it for the first appointments. I head upstairs, getting cross.

"What's going on?" I push open the door to her room and stride in. Her bed's empty. Her duvet lies on the floor in a crumpled heap. "Jessica!" I'm cross now. She is up, then, just messing about. "Jessica!" I start searching the room. "Come out. I haven't got time for this." Not under the bed. Not behind the chair. Not in the wardrobe. "JESS! This is not funny. Come out NOW!"

Fran appears in the doorway, hesitant.

I snap at her: "Where is she? Have you seen her?"

She shakes her head and looks blankly around the room as if she expects to find her there.

"Have a look in the bathroom, would you?"

She hesitates. "I was just in there."

"For God's sake!" I stand, hands on hip, looking round. "Go and check downstairs, then. When you find her, tell her to get on with breakfast."

I do not need this right now. I pour my anger into searching the house, cursing under my breath. I do a quick check of each room, bedrooms, bathroom. Nothing.

"Jessica! We're really late!" I go back through the bedrooms and go through it all again. Looking under each bed. In wardrobes. Behind chairs. My heart pounds. Where the hell is she? Time is slipping away. Each time I turn quickly, I almost see her, a crouching shadow in a corner, the humped back of a chair.

"JESSICA!" I head back down the stairs. She's hidden in some strange places before: I had an emergency team searching a shopping center once, after she somehow rolled herself into a tiny enough ball to curl, invisible, inside an upturned box.

Fran appears in the hall.

"Found her?"

She shakes her head and her eyes slide away from mine. Her shoulders are hunched. She's going to be late too, and it's not her fault.

I take a deep breath. "Don't worry. You go."

She grabs her coat and bag and heads off without a word.

"Jessica!" I rush through the sitting room, then the kitchen, then check the downstairs loo. I start all over again, back up the stairs, second floor, then up to the third. "Jessica! Jessica! Come on—that's enough!"

No sign of her. Slowly, my anger turns cold. I sit, breathless, on the stairs. The house feels utterly empty and silent. I think about the way she turned away from me last night, onto her side.

I run back down to the hall. Her shoes are there, her tiny pink wellies and outdoor shoes lined up neatly against the skirting board. Her coat is on its hook. The front door is closed. Fran shut it after she left. But was it properly closed before that? Could she have run out, unseen? Or could someone have got in?

I wrench the door open and head out, scanning under the bushes in our tiny front yard, lifting the dustbin lid and replacing it with a clatter. Beyond, the only figures in the street are solitary commuters, ears attached to their phones, hurrying toward the high street.

I start to shake. I run back inside, grab my phone, and call Craig.

"Have you got Jessica?"

"Jessica?"

"Is she with you?"

"With me? Why would she be with me?" He sounds impatient. "I'm at work."

"She's not here. She's gone."

My insides twist and tighten. It sounds real, now that I've told someone, now that I've said it out loud. *I've lost my daughter, my little girl. She's gone.*

A pause. He seems to hear the edge of hysteria rising in my voice and speaks steadily.

"Calm down. Where are you?"

"I'm home. Her bed's empty. I can't find her. Oh, Craig…"

As we're talking, I keep moving, running from room to room, floor to floor, half seeing her round every corner I turn, as if she's a spirit I can never quite catch. She must be here. She'll pop out any minute and shout "boo!," her face all smiles.

"She'll be hiding." He doesn't get it. "Don't panic. You know what she's like."

I stop and take a deep breath. "What if someone's taken her?"

Silence. "Taken her?" His voice is careful and considered.

I sit heavily on the floor in her bedroom, look around at the neat furniture, the elves and fairies framed on the walls, at the neat row of dolls on the shelf. It all feels like evidence that she really exists, that she was ever here at all.

"What do you mean?"

"I don't know. People traffickers! Pedophiles!"

It's all my fault. Because I'm a bad mother and I shout at her and I slapped her and now I'm being punished. Now it will all come out.

"Tess?"

I bend over and put my hands to my face and start to cry—wet, sloppy crying. *Jessica, my sweet girl. I'm sorry. I am. I didn't mean it. I'll make it up to you. I will. Just be OK. Please be OK.*

"Tess? Are you there?"

He's a distant voice, shouting from the floor. I wipe my face and pick up the phone again, sniff into it.

He says: "What makes you think she's been taken?"

"Because she's not *here*." I feel different now that I've cried. Exhausted in body and soul. As if I know I deserve whatever misery lies ahead.

His tone changes. He sounds worried too, taking me seriously at last.

"You're sure she's not there? Have you looked under the beds? In the wardrobes?"

"Of course I have."

"Stay there. I'm on my way." There are rustles in the background. He's moving, leaving whatever he was doing and coming to help. I feel a surge of love for him. I want the comfort of his arms around me and to press my face into the solidity of his chest. I want him to make it all OK.

He says: "If you find her, call me at once, won't you? She

might pop up. I'm going to hang up now. I'll be with you in twenty minutes. You OK?"

I don't want him to go but I manage to say yes.

"I'll call the police right now. OK? Just in case. They might get to you before I do, so don't stress out if they're at the door."

When the line goes dead, I drop the phone on the carpet and reach over to the shelf closest to me, and scoop up the nearest doll with its hard, plastic face and stiff skirts. A doll without a name. I sit hunched forward, my arms clutching it to my chest, sobbing. The house sits heavily around me. Silent and empty.

A voice cries: "Jessica!" It's a woman's voice but high-pitched and disembodied. It comes again, screeching now, splintering the silence: "Jessica!" The sound dies away and, after a moment, strained, listening, I realize it was my scream, my madness filling the room.

I pull the doll so tightly to my chest that my nails dig into my palms and I moan, a low drone that vibrates through my head. I bury my face in its dead hair and start to rock, mindless, to and fro, aching to hold my baby, my lovely daughter, imagining her warmth in my arms, her solid heaviness, trying to conjure up from sheer will the sweet, childish scent of her, my own girl, my Jessica.

I shake as I cry and I hear myself start to babble: "I'm sorry, Jessica." I barely know what I'm saying. "I'm sorry." Then I repeat, again and again: "Come back to me, please, my love. Jessica. Just come back."

CHAPTER TWENTY-FIVE

ANGIE

When the doorbell rings, I hesitate. My stomach clenches. I don't answer straightaway, just shout: "Coming!" down the hall.

I'm making a batch of banana muffins and I go back to spooning the mixture into the liners. My hand shakes and a blob of mixture hits the side of the liner, spills over onto the baking tray. I tut, use my little finger to wipe it off.

The doorbell sounds again, for longer this time. Insistent.

I set down the mixing bowl and spoon and go down the hall in my slippers, wiping my hands on the kitchen towel before I open up.

I pull open the door and freeze when I see two police officers standing there. Without thinking, I try to close the door in their faces, to make them go away.

One of the police officers puts out his hand and stops me.

"Angela Dodd?"

His face is hard. He looks only about thirty and the other one even younger, barely out of school. They tower over me, both in uniform.

I nod dumbly.

"Can we come in? Just a few questions."

They might as well have punched me in the stomach. I manage to stand to one side and they push in past me and stand there, broad and large, filling the hall. One, the older one, watches me as I press myself against the wall, the kitchen towel forgotten in my hands. The young one gazes around at the peeling paint, the worn stair carpet, the old radiator shelf with a few of my mum's cheap knickknacks.

I feel sick. I want them out of here, out of my house.

I manage to say: "It's not a good time, actually. I'm just in the middle of something. Baking."

"Shouldn't take long."

The older one closes the door and cuts off my escape route. I take a deep breath and draw the edges of my cardigan together across my chest. *Calm down, Angie, my girl. Keep your wits about you.*

"May we?" The older one invites himself into the sitting room and they sit side by side on the low, lumpy settee, their legs sloping back from their knees.

I don't sit down. I want it over and them out. I can't speak. I just stand there, leaning against the side of the armchair, and wait.

He gives me some official nonsense about who they are and which department they're from but I'm not really taking anything in. The first part I really hear is when he says: "You sometimes look after the children next door, Mrs. Dodd? At number thirty-six."

I don't answer. *If he knows, why's he asking?*

He waits, then prompts: "Jessica and Francesca?"

"They've been round when their mum's at work. No harm in that, is there?"

My legs shake under me. I hate policemen. Always have. And the sight of them, here, in my home, asking questions, hits me like a tidal wave. They smell of boot polish and cigarettes.

The older one considers me. He's reacting to my tone. Difficult. Uncooperative. I know all the words. I take a deep breath and say to myself: *Careful now, Angie, watch your step.*

"Mrs. Dodd, do you know why we're here?"

I can hazard a guess but I don't say that; I just shake my head, play dumb, and let him show his cards first.

The young one takes a notebook out of his top pocket, flips it open, and gets ready to write.

The older one says: "It's about Jessica. She's been reported missing."

My legs buckle and I sit awkwardly on the arm of the chair. My mouth makes a breathy noise as I go down, something like: "Oh!" The room sways away for a moment and comes back again.

"Missing?"

The young man writes in his notebook. I think: *Do I need a lawyer?* Then: *I can't insist. I'll look guilty.*

"Her parents say she was asleep in bed when they checked on her last night. She wasn't in her room this morning."

I blink. "Well, she's not here."

The older man shifts his weight. His belt, loaded with equipment, creaks as he moves.

"When did you last see her?"

"Yesterday."

"How did she seem? Anything troubling her? Anything unusual?"

I think of the bruises a few weeks earlier. Of the way Fran blushed when I asked her about them.

"She's a sweet kid. We get on well, me and Jessica."

The young one stops writing and looks up and they both consider me. I swallow hard. *Careful, Angie.*

"I'm just saying. She's a lovely girl, that's all."

"But is there anything that you can think of that might help us find her?"

I run my hand across my forehead. I don't know what to say.

"Mrs. Dodd, she's very young. We're just concerned for her welfare. That's all."

I should offer them a cup of tea, charm them a bit; maybe then they'll leave me alone. I just can't. I feel sick. I just want them out.

The older one heaves himself to his feet and the young one, taking his cue, jumps up too and stows the notebook.

As they go out, the older one peels off a business card and puts it on the radiator shelf, next to Mum's old knitted dog. It hits the wood with a smack, as if he's playing an ace.

"If you think of anything, anything at all that might help, please get in touch."

I close the door on them and lean against it, as if I can keep them out that way. I put the chain on and walk shakily through to the kitchen. The silence is ghostly. I snap on the radio, then turn it off again a moment later.

I fish out the spoon, half-sunk now in the muffin mix, wipe off the handle, and go back to filling the paper liners. My hands tremble. I try to remember exactly what they said and what I told them. I wasn't natural. Not convincing. I should have asked more questions. I should have played it cool, told them how worried I was, offered to do anything I could.

I open the oven door and slide in the baking tray, then run the water until it comes hot and wash out the dirty bowl and spoon.

I close my eyes and at once I see that image again, the one that came to me when I went snooping in their bedroom. The picture of little Jessica, that sweet little kiddie, cold and pale, packed inside a coffin. Of the lid being screwed on, plunging her into eternal darkness.

I promised myself I'd save her. I shudder. I promised. *Never make promises you can't keep.*

CHAPTER TWENTY-SIX

TERESA

It all happens so quickly.

One minute, life is normal. I'm at home, pouring breakfast cereal, thinking about getting off to work and the salon and the problems waiting for me there; then, for no reason, the world collapses around my ears.

It's all unreal. The police are here, their cars clogging up the road outside. Officers are pacing up and down in heavy boots as if they own the place. Doors open and close as they let each other in. I've lost track of who's who. Radios squawk. Their eyes, looking over the house, looking over me, are cool and suspicious. And, in the middle of it all, the black hollow center is this: Jessica's missing.

I sit on the settee and my head roars with white noise and my body shakes. I've lost control of it all. Of my legs, of my head, of my daughter. A broad-shouldered police officer, made wider by the equipment hanging from his belt and bulging in the pockets of his uniform, sits across from me. His mouth is moving, asking me questions. I want to help, I do, but I can barely force my mind to focus, to understand.

"What exactly happened, Ms. Law?" He speaks slowly and clearly, as if to a child. "Take me through the events this morning. Has she ever gone missing before?"

I answer by nodding or shaking my head. I don't trust myself to speak. My mouth is a tight line as I struggle to stop myself from crying. I want to wake up and find everything is normal again, as it should be. I want Jessica back. *Just come back, my love. Give me another chance. I'll be kind. I'll be the best mummy. Please, Jessica.*

The police officer's voice comes again. He has broad lips and they're dry and crack into shapes as I watch them and try to understand. He says: "I know it's a difficult time, Ms. Law, but please try to cooperate. Anything you can tell us, anything at all—you never know how it might help."

It feels like a reprimand. Jessica is missing and it's my fault. It must be. *It's me. I'm a terrible mother. I drove her away with shouting and scolding and I deserve this pain, I do.*

I keep my mouth closed and turn my eyes to the floor and the settee shivers underneath me as my body shakes.

Voices in the hall. Craig. He pounds in, rushes over, and sits beside me, reaches his arms around me. I'm too rigid to respond and he hesitates and pulls back after a quick hug. I sense the police officer watching us and then I worry about how we're behaving, about how it looks.

Craig turns to the police officer. "I'm her partner. Craig Fox."

The police officer nods and looks him over and I sense the tension between them.

A new man is in the room. I didn't sense him come in but I see him now, a tall shadow by the door, watching us and listening. He's in civilian clothes.

The police officer starts again. "Tell me about the property, Ms. Law. The front door—was it locked overnight?"

Craig says: "Of course it was."

The officer's face doesn't change but something in his posture tightens. "The double lock was engaged? I see there's a safety chain—was that on?"

Craig nods. He looks cross. "I was the first one out this

morning. Everything was normal. I'd locked up the night before."

"And the back door?"

"I didn't check the back door. Why would I open the back door at seven in the morning?"

The officer writes something. "Is that the time you left the house, Mr. Fox?"

"Well, about five past seven. I put the radio on and I remember hearing the pips and the headlines."

"Was Jessica asleep in bed at that time?"

"Yes." He hesitates and realizes what he's said. "Well, I don't know. I didn't look in on her. I don't, in the morning. Tess gets the girls up."

The police officer turns to me. "Did you see her?"

I swallow. "No. It was all quiet so I had a shower and came down to get breakfast ready. When she didn't appear..."

I break off, remembering how cross I was as I stormed around the house, shouting for her, telling her to stop hiding, to hurry up. I bite my lip and the corners of my mouth pull and twitch as I struggle not to cry.

The police officer says: "Did you notice anything odd?"

I shake my head.

"Do the windows lock? In the bedroom?"

"They all do. But they'd be open, at night."

"Open?"

I nod. "Ours. And the girls' bedroom windows. Just the top one, in Jessica's room."

The police officer looks surprised. "It was quite cold last night."

Craig says: "What's that supposed to mean? We like fresh air, that's all. We keep the bloody windows open a few inches. What's the big deal?"

I look across at the silent man in civilian clothes, still by the door. He hasn't moved a muscle. His eyes are on us, absorbing everything. I look quickly away. His face is impassive but he frightens me. *He knows*, I think. *He knows about people. He knows about me. I can't hide anything from him.*

The police officer folds away his notebook and gets up. "We'd like to search the house, if that's all right?"

"No." Craig sounds riled. I turn to stare at him. His face is tight and closed. He gets like this sometimes with other men, when he feels undermined. I had to drag him out of a pub once when he got into an argument.

The police officer says at once: "Mr. Fox, I really—"

The air in the room changes. I open my mouth to say: *Craig, please.* Nothing comes out.

Craig says, "Check down here. The back garden, if you like." He sounds sneering, and I reach out and put a hand on his arm. "And Jessica's room, I suppose. But that's it. Right? This is our home."

I lean closer and try to whisper. "But, Craig, please. Why can't they—"

"Why?" He reaches for my hand and grips it tightly. "I'm as worried as you are. But we've got rights, Tess. They can't turn the place over."

I shake my head. "Why not?"

He frowns. "What's the point?"

A calm voice comes from the door. From the quiet man who seems to be the boss. Detective.

"That's a nasty cut, Mr. Fox. Been in a fight?"

Craig puts a hand to the gash on his cheek.

"That's nothing," he says, turning away. "Just clumsy."

I close my eyes and the room sways, then takes a moment to right itself. I feel suddenly very sick.

*   *   *

Later, a female officer arrives and comes through to the kitchen to find me there, sitting vacantly at the table. My head aches from crying and I stare out at the garden, at the untidy square of lawn and the empty flowerbeds. I wonder why any of it ever seemed to matter. Jessica got filthy once, playing in the mud. I screamed at her. *No wonder she's gone.*

The officer makes me a cup of tea and sets it in front of me on the table. I don't move. I'm too sick to drink a thing.

"I'm your family liaison officer," she says. "I'm your point of contact."

She sits next to me and I see she's helped herself to tea, too.

I don't answer. I don't want a point of contact. I don't want the police in my house. I just want Jessica back.

She continues: "Have you had breakfast? Can I get you anything?"

The police have been up in Jessica's room. Craig went with them, to keep an eye.

I say: "Have they found anything?"

She shakes her head. "Not yet." She sips her tea. We look out together at the back garden. It looks very small. "The back door was unlocked. Did they say?"

I stare at her. My head is dull and it's a struggle to grasp what she's said, what it means. "The girls play out there sometimes. They might have left it unlocked, I suppose."

She shrugs. "Maybe." She peers out at the fence. "Is that your childminder, that side?"

I nod. "Angie."

"Handy." She considers. "You're lucky."

I breathe in. I think of Angie and her slow, heavy body, of the way Jessica throws herself against her legs when she opens the door each morning, and of the way I have to scold and to shout to get her out of there each evening, to get her to come home with me.

"Actually, she's a bit strange…" I say at last. "I can't prove anything but I've lost things, you know? Before all this happened, I wondered if she might be, well, a bit light-fingered?"

She turns to look at me.

"Like I said, I can't prove it," I say. "But I'm just saying, just in case…"

I get to my feet, leave the tea cooling on the table, and walk back through to the sitting room. I can't stay anywhere for long. I can't sit still.

CHAPTER TWENTY-SEVEN

ANGIE

The sitting room fills with mechanical wailing and the strobe of a flashing blue light. The sight of it makes me feel sick. I go to the front window and part the lace curtain and peer out.

There's another police car out there in the road, parked messily at an angle. A group of police officers stands out there on the pavement, talking in low voices. They hitch their belts and rest their thumbs on the bulky pouches hanging there.

One is in plain clothes and stands for a moment, his face thoughtful, looking up at next door's house as if the new windows and freshly painted sills are some sort of clue. He starts to turn back toward the path, to go back into their house—and I let the curtain fall from my fingers as if it were suddenly hot, taking a sharp step backward and catching my ankles on the hard frame of the armchair.

I creep into the hall and quietly put the chain on, just in case they try any funny business. Then I head upstairs and run a hot bath. I don't know why. It's just the comfort of it, the sudden need to be safe and warm and clean. The bathroom clouds with steam.

I switch off the taps and go into my bedroom to get clean clothes. Instead, I forget, and walk in a daze round my big, old bedroom, touching things as I pass for no reason other than habit and the relief of their solidness: the big, wooden brush and mirror set on the dressing table that belonged to my mother;

the fraying candlewick bedspread; the silver picture frame with a portrait of my grandparents' wedding: a group gathered together so long ago that everyone in it is already cold, their lives forgotten.

When I walk back into the bathroom, the mirror, thick with steam, shows a child's scribble. The grease from Jessica's finger, last time she was in here and drew on its surface. I bend forward, my arms wrapped tightly round my stomach, and choke on a rising wave of sickness.

I only stay two minutes in the bath. I can't settle in the water; I'm too restless and, besides, what if they come back to visit me and I'm all wet, what would they think? I need to act normal so I don't arouse suspicion.

I climb out of the bath, fleshy and red, and rub myself down, dress in the same clothes: not the clean ones I carried through from the bedroom. They notice things like that. I imagine their questions. *I see you've changed. A bath? Why did you have a bath? Is that usual, at nine o'clock in the morning? What were you trying to hide?*

I make myself a cup of tea but I can't settle to drink it. Male voices outside. I hurry through and peer around the edge of the sitting room curtain. Two police officers are standing on next-door's path, talking in low voices. One seems to sense me there and pauses, looks across. I shrink back but his eyes catch mine and they look sharp. I curse under my breath. I stride up and down the sitting room and back into the kitchen. It smells of baking, of sweet, cloying banana. The muffins are still warm and I pack half a dozen into a tin, then lift the flowers from the vase on the windowsill—Jessica loves Michaelmas daisies—and wrap them in paper towels, then head next door to find out how much they know.

CHAPTER TWENTY-EIGHT

I feel like an intruder. Their house has already been taken over by police. The front door is partially open and I peer into a hall cluttered with thick-set men in uniforms, made bigger by their hats and helmets.

I take a deep breath, steady myself, and step inside. I hesitate, there in the hall, waiting for them to notice me, unsure how they'll react.

The plain-clothed officer who spotted me earlier, when he was outside, is briefing a colleague and he looks past the constable and his eyes fall on me. They are the sort of piercing eyes that say little but see a lot.

"I live next door." I swallow hard. "I'm their friend."

I gesture to the tin, to the flowers. The wet stalks have soaked through the bottom of the kitchen towel and drip onto the toe of my shoe.

He lifts a hand and waves me through and I'm too nervous to look as I pass him, in case he's scrutinizing me.

Craig sits in his shirtsleeves at the kitchen table, his suit jacket draped on the back of his chair. He's busy, his phone pinned to his ear by a raised shoulder, his pen scribbling on an A4 pad. I glare at him, hardly able to believe my eyes. That little girl's missing and he's still focused on work?

"I'll do the design," he's saying. His voice is brisk. "A5. One image. Color. If I email it to you by"—he breaks off, twists to look round at the kitchen clock—"let's say by ten, when can you have them ready?"

He listens, notes down a few figures.

"And for a thousand?"

He only seems to see me when he comes off the phone. He stares as if, for a moment, he can't remember who I am and how I've appeared in his kitchen. His eyes go to the soggy paper around the daisies.

"I'm so sorry." I don't know what to say. He frightens me, this man, with his briskness and his eagerness to sell death. "Is there any news?"

He shakes his head. "If there is, no one's told me."

I pause, thinking about little Jessica and the bruises and the screams, late at night. About the documents, hidden under the floorboards, that pave the way for her funeral.

I say: "Don't they know what's happened? I mean, what do the police say?"

He shrugs. "The first few hours are crucial. Apparently." He looks past me to the police officers in the hall and, through the open plan, into the sitting room. "They've got men out, walking the streets." He looks harried. "Knocking on doors, you know, asking if anyone's seen her."

I turn to look, too. Teresa is sitting on the pristine white settee. She's leaning slightly forward, as if she's studying her feet on the polished wood floor. Her shoulders droop. A female officer sits beside her and another across from her, on an armchair. Their stillness and their sorrowful attitudes remind me of a scene from some old oil painting.

Craig is back on his laptop now, his face intent. "I thought maybe this one?"

I put the flowers in the washing-up bowl in the sink and go to stand beside him to look at the screen. A big photo of Jessica, smiling. Her mouth open and daubed with chocolate.

He hesitates, clicks to bring up a second. Jessica sitting in a pile of ripped wrapping paper at Christmas, her head turned back to the camera, as if someone had just caught her attention.

"Maybe that's clearer? The features?"

I don't understand. "What's it for?"

He frowns, as if I'm deliberately wasting his time, pulls the screen away from me, and starts to type. Embarrassed now and feeling stupid, I say: "Maybe the second one," but he's absorbed in the screen again and it's too late.

I fill the kettle and put it on, get out a tray while it comes to the boil and set out mugs from the cupboard, find a small jug that will do for milk.

"Cup of tea?"

He doesn't answer. I want to make myself useful, to blend in, somehow. I cut the muffins into quarters and find a big plate. When the tea's ready, I pour as many cups as the kettle allows and set them on my tray, ready to carry out to the men in the hall and the women in the sitting room. I set a mug at Craig's elbow with a couple of pieces of muffin. His hand reaches for it and lifts it to his mouth without his eyes leaving the computer screen.

As I draw away, I see the flyer taking shape there. The large bold letters across the top, reading "MISSING" and, below, the picture of Jessica, looking out with her large eyes from the past. My legs buckle and I find a chair, sit heavily.

"Did they tell you to do that?"

He bends low to the screen, fiddling with the letters, changing the sizing. I don't know if he even hears me. His jaws munch and he doesn't answer.

All morning, police officers come and go with solemn faces. Radios squawk. Men murmur in low voices in the hall. Craig makes lists and a series of efficient phone calls, re-arranging meetings, canceling visits, organizing offers of help. Every now and then, I go through to the sitting room, head bowed, gather up dirty mugs and plates, and carry them through to wash in the kitchen sink. No point putting the dishwasher on for that. Besides, I want to look busy. Hide in plain sight, you might say. Teresa's face is soft and puffy with crying. She doesn't eat or drink a thing. She sits in silence, in a world of her own. Her knees keep juddering.

At one o'clock, a young woman with big hair and high heels appears in the kitchen doorway and hands me a supermarket bouquet.

She nods at me. "For Teresa."

I say: "Cup of tea?"

She shakes her head, embarrassed. "Any news?" Her voice is a whisper.

I shake my head and she creeps out again.

I put the gift card on the windowsill and the new flowers in the washing-up bowl with the sad daisies. That policemen's sharp eyes follow everyone and everything and, throughout it all, as I make tea and wipe down surfaces and listen to Craig in action, it seems that we're all, always, under observation.

CHAPTER TWENTY-NINE

Craig likes the police about as much as I do and he doesn't make any effort to hide it. He packs away his laptop just before lunchtime, grabs his coat, and goes striding off down the hall.

The police officer at the front door moves to block his way and he pushes past him. I don't catch what either of them say but I see the look on the officer's face. Raised eyebrows, set jaw, frown. He nips into the sitting room and, a moment later, a young officer slips out of the house. Tailing him, that's what.

I have a look through the kitchen and make up a few rounds of ham and cheese sandwiches for lunch. Teresa's in no fit state. The police officers seem pleased, anyway, when I offer them around. *Always take some food round*, that's what my mum used to say about a crisis. She'd cut up a fruit cake if there was bad news in the street. Or make a pot of soup.

I sit in silence at the kitchen table, eating a sandwich and drinking tea. I'd rather be at home, hiding away from it all, but I steel myself to stay. I'm better off here, keeping in the loop. Listening.

Now and then, radios sound. Every time they do, Teresa looks up as if she thinks it's god calling, bringing good news. Nothing of the sort. I see down the hall, and the police officers' faces are tight and serious as they murmur together in low voices.

Craig comes back. His hair sticks up in clumps and I wonder where he's been, if he knows the police followed him. He shrugs off his coat and strides into the sitting room and the mood changes at once. It's like someone dive-bombing a still, sad pool of water, churning everything up.

Teresa's on her feet and she's crying again and pawing at Craig and one of the police officers steps forward and suddenly their voices are raised, his and Craig's, arguing.

I sit, frozen, at the kitchen table and strain to catch what I can. I don't want to creep nearer and be seen listening.

Craig sounds accusing. "Well, what ARE you doing? Why haven't you found her? I just want to do something—"

They keep talking over each other and Teresa's caught there in the middle, clinging to Craig, sobbing.

The officer's voice is softer but I hear bits. "We're doing everything we can," and "Sir, please—" and he's got an arm outstretched toward Craig as if he's stopping traffic.

After a while, Craig sits down beside Teresa and the voices are quieter now, and I rush to get a tray and head through to gather up the last round of mugs and plates and see what's going on.

Craig's sitting half turned to Teresa and he's got her hands between his own and his eyes are on her face as if he's about to propose. But it isn't that. He's trying to persuade her to do something.

"It can't hurt," he's saying. "Maybe they're right, they won't need it. But what if they do? It'll spread the word, right? Get her home. But it's got to be you. Her mum."

She's crying and her head hangs forward as if it's too heavy for her neck and she's shaking her head, saying: "I can't, Craig."

The plain-clothed officer stands in the shadows, near the door. Watching, always watching. His eyes are cold and shrewd.

The atmosphere is even more strained after that. Craig helps Teresa up the stairs. She leans on him as if her legs can't take her weight anymore. The female officer goes too, taking her other arm, until they all reach the top and then Craig says something to the policewoman and she steps back. She doesn't look happy. She stands there in the hall, watching, until they disappear from sight.

Time passes. A young officer comes through and finds me sitting there in silence and gives me an odd look.

"You related?"

"I'm from next door."

He shrugs and goes out again and I feel my cheeks burn and wonder if he's gone to tell on me and what might happen next but nothing does, just the clock hands slowly moving and the light in the garden shifting across the grass.

It's nearly three when the doorbell rings. A murmur of low voices creeps through to the kitchen. Craig's heavy tread sounds on the stairs and he appears in the hall and waits there as the police open up. He ushers the new arrivals through to the sitting room. A young woman comes first, followed by a middle-aged man. He carries a bulky metal tripod in one hand and, with the other, steadies an enormous camera hoisted high on his shoulder. Something's happening at last, and I get to my feet and hover at the back of the sitting room for a better look.

The young woman turns to Craig with a fake smile. She wears too much makeup for a girl her age. *No better than she ought to be.*

"I'm so sorry about your little girl." She doesn't look sorry. She looks pleased with herself. I check her out as Craig nods and tells her quickly what's happened. I try to decide what makes her look so obviously a reporter. She's dressed in smart black trousers, a scoop top that reveals cleavage, and a well-cut jacket. A gold chain sits just above the scooped top, echoing its line.

My eyes move to the cameraman. We are both extras, he and I. No one shakes hands with us or introduces themselves to us or exchanges pleasantries: we are invisible people. As Craig and the reporter chat about Jessica, the cameraman moves quietly about the room, judging angles and light with a professional eye. I go forward to help as he starts to shift the furniture.

We push back the settee and pull two armchairs forward to face each other. He stands back, hands on hips, and looks round, then darts forward to pick up a low side table and set it beside one of the chairs, dressing the shot.

He turns to me. "Any flowers?"

I nod and go to fetch the supermarket bouquet. There's an empty vase on a shelf and I arrange them in there and take them back to take their place on the side table. The cameraman has set up his tripod now and clicked his giant camera on the top.

"Could you just sit in?"

He points to the chair, then takes up his position behind the camera. I hesitate, suddenly rigid with embarrassment, then step forward and sit on the chair. Everyone must be staring at me—I feel their eyes, feel acutely conscious of the shabbiness of my jumper. When I look down the barrel of the camera, it's an endless black hole and I think of space and swirling nothingness and Jessica. I do my best to stay calm, and straighten my back. I try to think what to say, what message I could give the nation if the red light went on. My hairline pricks with sweat.

The cameraman darts forward and hands me a white sheet of paper. I think he's giving me lines to read but when I unfold the paper, there's nothing on it.

"Just hold it up. Like this."

He disappears behind the camera again and I hold up the blank paper under my chin, as if I'm a convict getting a mug shot. The paper rustles as my hands shake.

"Thanks." He stands again and looks around, his attention as quickly lifted from me as it descended.

There's a noise in the hall. The door opens and Teresa's standing there. I jump up in embarrassment and get out of her way. She looks ill. Her hair is a mess and her skin has a horrid gray tinge. Her eyes pass over the room, over the people, the rearranged chairs, the tripod, but her gaze seems dead. For a moment, no one moves.

Finally, the reporter steps forward. "Mrs. Fox?"

Teresa blinks as if she's trying to remember. "Teresa Law. I'm Jessica's mother."

"Of course." The reporter and Craig guide Teresa sideways toward the chair. She moves as if she's in a trance. "What a worrying time," the reporter says. "I can't imagine."

Teresa is staring right into the camera lens. She turns to Craig. "I don't know if I can do this."

"You'll be fine." He pats her arm, crouches down at her side, and whispers something.

I go to join the cameraman. He's looking down the lens and making small adjustments. There's a flip-out screen on the side of the camera, a mini TV, and I watch the small Teresa on screen shuffle a little in the chair. She looks uncomfortable. She tries crossing her legs, then uncrosses them again, her knees and ankles all wrong. None of it looks natural. The cameraman adjusts the shot, moves the side table farther forward.

I whisper to him: "The flowers look nice."

The reporter sits in the other chair, with her back to us, and lifts a long, furry microphone, angling it from below to catch Teresa's soft voice without it being in shot. Teresa looks lost.

"It's just a shout-out," the reporter says. "Not long. We might only use a clip. Just think what you'd like to say to anyone who might be watching. Who might have seen Jessica or know something. That's all."

Craig chips in. "They've got a photo of Jessica. It might jog someone's memory."

The reporter looks at the cameraman and he nods. She says: "So, what would you like to say, Mrs. Fox?" She adopts a hushed tone. The careful voice people use to address the recently bereaved.

Teresa puffs out her cheeks with a sigh and the woman I'm watching in the mini screen looks suddenly very small and far away and very frightened.

"My daughter's missing. Jessica. She's only three."

She stops and presses her lips together in a tight, jagged line. The reporter holds her breath. The air seems sucked from the room and the tension is suddenly unbearable. No one moves.

A moment later, Teresa's mouth puckers and breaks and her face folds into tears. Craig plucks a hankie from his pocket and leans forward to hand it to her and she buries her face in it. The reporter twists to look back at the cameraman and some signal passes between them that I don't understand.

Teresa, swollen-faced, gulps air. As she recovers and mops her eyes, the reporter gets to her feet and comes to peer at the TV world in the mini screen. She and the cameraman whisper.

"Actually, as we've stopped anyway, we just wondered, is there a teddy bear or something? A toy you could hold?"

Teresa blinks.

Craig comes forward to intervene. "A toy?"

The reporter looks awkward. "Well, if there's something the little girl loves. You know. It personalizes, makes it all more real. Is there, you know, a bear or monkey or something, something she dotes on? It would help."

"They're in her room. Her toys."

The reporter turns back to look at me as if she hadn't noticed my existence before. I feel my cheeks flush.

"Upstairs…"

The cameraman nods to the reporter, who says brightly: "Perfect."

Craig turns and heads up to Jessica's room. I pound after him, trying to keep up. By the time I get there, he's standing in front of the shelf, looking over the hard-faced dolls. He plucks one at random and heads back downstairs with it.

I don't follow. I stand there in the middle of the bedroom, quiet, thinking. He doesn't know the first thing about Jessica, that man. Those showy dolls weren't made for cuddling, they were designed to appeal to adults, not for children to love. Jessica never cared two hoots for them. Rabbit, that's the only toy she loves.

I sit heavily in the bedroom chair and look around at the pristine fairy pictures, the white-and-pink shelves, the jewelry box with its dancing ballerina. I look at Jessica's crumpled bed, the duvet heaped on the floor. She screamed out here, late at night. I think of the bruises down her side, the way she folded into herself when her mum came to the door to take her home and how she slowed herself down, delaying the moment when she had to go.

I think about Rabbit. No one else seems to realize that it isn't just Jessica who's gone missing. It's Rabbit too. If they had, they'd get to thinking about that. About the fact that Jessica can't have been spirited away by a stranger. She can't have been lifted, sleeping, from her bed. Jessica was awake. She must have been. Because she had time to find Rabbit and take her too.

CHAPTER THIRTY

Whatever inquiries the police are making, they certainly spread the word.

After the TV crew leaves, the vicar from the local church, St. Andrews, appears on the doorstep. I've seen her around: she's a thoughtful-faced woman with sensible shoes. I'm not a church-goer myself but I've nothing against it and I offer her a cup of tea and a muffin. We sit together in the kitchen for a while.

"How's she doing?"

The vicar doesn't need to explain who she means. She just nods discreetly toward the sitting room.

I whisper: "Not too well."

Teresa sits there, deathly pale, her hands twitching in her lap. Every time someone comes in, she looks up sharply and it's painful to see the flicker of hope in her face that gutters as soon as she realizes there's no news.

She's started saying: "What can I do?" every five minutes. "There must be something."

No one wants to tell her straight that she's in no fit state to do anything useful and she's just getting in the way. In the end, the policewoman helps her to her feet and they head upstairs together and it's a blessing to have her out of sight.

Craig paces up and down, making and taking phone calls. His shoulders are hunched and his face is dark with anger and he barely acknowledges the police. They've rowed again about the reporter's visit and whether the appeal can go on the telly just yet. She's only been missing for about nine hours, it just feels like more.

I quite like the vicar. She isn't the preachy kind and she doesn't make a meal out of being holy; she just sits quietly and drinks her tea and eats half the muffin—not all of it, thank you, she's dieting—and keeps watch with me.

A man appears in the hall and stands there for a while with a large cardboard box in his hands until Craig rescues it and sends him off with a signed paper. Craig plonks it on the kitchen table, right where we're finishing tea, and cuts through the tape with a blade.

"What do you think?" He pulls out papers and hands one to me, one to the vicar.

The sight of it makes me queasy. It's the sheet he designed that morning with "MISSING" printed in big letters across the top and a color picture of Jessica. A description underneath of her height and age and a plea for information. It has that pungent, heady smell of fresh ink and brings back a memory of school, all those years ago. I look at my fingers to see if they're smudgy with color but they're not. I open my mouth to say: *She's not a bloody cat*, then think better of it and shut it again and look out of the corner of my eye at the vicar, who has a thoughtful expression on her face.

"Well done." She seems the kind of person who often says "well done" to people. "How many are there?"

Craig checks the order form. "Two thousand." He hesitates, embarrassed. "It's a lot, I know, but it's the cost ratio, you know. In for a penny."

She hands him a card. "Just let me know, would you? When she turns up." As she leaves, she adds, almost under her breath, as if we can take it or leave it: "God bless."

I go through to the hall with her, to see her out, and Fran's there, standing at the gate, staring. She's in her school coat and her headphones are loose at her neck and her schoolbag hangs from her hand. She looks stricken. In shock.

Just then, Craig calls to the police officer in the hall, something about his leaflets—he wants the police to help—and the officer sighs and heads back toward the kitchen to deal with him.

I seize my chance and walk smartly out behind the vicar. I grab Fran by the arm. She turns to look at me and her eyes are frightened.

"It's Jessica." I keep my voice low and calm. "She's disappeared."

She doesn't answer. Just stares, then turns and tries to pull away, to go past me and into the house. I tighten my grip.

"No, petal." I twist her round and start pushing her along beside me, away from it all. Her feet drag as she tries again to shrug me off. I lean in close and whisper: "Stop it, Fran. Listen. I need you to be very grown up. Very brave. Now, come with me."

CHAPTER THIRTY-ONE

Fran was never what you'd call a big talker, but now she goes completely silent on me.

I walk her as fast as I can toward the common, pulling her along. The weather's turning and the clouds are darkening the sky, getting ready for rain. The image of the coffin is never far from my thoughts and every time it rises, I have to work a little harder to push it away.

When we reach the edge, I stop for a moment and stand there, looking out across the grass, smelling rain in the air.

"Let's cut across." I turn to Fran. Her face is pinched with worry. "It'll save time."

She runs with me across the grass. We find the path through the scrub and into the copse.

I think of Jessica and the day she slipped into the water here. Of those bruises. No kiddie deserves that. The light is fading. We're passing close to the cave now, picking our way over the rough ground. Fran stumbles and I reach out a hand to steady her. The rocks all around us look pitch-black and forbidding.

My foot kicks a plastic bottle in the undergrowth and it rolls out, clatters down the bank. Fran jumps at the sound, then hangs back. We're almost at the entrance to the cave now, and its sour smell, of foxes and cats, reaches for us.

I turn back to Fran. "Hurry up. It's getting dark."

I peer into the blackness of the cave and think of Jessica and the games we played there and all the other little ones I've brought here over the years. Children need make-believe and a little magic. They need a safe place to hide.

As I shake myself and move on, I realize Fran is standing still, lagging behind, watching me. There's a strange look on her face. She puts a hand to her mouth and, even through her fingers, I see it tug and crumple. Pellets of rain strike her forehead and burst there, run down her cheeks.

"You must be hungry." I retrace my steps until I'm at her side again, then take her schoolbag from her, put my arm around her shoulders, and ease her back into motion. Ahead, across the dark stretch of bushes and rocks and wiry grass, car headlights swing and flash on the road. "Let's find a nice, warm café, shall we?"

We're both faltering by the time we reach the far edge of the common. The nearest place to eat is a small Greek deli on a gusty corner. It's almost deserted inside. The stout, middle-aged woman behind the counter wipes down the insides of glass cabinets and wraps dishes of salad in cling film as a prelude to closing time.

We settle in the window, me with a cup of tea and Fran with a mug of hot chocolate. She looks chilled, inside and out, and I press her to drink it.

"Try not to worry." I look at her pinched face. She's just a child herself. "I know it's scary. But you need to be brave."

She doesn't answer. She licks cream off the top of the hot chocolate and sips it. We both know she doesn't really feel like it. She's doing her best to humor me and the sight of that—the child trying to look after the adult—makes me bite my lip, look past her to the road and the darkening mass of the common beyond.

The rain falls in sheets now, blown sideways by the wind. Cars slosh past in a steady stream. The café door rattles as a sudden gust knocks it about in the frame. The woman behind the counter stops, raises her head to look, sighs under her breath, then goes back to her work. She's dark-haired and I wonder if she's Greek herself and, if so, if she grieves for the sun.

I turn back to Fran. She's slouching, her face hanging forward over the mug.

"You hungry?"

She pulls a face. I think of Teresa and Craig, one hiding upstairs in her room and the other already launching a public information campaign, whatever the police think. Neither seems likely to remember to feed the daughter they still do have. I call across to the woman, who's lifted a dish of moussaka from the cabinet and is covering what's left.

"Could you do us some of that, please? With some bread, maybe?"

The woman pauses and looks pointedly at the clock. It's nearly half past five.

"No bread left."

"That's OK. Just moussaka then."

She doesn't answer, just makes a labor out of peeling back the cling film, cutting square portions of cold moussaka, and placing them into shallow bowls, then carrying them through to the back. A microwave door clicks and slams and there's a low whirr as it starts.

"Try to eat something," I say when the plates arrive. "It might be all you get this evening."

Fran pushes the remains of her hot chocolate to one side and picks at the food. I do the same.

"Didn't you know she'd gone?"

"No. Well, not really." She pauses, sunk inside herself. "She wasn't there at breakfast, you know. Her mum was doing her nut, as usual. I tried to help but she told me to go. I nearly missed the bus."

Something and nothing. She must have forgotten about it

during the day, busy at school, then come home to find no answer at my place and her own home in chaos. No wonder she looked stunned.

"Was everything OK last night?"

She shrugs. "About normal."

The moussaka is homemade and pretty good, even reheated. We sit quietly for a few minutes, eating. I think about what she said.

"What's normal?"

She snorts. "You know. Bit of a fight around bedtime. Usual stuff."

"Who, your mum and dad?"

Her lifts her eyes and glares: "She's *not* my mum." She pauses, eyes back on the plate, eats a bit more. "Anyway, Dad was out. He's always late nowadays. I never get to see him."

"So who was fighting?"

"Her and Jessica. They do that, you know? Jessica messes about and then she loses her rag."

I think of the bruises. "Does she ever hit her?"

She can't look at me. Her jaw stops moving but she doesn't go ahead and eat any more. Everything is suddenly too tense.

I say: "I won't tell, Fran. I'm just worried about Jessica."

She puts down her knife and fork and pushes her plate away. She's eaten maybe half. I do the same.

The woman behind the counter steps forward at once and interrupts. "Finished? Anything else?" She removes the plates and nods at the uneaten food. "I can pack it, if you like."

While she does, I turn back to Fran. "No one can hit a child. You know that, don't you? There's a law against it."

She studies the top of the table. It's gritty with sugar.

"Fran, you can trust me. You can."

She shakes her head.

"Why not?"

She squirms, reluctant to talk. I lean forward, arms resting on the dirty table between us.

"Fran, this is serious. Don't you see? The police are involved. They'll want to ask you questions, too. You might as well tell me."

She frowns. Again, she seems to shrink from me, to retreat inside herself.

"Is there something you saw? Something her mum said? Or your dad?"

She mumbles, her head down.

"You can't what?"

"I can't tell you."

"Why not?" I press forward. "Why, Fran? Are you frightened of getting into trouble?"

The café woman strides over and plonks a handwritten bill in front of me, then drops a paper bag beside it. I peer inside. A foil carton of leftovers. She stands there, waiting, while I get out my purse and pay.

"Take it." I push the doggy bag into Fran's schoolbag and hand it back to her. "You might want it later."

Outside, the gusts across the common nearly take us off our feet. We walk together, heads down, close to the row of buildings. Rain paints a wet stripe down the sleeve of my coat.

By the time we reach the corner of our road, my shoes are slopping water. Ahead, blue lights flash, sending sudden splashes of color across the wet street.

I grab Fran's sleeve. "Come and stay with me tonight."

She stares. "Why?"

I want to say: *To escape the police, to escape all of them. I'll keep you safe.* I take a deep breath and try to keep my voice level. "It might be a bit crazy at home. That's all."

She hesitates, her eyes trying to read mine in the darkness.

I shrug. "I just thought it'd be nice. You know. You and me. We get on, don't we, Fran?"

She pulls away from me and sets off briskly toward home. I have to hurry to catch up.

"What is it, Fran? You know I love you, don't you? And Jessica."

"Me, too." Her voice trembles. As we rush along, side by side, the hood of her coat blows off and the rain plasters her hair to her cheeks and drips down her forehead and nose. Her brow is knitted and she looks very young and very fragile.

She opens her gate and I follow her down the path, reaching her as she finds the bell.

A female police officer opens the door and, seeing Fran, hesitates.

Fran says in a cross voice: "I live here," and pushes her way inside.

I say: "Any news?"

The woman shakes her head and stands back to let me in too, but I turn and climb over the rail to my own path and fish for my keys. From their house, Craig's voice drifts out, raised: "Where've you been? You're soaking!" and my chest aches and I wish so much that Fran had said yes to me and come here where she could be safe and loved and away from all that madness. But, even as I hesitate, listening, their front door bangs shut and it's already too late.

CHAPTER THIRTY-TWO

It's dark outside but I don't bother to draw the curtains. I sit very still in the sitting room in my damp clothes and listen. I can't eat. Not even tea. Not even a glass of wine. My body is so heavy, weighted in the chair, that I can't move. I feel suddenly ancient and trapped inside myself and I think again of the solid wood of a coffin. I close my eyes and shiver.

I can almost hear Jessica's giggle and see her scamper across the room, joyful, eager to explore. I think of the way her ribs showed clearly through her skin as she breathed, her skin young and perfect, without a sag or wrinkle or roll of fat anywhere. Of the sweet, clean smell of her hair when she sat on my lap and the soft crush of her when she snuggled against me in the chair to read. I wonder if that vicar's praying for her. I'm beyond that. Prayer. I lost the way of it a long time ago.

Footsteps thud next door and the front door opens, sending out a cloud of noise, police radios and strange male voices and stomping down the path. The gate squeaks and clangs. It's all so close, it could be my house. It could be me. A car engine revs and blue light swings across the front of the house, bouncing off the wall. I want to get up, to see who's leaving and how many are left behind, spying on us through the night, but I can't move.

Later, the sound of the wind shrieking in the chimney and the dash of rain on the windowpanes reminds me of storms when I was a girl. My mum stuffed newspaper in the cracks but it never kept out the drafts and when it rained, the sitting room fire hissed with spots down the chimney and threw up steam from hot coals. That was before she had the gas fire put in. I haven't thought about that for the longest time and I wonder why it's come back to me now, and whether that too is a sign of getting old and close to dying.

Eventually, the darkness thickens. The sounds of movement next door subside and settle. In the silence, the house emits low creaks and sighs and scratches as the wind rages, and I think of the rats and poor Mrs. Matthews, who died in such squalor in the end.

After a while, I must doze off, because I have strange fancies, that the noises around me sound like the remnants of all the strangers who lived here before me and Mum and Susie, in the 110 years since these walls were built. My ears throb and I wonder if I'm coming down with something, a fever perhaps from the soaking and the shock, the way I'm mixing together the past and present like this, the dead and the living.

Somehow, I find the strength to heave myself to my feet and pull myself, step by step, up the stairs. The bedroom is cold and I hunch under the covers, my feet numb, feeling the last remnants of warmth ebb away from my body. Slowly, I start to sink into the mattress as my body gives way to exhaustion and, as I do, my worn old skeleton starts suddenly to shake, rocking the tired bedsprings, there in the darkness. It's the terror I've been trying all day to suffocate. The rising horror of what's to come.

I see the cold-eyed police officer with his plain clothes, watching from the corner of the room. And it seems, all at once, as if he's always been there, all my life, silently waiting for me, around every corner, in every park, on every street. I huddle into a ball and moan and the voice in my head says, clearly now: *The game's up, Angie. They're coming for you, my girl. They're coming.*

CHAPTER THIRTY-THREE
TERESA

Jessica loves a story about a wolf with stones in its stomach. Heavy, hard weights. It dies in the end. It creeps into my mind now, that story. I never thought before how the wolf must feel; its pain as it drags itself around, trying to get relief. Its fear. Its sense of its own looming destruction.

It hurts so much. Not just my mind but my body. The pounding head, twisted intestines. *Innards*, isn't that the word people used? Rocks in my stomach. I can barely move for the weight.

I lie now in bed, the bedside light on, curled sideways into a ball. Jess likes to sleep on her back, arms thrown out above her head, a line of stomach exposed between her pajamas. Safe. But she wasn't. I didn't keep her safe. The mattress sighs as I shudder. A trembling I can't stop. I'm in the grip of some giant, invisible hand that reaches down and shakes me.

Wind rattles the glass in the windows. Gusts, out there. Arrows of rain. I hope she's sheltered, wherever she is. She'll be freezing, in her pajamas. Soaked to the skin. I see her huddled somewhere, whimpering.

Noises drift up from downstairs. A man's voice in the hall. The bang of the front door. Heavy boots. Male. I hunch forward and tighten my arms around my body. My hands press down on ribs that keep rising and falling, rising and falling, despite everything. A moan comes into the room, an animal cry, and I realize it's my own.

I try to close my eyes but I see such pictures there. They lie in wait for me. Jessica, lying still in undergrowth, her pale face smeared with dirt and leaves. Her cheeks cold. I bite my lip and twist onto my other side. Jessica, carried out of the house and away down the street in someone's arms. Driven away in the back of someone's car. Hurt. Abused. Crying out for me. Why can't I hear? I stiffen and concentrate on listening. Was that her? A small, high voice. *Mummy!* The way she calls for me in the night, in her sleep. My shoulders sag. Just the voice of the wind, shaking the windowpane.

A soft tread on the stairs. The bedroom door creaks open. I catch my breath and listen.

"Teresa?"

A low voice, barely more than a whisper. That woman from the police. I forget her name. I don't want her. I don't want to be carefully handled. Mother of the missing. Mother of the victim. I know what they really think: *Keep an eye on her. Maybe she did it. She used to shout at her child, that poor little girl. That's what people say. She slapped her. She hit her partner. If she did that, what else might she have done?*

"Are you awake?"

Stealthy feet across the carpet. A faint smell of perfumed soap.

"Can I get you anything?" Low, calm tones. They train them to talk like that. She knows I'm awake. She knows everything. Except the one thing that matters. Where Jessica is.

"Any news?" I open my eyes. Her skin is lined but her eyes are blue and very clear and they hover close to mine as she stoops to see my face.

"Not really. They've got a few leads. They're checking them all out."

"What leads?" My eyes widen. The sudden pain in my chest is suffocating.

"Sssh." She pats my shoulder. "Just from people around here, people who think they might have seen her. Everyone's doing what they can. But it takes time."

Time. Low light presses in through the gap between the curtains and confuses me. I struggle to piece it together. It's evening. It was only this morning that she went missing. Less than twenty-four hours. Already, it seems a lifetime. "What if I forget what she looks like?" I stare out at her. "What she smells like?"

I start to sob and she puts a hand on my shoulder and pats it through the duvet. Pat, pat. Slow and steady.

When I quieten, I say: "What time is it?"

"Just after six."

I start. "Where's Fran?" She should be home by now.

"She's fine." The soft voice. Never ruffled. I should have been a mum like that. "She's downstairs. She got wet out there but she's all dry now."

"Has she eaten?"

"She's fine."

Rain peppers the window. It's the wolf again, huffing and puffing. Trying to blow down our house.

She says: "What about something to eat? Some toast, maybe? Or a little sandwich?"

I shake my head. "You'll tell me, won't you? The slightest thing?"

"Of course."

I let my eyes fall closed again. The woman's joints creak as she stands up and retreats. Her soft footfall on the stairs. Back into the fray.

Leads. I try to imagine what that means. What did they see, these strangers? What do they know? I don't trust them to tell me the truth. I can't trust anyone.

Downstairs, Craig is pacing up and down the hall. I know his voice, quick and efficient on the phone. All day, he's been organizing people, arranging things. He seems so—I hesitate, struggling to think—so *normal*. I think of his hand on my arm, guiding me. Of his eyes, watching me. Of the tightness in his face every time a police officer tries to talk to me. My eyes stare up at the shadows on the ceiling. He hasn't cried. All day, he hasn't cried.

I twist into the pillow and start to cry again, howling. My eyes are hot and wet and my nose runs and I cry until I'm exhausted. Memories come from nowhere, surging into my head. For the first time in years, I think about Jessica's father, about calling him, tracking him down across the Atlantic. He should suffer, too. *You had a daughter, you didn't know that, did you? She had your eyes. Your lopsided grin. Where were you when she was taken? When she was stolen from her bed in the middle of the night?*

I squeeze my eyes closed, press my palms into the wet sockets. It's not his fault. I know that. It can't be his fault if he never knew. I didn't want him to. He was a one-night stand—he didn't have any claim on me or on her. I had some pride.

I think back to those first weeks and months after Jess was born. It was hard. Harder than I ever imagined. The sleeplessness, the crying, the suffocation of being always with her, always, with no chance of escape. But there was goodness, too. I suppose I'd almost forgotten that.

Before, I'd had a fast-paced, anonymous life as a young, single woman. I was never a party girl but I dated, I had fun. I knew people. I knew people my own age, all over London. But no one close to my flat, in the part of London I happened to live.

Then I was pushing a buggy with Jessica inside, that tiny baby girl who seemed to see right through me, who seemed to judge me from the start. Who knew me for the failure of a mother I really was. All those single friends my own age melted away as if they'd never been. How could I blame them?

And something else happened. A veil that had parted me from my community suddenly lifted. I swam into their vision and they into mine. When did I ever talk to random strangers before becoming a mum? Strangers don't stop a smartly dressed young woman as she marches to and from the station, to and from the office. I didn't have time, anyway, to talk. I was too busy. But now I walked down the street with baby Jessica and people I'd never seen before would smile at me, stop to chat, peer into the buggy to see.

"Little girl? What's her name? Jessica? That's lovely."

Warm smile. Kindness. I was grateful but inside I felt like such a fraud. I was too afraid to say: *Help me, please. I'm drowning.*

"Hello, little Jessica. Aren't you gorgeous?"

Then back to me. "Well done, you. How are you doing?"

How could I possibly say?

Now, remembering what a mess I made of it all, right from the start, what a wretched mother I've been, I press my face back into the pillow, utterly bereft, and sob.

CHAPTER THIRTY-FOUR

I doze. I wake with a dry mouth and crusty eyes. The room is dark. The wind still splatters rain against the windows but with less force. For a moment, my mind hangs, suspended, catching up. Then it hits me. *Jessica, my baby girl. Where are you?* I start to shake all over again. The nausea. The aching. The stones, weighing me down.

The front door bangs again. Someone with news? I stiffen and listen. Nothing. Someone must have left. Fran's door, above me, shuts and the low bass of her music sounds for a moment, then disappears.

The room sways when I try to sit up. I move like an old woman, feeling for the end of the bed and using it as a lever, a prop. Easing myself to my feet and heading for the door. My body feels sweaty and rank inside crumpled clothes. I creak slowly up the stairs, one by one, leaning heavily on the banisters.

A line of light shows under Fran's door. Jessica's room, alongside, is in darkness. I go inside. The curtains are open and the window glistens with streaks of light from next door. I cross to them and pull them closed.

I stand for a moment, with the edges of the curtains in my hands, straining to think back. I did exactly this twenty-four hours ago as I put Jessica to bed. I drew the curtains, standing right here at the window.

I turn and go back into the middle of the room, looking, remembering. Trying to bring back the details. There must be something. I helped her into her pajamas, tucked her into bed, and read her a story. I look over at the shelf. That picture book about the bears, there it is, lying on the top of the pile.

I sink down onto the carpet and sit with my back against her bed. Then what happened? Isn't there anything I can remember that might help? She hunched over on her side and I leaned down and stroked the hair from her face and kissed her goodnight. Then I went downstairs. She didn't even call for me. She seemed calmer than usual, and tired out. When I looked in on my way to bed, she was fast asleep, sprawled on her back with the duvet kicked off. I remember straightening it to tuck around her again.

I shake my head, rub my cheeks with my palms. *What was different about last night?* There must be something, some clue of what was to come. I close my eyes, trying not to cry. Nothing. It was so very normal. Just another ordinary bedtime.

It's quiet downstairs. After all the people, all the commotion, it feels deserted.

When I cross the hall toward the kitchen, Craig's there at the sink, scrubbing at something on the draining board. His hands are thick with suds.

"What're you doing?"

He jumps. "I didn't hear you."

I go across to see. He's pounding at a shirtsleeve with a scrubbing brush. I've never seen him do that before.

"What happened?"

"Just keeping myself busy." He shrugs, bundles the shirt up in his hand, and takes it through to the washing machine. It's inside and the machine switched on before I can get a closer look.

I stand there, thinking about it. It bothers me.

He comes back and says: "Shall I put the oven on? There's chicken in the fridge."

"I'm not hungry."

He gives me a strange look. "You've got to eat."

My throat aches. I turn away from him and put the kettle on. "Tea?"

"Sure." He looks uncertain, trying to read me. He puts bread in the toaster and gets butter and a slab of cheddar cheese from the fridge. Comfort food. Normally I'd offer to cook him something more substantial. But this isn't normal and I don't.

I make tea and stand against the worktop to drink it, cradling the mug in my hands as if I need its warmth. My eyes are sore. I can't face going through to the sitting room. I don't want to sit down, to be comfortable. I can't settle. I'm in too much pain.

I feel Craig's eyes on me but I don't look back. I screen him out and the silence between us is hostile. *Serves him right.* I think of the lonely evenings in this house and Lorraine and the misery he's caused me. And now this. Now Jessica.

Finally, when he's eaten his first slice of toast, he comes across to me and tries to put his arms around my waist. I keep my eyes on my tea and don't respond.

He kisses the side of my face. "It's unbearable. I know. I can't imagine what you're feeling."

"No," I say. "You can't." I nearly add: *Because it's not your daughter, is it?*

"But she'll be OK. Wherever she is. I know it."

He hesitates and I don't help him out by responding and he carries on, his voice murmuring. It isn't natural for him, this emotional stuff. He's struggling, and I let him.

"This time tomorrow, we'll be back to normal. You'll see. Jessica asleep in bed and the two of us having dinner as if nothing ever happened."

I say: "Really?" My voice has a hard edge. *As if nothing ever happened?* Everything's happened. It can never be the same again.

I go back to drinking my tea, pretending not to notice that

he looks forlorn as he returns to the breadboard and his second slice of toast.

"Word's getting out, that's the thing." He scrapes butter on the toast, slices pieces of cheese with care, and makes a jigsaw of them on top. "We could hear any minute. And if we don't, well, I'll keep fighting to get it on the telly. There's the flyers. Someone must have seen something."

I think about the police family liaison woman. "They've got leads already. Did they tell you?"

He nods, crunching toast, swallows. "She can't just vanish."

I feel suddenly light-headed and grope my way to the kitchen table and a chair. I sit there, looking at Jessica's paintings on the fridge. Wild brush strokes in thick paint, the colors bright. Orange is her favorite. And red. Underneath, a small smudged handprint on a piece of card. My lip trembles.

I turn on him. "Why can't they search the house? What's the big deal?"

Craig comes and sits beside me. "It's a waste of time, of resources. See?"

I look away. "But why not? We've nothing to hide."

He sighs and tries to move closer. "Of course. I know that. But think. They're short of people as it is. They need to be out there, gathering information and finding out where she is, not poking through our drawers."

My body is stiff, holding itself away from him, from this man I thought I loved. His cheek is a mess of dried blood and yellow bruising where I hit him. I turn away.

I say: "It's weird. Not letting them."

He lifts a hand and rakes it through his hair.

I persist. "It's suspicious. I don't mind them looking through our stuff. Who cares?"

He blows air from his cheeks. I see for the first time how tired he looks, how gray his skin is.

"I just think they should do their job properly. That's all. And the last thing we need right now is coppers crawling all over us, right?"

"I just want her home."

I crumple and start to sob. He moves in a heartbeat, taking the drooping mug from my hands and pressing me against him. His arms are strong and warm and the familiar male smell of him, of Craig, breaks me into pieces.

"Where is she?" I'm weeping now, gulping and messy. "What if someone's taken her? Some pervert or trafficker or..."

"Don't say that."

He rocks me in his arms until the crying subsides. Afterward, I cling to him, my face in the spreading wet patch on his chest. Behind us, the washing machine whirrs and spins. When he pulls away from me and reaches in his pocket for a hankie, his eyes are wet too, and I'm relieved. He should cry. "We need to stick together, Tess." He wipes my eyes and runny nose as if I'm a child. As if I'm Jessica. His hankie smells of fresh ironing. "I don't want to alarm you, but we're all suspects, until they find out what really happened."

"Suspects?" I frown, pulling away from him. "I haven't done anything."

I feel my cheeks grow hot as I remember the things I don't want anyone to know. The slaps and the shouting and the bruises down Jessica's side from the times we've fought. I never mean to be rough. She just bruises so easily. I have to wrestle with her sometimes to get her moving.

"I know. Neither have I. But they have to figure that out. They'll look for things. And the longer it takes to find her, the more pressure they'll pile on." He reaches forward and kisses the tip of my nose. "That's what they're like."

I think of all the questions they asked this morning, going over and over the same ground until I wanted to scream. When

I'd last seen her. How she'd been behaving. All about my working hours and what happens to Jessica during the day.

"I can't bear it."

"I know." He puts his hankie back in his pocket. "But we have to."

He gets to his feet and goes back to the worktop, brushes the crumbs from the breadboard into the bin, and puts the knife in the dishwasher. It looks odd, seeing him potter around the kitchen.

"They kept asking me about Angie, next door."

"Me, too." He doesn't look surprised. "Why was she here? Did you ask her round?"

I shake my head. He's right. She was hanging around all day. It hadn't really registered.

"Maybe she's just worried." I think of Jessica, sitting happily at her battered kitchen table. "She's very fond of Jessica."

He hesitates and then says, without looking at me: "You had references for her, didn't you? I mean, they all checked out?"

"Of course." I say it too quickly, repeating the same lie I told the police. I had meant to. There just wasn't time. I mean, the girls clearly liked her. She seemed fine. Her references said all the right things. Who actually cross-checks something like that? Life's too short.

He says: "That's what I thought. They asked me and I wasn't sure, that's all."

Then his phone rings and he's off, striding away into the hall and murmuring.

I shout after him: "Who is it? Is there news?"

He turns and cups his hand over the receiver for a moment and shouts back: "No. Just work. Sorry."

He moves farther away and hunches near the front door and all my doubts about him come flooding back in a moment, about his secrecy and the lies about where he's been, who he's been with.

I get to my feet and drop the mug in the dishwasher and go through the hall on my way upstairs. As I do, he walks past me into the sitting room and I can't help wondering if it's to stop me from overhearing his conversation. I hesitate for a moment, trying to listen, but I can't make anything out.

I go wearily up to our bedroom, then into our bathroom, where I run a hot shower and stand under it, letting the water stream over my shoulders, watching the steam rise and cloud the tiles, tense and sick and trying to stop myself from trembling, all over again.

I soap myself down and my flesh flushes red in the heat. I think: *What was the real reason he stopped the police from searching the house?* Was it really just to stop them from wasting time, as he said? To protect me from feeling invaded?

I switch off the water, step out, and wrap myself round in a towel. The steam billows around me as I enter the bedroom. The bed is crumpled and uninviting but I don't want to go back downstairs again, to be with him. I want to be alone.

I rub myself down and climb under the covers, glowing from the hot water. I lie very still and feel the coolness of the sheets and study the ceiling. My insides twist and knot.

Why else might he say no? I stare up blankly, miserable and afraid. *What could there be that he doesn't want them to find?*

CHAPTER THIRTY-FIVE

It isn't easy splitting yourself into two people. I can do it—I'm smart—but it's tougher than I thought. There's the outside me, all horror and grief and oh my god, what's happened to poor little Jessica, boo-hoo, why can't they find her? And there's the inside me. The one trying to keep control in a different way. I knew I was a good liar but I never knew how good until now. I guess it's a skill.

I'm scared. I admit it. I never thought it would blow up in my face the way it has. I mean, TV reporters and police all over the street for a three-year-old who's only been gone a day? It's not as though they've found a body. She's just logged as missing. Don't kids go missing all the time?

There's talk of a search party tomorrow, to comb the common. I'm almost proud. Maybe I could even volunteer.

Regret? No point going there. What's done is done. I can't afford to fall apart.

So I don't sleep much. The next morning, I see myself in the mirror and I look wretched. That's when I figure it out. That the trick to being convincing isn't to fake emotion, it's to use what comes. Take it, run with it, just dress it up as something else. So I look red-eyed? Good. I can say I was awake half the night, listening to the sound of the rain against the windows and worrying about her. Boo-hoo, poor little baby.

After all, people acting strangely in a crisis is actually normal, right?

I should've realized there'd be a fuss. I suppose I did. I just never expected it to get so big, so fast.

CHAPTER THIRTY-SIX

ANGIE

I'm sitting in the kitchen over breakfast when they bang on the door. Two police officers are in uniform. A third, in plain clothes, stands between them. As I open the door, he's looking the other way, back down the path, but then his face swings around and I know him at once from yesterday. Those sharp eyes that see everything. He's the one who kept watch next door as people came and went, who sniffs out guilt.

I try to smile but my mouth is suddenly tight, and it feels more like a grimace.

"Any news?" I look from one grim face to another.

The plain-clothed man shakes his head and his eyes stray past me into the hall. *Yes*, I think, *a bit different from next door, isn't it? Shabby. Cluttered. Needs work*. I lift my chin. Being short of money isn't a crime, not the last time I looked.

"May we come in?"

It's more of an order than a question. We sit awkwardly in the sitting room, the plain-clothed officer, one of the constables, and I. The other constable stays out in the hall as if we might need guarding and it makes me feel sick, not knowing what he's up to, where he might go.

The sharp-eyed one does the talking. The constable opens a notebook and writes.

"Just need to go over a few details, Mrs., er, Dodd?"

"Angela Dodd." I told them that yesterday morning, the first time they came. He's playing a game, asking questions when he already knows the answers. It's a trap. My chest is prickling and I'm starting to get those feelings again, my feelings of being chased, of being cornered. *Anxiety*, that's what the doctor said. *Depression*. Of course, I never told her the whole story.

"Mrs. Dodd, what exactly is your relationship with Jessica Law and her family?"

I shrug. My hands find each other in my lap and when I look down, one set of podgy fingers is picking at the other set, a restless, punishing movement, like rats gnawing through thick rope.

"They're neighbors." I stutter. "Friends. You know."

When I falter, the only sound is the scrabble of the constable's pen across the paper, the rustle of a turning page. I want to see what he's writing. Is he just taking down what I say, or is he making notes about me?

The silence stretches and finally I falter on: "Well, like I said before, I look after the children sometimes. Jessica's only three so she's not in school yet. Her mum drops her around at mine sometimes when she goes to work. And Fran, well, Fran's eleven. She stops by after school and joins us for tea sometimes."

"Sometimes?" He pauses. "How many days a week, would you say?"

His eyes are on mine and he has the unblinking stare of a snake. I wonder what Teresa has already told him.

I mumble: "Don't know. A few."

"Ms. Law says you look after the girls every day during the week because she works full-time. Sometimes, that lasts until well into the evening."

I don't say anything. What's the point? Anything you say, they use against you, this lot.

"Are you a registered childminder, Mrs. Dodd?"

I shake my head. "Didn't see the need. Just being neighborly, you know."

He narrows his eyes. "Cash in hand?"

My eyes slide down to the carpet.

"Are you aware, Mrs. Dodd, that anyone providing childcare for more than two hours a day in return for reward is required by law to be officially registered?"

The carpet is speckled with biscuit crumbs and a few dried apple pips. Jessica loves a biscuit. Likes making them, too. I can see her now, kneeling up at the kitchen table with my red apron's strings looped twice around her waist, sticking her finger in the mix every time she thinks I'm not looking.

"It's quite a business, getting registration." His voice has a hard edge to it. "Lots of checks." He pauses and it's a warning, a "you know and I know" going on beneath the words. "And they need to approve the place of care, too, of course. Make sure the paperwork's up to date. Such a lot nowadays. You need certificates for everything. Electrics. Appliances. Smoke alarms. Gas safety." He turns his head and looks pointedly at the ancient gas fire. "Which in your case..."

"I haven't used that in years." I'm flustered.

He raises his eyebrows. "Carbon monoxide is deadly, Mrs. Dodd. Wouldn't want to poison the kids, would you?"

The constable pauses with his writing and looks up, suddenly alert.

"I'm just helping out." I lift my eyes and look back at them both, trying to pretend I'm not frightened. "It's not easy, being a working mum. I've done it myself."

He gives a thin smile. I feel a sudden chill and lower my eyes again at once.

"Of course, we're not here to investigate all that, are we?" His tone changes from stern to conciliatory. "We're not from the benefits fraud department. We're not from Her Majesty's tax office. We're police officers. And all we want is what you want, I'm sure. To find little Jessica. Safe and sound." He plants his broad hands on the arms of the chair and pushes himself to his feet. "So, would you mind, Mrs. Dodd, if we have a look around?"

What can I say? I know blackmail when I hear it. I don't suppose the constable wrote that bit down. I take a deep breath and shrug and in my lap, my hands clasping each other.

"Help yourself."

CHAPTER THIRTY-SEVEN

Four constables search the house. The plain-clothed one walks from room to room, watching. Those eyes miss nothing. They turn on me too every now and again as if he can tell from my face where they need to dig deep and where they needn't bother. I keep thinking of that game I play with children. Hotter and colder. The police officers go through the cupboard under the stairs. Cold, very cold. Freezing. What on earth do they think they'll find in there?

Then they head upstairs. I hate watching but I can't do anything else: I can't sit down in my sitting room on my own, can I, while those men stick their hands in my wardrobes and drawers—going through my mum's stuff, too—handling everything with plastic gloves, and rummaging through the bags and boxes packed away under the beds.

At times, they split and search two rooms at once. He watches me as I dash from one to another, trying to keep check on them. They find a load of papers, official stuff, you know, from the council and the gas company. Private. I walk in just as one of them has them spread out on top of the dresser and is taking pictures of them with his phone.

"Hey! Stop that!"

The plain-clothed man appears at my side in a moment. "Problem?"

His smells reach for me. Fresh male sweat and lemon detergent. I wonder who washes and irons those shirts.

I glare at him. "That's personal."

He steps up to have a look over the constable's shoulder and see the papers for himself, says something in a low voice. The man shoves it all back into the file and sticks it back in place, then carries on rummaging. No apology. No move to delete the pictures he's already taken.

They've no right, poking about in here. I want to say to them: *Go and have a nosy next door. Dig into their secrets. That man, flogging funerals for a living, and that woman who doesn't have time to care for her own little girl. Ask them about the crying at night, about the bruises.* But I don't dare. I don't say a word.

They move to the back bedroom, the make-believe room. The plain-clothed man stands for a moment in the doorway, peering into the gloom.

"Photography?"

I blink, then realize what he means. "No. It's for children. It's a playroom."

He gives me an odd look. "Why's it so dark?"

I tut and just shrug. What's the point? How do you go about explaining make-believe to a policeman? The magic of letting go of what's real and escaping into fantasy, into being and doing anything you can imagine? One look at this man and you can see his heart shriveled a long time ago, if it was ever alive at all.

He lifts a hand and gestures to his men to go inside. They switch on torches and pick their way through to the window, start ripping off the tape holding the blackout blind in place.

"Careful." I can't help it. "Don't tear it." What would little Jessica say? She loved her magic room. "Make sure you put it all back afterward. Just like you found it."

The officer in charge raises his eyebrows and picks his way farther into the room, those eyes scanning left and right. It's been a while since light streamed in here and it's a shock. It penetrates dark, shadowy corners that are better left unseen.

The columns of air are thick with dancing dust and it multiplies, sending clouds through the air as the men part the hanging curtains of material with their coarse hands. Their faces are incredulous and slightly disgusted, as if they suspect me of something perverted.

I bite my lip, pained by the sight of them, trampling over the children's cushions and scraps of magic carpet. The air seems suddenly stuffy and stale with a hint of damp. Everything— the tails of chiffon draped from the ceiling, the old lengths of sequined velvet, the wisps of cotton—looks faded and worn in the strong sunlight. I shake my head. They don't understand the first thing, these men. It might look tatty to them but it's powerful to little ones. They get it at once.

One man examines the string of colored fairy lights up close. Another pulls the blanket off the old puppet theater and coughs, shielding his mouth with the back of his hand and grimacing. A third stoops to the wicker basket and lifts the wolf puppet by the tail between a thumb and forefinger, turns it slowly in the light, his mouth tight, then lets it fall. He does the same with the old grandma puppet, then with the squirrel and mouse.

The first man moves on to the doll's cot. He eases the blanket off the ragdoll and moves it to one side, probes underneath it with his adult fingers.

I hear little Jessica's voice in my head, close to a sob: *Stop it! They're ruining everything!*

I know, petal, I say back to her. *I know. There's nothing I can do.*

All this time, the plain-clothed man is standing motionless in the middle of the room, watching, looking, seeing it all through his own joyless eyes.

I don't know what they expected to find. They seem dispirited as they come away, and I'm glad.

I stand on the landing and watch as they climb up the ladder to the attic. Their footsteps crash overhead as they disturb the dust, peer in boxes and cases and run their fat fingers through my mother's things.

Later, downstairs, a constable searching the kitchen pulls down the list of rules from the fridge and presents them to the boss as if it's evidence.

He reads it through, raises his eyes to mine. "Anything can happen?" He reads my face. "Everything is secret?"

I shrug. "What's wrong with that?"

He narrows his eyes. He will trap me if he can and I sense it, fear it, look quickly away.

He leans closer to me and the smell of male sweat is stronger than before, and sour now. He says in a low voice: "And what secrets did you make little Jessica keep?"

CHAPTER THIRTY-EIGHT

When I can finally shut the door on them, I go quietly to the window and peer out, keeping my distance from the curtains so they don't stir and give me away. The constables go out of my gate and turn back on themselves at once, back through next door's gate and toward their front door. Crime scene HQ. Only the one in plain clothes heads off to one of the cars, pulling his phone from his jacket pocket as he walks. He opens the back door and climbs inside, already talking, then disappears from sight. I imagine him checking in with someone. Reporting back. Plotting their next move.

He's in one of a line of police cars now standing outside— not even parked properly, just abandoned in the road. A few hundred yards farther down, police tape is tied right across the street, from a lamppost on our side to one on the other. Such a nuisance. There's a policeman guarding the cordon. Half the street is blocked in, people unable to get their cars out without permission.

Beyond, there's a TV truck with a mast sticking out of the roof and a set of steps on the side. Huddles of men and women— reporters, I suppose—stand about in twos and threes, hands in pockets, shoulders hunched, chatting. Some have takeaway coffee cups in their hands. Some have notebooks or tablets. They're all angled roughly the same way, facing down the street toward us, like sunflowers toward the sun.

My knees buckle and I make it back to the kitchen and sit

heavily. The last piece of toast, still half-buttered on my plate, is hard. My tea's stone cold and the milk has separated into swirls on the surface. I need to get up again and clear away and wash up the breakfast dishes and maybe make myself a fresh pot, but I'm shaking all over and I haven't the strength to move. Not yet.

I look around the kitchen. It's safer here. Farther from the street. Harder for them to spy. But the sense of violation is everywhere. In the tea-towel on the floor, swept off the radiator by some clumsy, passing constable; in the faint traces left by muddy boots on the tiles; in a half-open cupboard door that bulges where casseroles and pans have been shoved back out of place.

My head's muzzy. I lower my face to the mesh of my hands and close my eyes. It's all coming back. The male sweat and uniforms. The faceless officers, tramping back and forth, prying, photographing, gathering evidence. The helplessness. The guilt. The grief.

I sit, trembling, for a long time. When I summon the power, I manage to pour myself a glass of wine and drink it off, hoping to stop the shakes, to blur the pictures in my head, to deaden the noises in my ears. I don't need to move. I just listen. And wait.

The knock on the door sounds like the blow of an ax on the wood. It reminds me of something and I pause, trying to find the memory from long ago. A play in church when I was a child. A bunch of knights, loud and frightening in chainmail, burst in to murder a priest. I understood very little of the play but I understood that. The terror of being taken.

I open the door to find the plain-clothed officer there. He's come back for me, as I knew he would. Flanked again by his men.

He doesn't speak for a moment and I feel as if a thought passes between us without words: *I know why you're here and you know I know and what else is there really to say?*

Then he says, firmly but politely: "Please would you come down to the station with me, to answer a few more questions?"

I say: "Can't you ask them here?"

He answers with a look that says: *Come now, you know better than that, but I don't blame you for trying.*

I say: "Am I under arrest?"

He gives his thin smile. "Just helping with inquiries. That's all."

That's all.

I get my coat and bag and fumble about looking for my keys and make a performance of locking up, then realize how absurd that looks when the place is swarming with police.

He leads me out and opens the back door of the patrol car and it's been a long time—years—since a man held open a car door for me. Someone's at an upstairs window across the street, watching it all. I keep my head low and get in. A moment later, the car swings forward and out into the road.

A constable lifts the plastic tape as we drive toward it and the reporters on the other side stir and scurry into action. They press around the back of the car as it pushes through and I see a blur of faces and hear voices calling questions and bursts of camera shutters and then we're through.

I close my eyes. A scream starts, deep inside me, cutting up through my body into my throat. I fight it back and try to take deep breaths and remember what the doctor taught me. From the stomach. Not the chest. *Slowly now, Angie. In. Out. In. Out.*

For a moment, time folds and creases and I'm here but also back there, in the thick of it, scrunching up my eyes against the flashes, shutting out the angry voices, forgetting, for a moment, where I am and who I am, who's alive and who's dead.

CHAPTER THIRTY-NINE

At the police station, they lead me into a boxy interview room and sit me down at a table. There's a large, old-fashioned clock on the side wall. Eleven minutes past eleven o'clock. Time moves at a different speed in these places, I remember.

A young woman puts a plastic beaker of water in front of me. Thin plastic, the kind you pull down from a tube and throw in the bin afterward.

My mouth is dry but I'm afraid of drinking their water. They watch everything, try everything to catch you out, every little thing. *Be careful, Angie, my girl. Keep your wits.*

They make me wait. Somewhere, through that mirror or that black square of window, they'll be watching me. Talking about me. It's hot and airless in the room and sweat pricks along my hairline. I loosen my coat and look at the water. My lips are dry. The tricks they play, these people. The traps they set. I remember it all.

Finally, the same plain-clothed officer comes in, pulls out a chair, and sits on the far side of the table. The young woman follows and sits beside him, directly opposite me. That confuses me. I had her down as a novice, but she must be more senior than I thought. I take a quick sideways glance at the clock. Eleven forty-three.

"So, Angela." She has a low-pitched voice. Authoritative and calm. She smiles as if she wants to be my friend. "Dodd isn't your real name, is it?"

The sour aftertaste of the white wine I drank earlier rises in my throat and I swallow hard, reach for the thin beaker of water. My hand trembles on the plastic and I see them looking but am powerless to stop.

"We know who you really are, Angela. We know what happened." She pauses, watching my face as it crumples. "So how about you start telling us the truth, OK?" She leans forward. Her eyes bore into mine. "Where's Jessica?"

CHAPTER FORTY

TERESA

They're asking me questions again. I wonder if they're beginning to suspect me. Of what? Of killing my baby girl? My Jessica?

I'm so tired. Maybe it's true. Maybe it was me. Maybe I just don't remember. There are moments I feel like confessing. I don't know anymore what happened that night. I remember drinking. I know I have rages. I have hit her. She's had bruises because of me. Craig, too.

She fell once against the taps. We were fighting. I tried to grab hold of her soap-slippery arms and drag her out of the bath and she struggled, then lost her footing and crashed sideways onto the metal. She bruises so easily. There were other times, too.

I put my face in spread hands and sob, thinking about it, about her. It's been more than a day now since I felt the press of her little body against mine, since I heard her high voice, chattering away, always, like background music. I'm a bad mother and I'm being punished. I never mean to shout. I never mean to hurt her. It's just a struggle, sometimes.

The family liaison officer plucks a tissue from the box on the coffee table—I don't recognize the brand, they're not mine—and pushes it into the sieve of my hands.

"The more you tell us, the better our chances of finding her quickly."

I gulp hard and try to steady my breathing and stop crying. I use the tissue to mop up my messy face and blow my nose.

The detective, the sharp-eyed one in plain clothes, is in charge. He's charmless. Direct. They work as a team. *Good cop, bad cop*, I think. That's what Craig used to say about us. No prizes for guessing which parent I was.

"So, Ms. Law," he says. No nonsense. "Let's go over it again. You put Jessica to bed at what time on Tuesday night?"

And the memory breaks open and bleeds all over again.

Later, Craig comes to see me. He looks pale. He retreated to the spare bed in his study last night. He said he couldn't sleep and didn't want to disturb me.

"They're organizing a search." His eyes are red-rimmed. "On the common."

I'm startled. "Why?"

He looks down. He's wearing his old golfing shoes. They need a clean.

"She played there sometimes, didn't she? I suppose they have to start somewhere."

I try to think about that. I never liked the common. Too many roads crisscrossing the land, cars speeding suddenly from between bushes. Too many streams and culverts, heading toward the river. Did Jessica play there? I hear myself sigh. My head is thick and clotted.

He says: "I said we'd go and help."

"OK." It's all unreal. I can't think about it.

"I don't want to." He looks miserable. "But, you know, I think we should show willing."

I don't have the strength to argue. Let him. In the end, I just say, "Wrap up warm." A little later, when the front door bangs behind him, I stand back from the window and watch, without being seen. A ragged group of people has gathered in the street. Hushed and awkward, with somber faces. I recognize several neighbors there and a woman from the supermarket and another who works in the library and there's a vicar too.

Craig leads Fran down the path and the group turns and shifts to make room for them to join. Someone lifts a hand and pats Craig on the shoulder. A man I don't even know. A police officer takes charge and they move away, silent and sad, following the uniforms toward the common.

The HR woman at the salon headquarters has left a string of messages on my phone. They sound cross at first. Officious.

"I understand you haven't attended work today. Please call me back."

Later, by yesterday afternoon, the messages are more careful. As if she suspects the police may be listening. Her voice sounds different, a little posher.

"So sorry to hear the sad news about your family. Please could you call at the earliest opportunity? We need to arrange handover to an emergency manager. With thanks."

Sophie must have told her. She brought flowers, apparently. Someone's put them in the old vase from my mother's, the one that leaks. There's a sad bunch of daisies too, from somewhere. Half-dead.

Outside, the sun moves and the light shifts and somehow, minute by minute, the day tilts toward evening. The second day. I have sudden moments of utter panic. What if I forget what she looks like, what she feels like?

What if they never find her?

I stay in bed now, out of the way. My body is rigid and shakes, and I observe the way I'm already falling apart physically with detached curiosity but little interest. All this is a dream, a nightmare, happening to someone else. I want to sleep. I need to. But it won't come.

Even here the noises find me. The bang of the front door. Strangers tramping up and down the hall. Men's voices. Once, male laughter, quickly suppressed.

From outside, shouts in the street and chatter.

I can't eat and when I try now to sit up, the room tips and sways. The headache that has steadily grown under my eyes is blinding. I keep the curtains closed. I listen for sudden cries and commotion in the hall that might mean news but that never comes. I crawl to and from the bathroom on my hands and knees.

Another message from headquarters. They're sorry to intrude at this difficult time, they can't imagine what I'm going through, but could they at least send someone to the house to collect the master keys? Pause. They need permission, you see, to get through the cordon. The police. Or if someone could drop them round?

I count down the hours until closing time and then start the painful process of getting myself washed and dressed. I don't want them coming here. I don't want to face anyone. And, in truth, I want to do something, to escape from this home, which is now a police prison.

The family liaison officer is sitting in the kitchen in front of a takeaway, plump and greasy in its paper. Her elbows are on the table. Her hands are either side of a bulging burger, pressing it together as she bites. Mayonnaise spills in blobs at the corner of her mouth.

Fran, bright-eyed, sits opposite her with a soft-drink carton, a protruding straw between her lips. The remains of a burger and a packet of fries, torn open, is strewn on the table.

She looks up and starts when she sees me. I don't know if it's because I've caught her eating junk or if it's the sight of me, gaunt and shaking.

"I need to go round to the salon."

The family liaison officer hesitates, swallows. "Shall I come with you?"

She looks relieved when I say no.

CHAPTER FORTY-ONE

I head out with a wooly hat low over my forehead and my coat collar turned up.

I don't go the obvious way, toward the high street. TV trucks and cars are parked there and I'm frightened of being accosted by the reporters. Instead, a police officer at the cordon on the other, sleepier end of the street lets me slip out and I walk all the way through the residential estate and emerge to the north.

It's a relief to be out. I walk slowly, like an old woman, my shoulders hunched and steps careful. My head throbs but the air is damp and cool and the rain has stopped. I fill my lungs with the freshness and feel a moment's pulse of pleasure, followed by guilt.

A black-and-white cat zips ahead of me and disappears into a garden. A young man, one hand in his pocket and the other swinging a briefcase, walks quickly down the other side of the road and turns off into a side street. His footsteps echo, then fade.

The Victorian terraces down here are a mixture of family houses and flats. Many are dark. In others, light gleams round the edges of curtains and presses through the slats of half-closed blinds. Every now and then, the curtains are left open and I slow down as I pass and see straight into a lit sitting room and feed on the stillness of the scenes inside. Bookshelves and mantelpieces and coffee tables with papers and fruit bowls and, on the walls, framed posters and modern, wall-mounted television screens.

Places designed for uninterrupted, normal routines, lived in by strangers with no idea how precious a gift their quietness is.

The salon is in darkness. I fumble the keys and punch the numbers into the keypad and then sink into one of the black swivel chairs and feel my shoulders drop. The face in the silver-and-black shadows of the mirror is pinched. The eyes are sunken and the hair tangled. I sigh and put down, just for a moment, all the fear and grief of the last two days and creep into the skin of my other self, to rest.

The floor is swept and the debris of the day cleared away. But the smells linger. The sweet scent of conditioner and shampoo and the sharp pungency of setting lotion and color. The face in the mirror gives a small, cracked smile.

I go through to the staff area and make a *cafetière* of coffee. While it brews, I find myself tearing open the little packets of cinnamon biscuits, one after another, and devouring them.

The manager's tray is overflowing with post. Junk, most of it. Product promotions and special offers. A meter demand. A couple of thick envelopes from HQ.

I freeze. There's a noise in the salon. The rattle of a key in the lock.

I creep to the door and peer out. A figure, a woman in a short coat, is crouching on the far side of the door, low on the pavement. She's fiddling with the lock, trying to twist back the bolt, which is already open. As I watch, she realizes the mistake and tentatively pushes the door, steps in as it swings open.

I reach my hand round toward reception and snap on the lights and the spots flood the salon, leaving us both blinking.

"Helena!"

Her hand goes to her mouth at the sight of me. The nails are neatly manicured and painted a rich red.

"Oh my goodness! Look at you." She comes toward me, her

eyes climbing all over my messy hair, pale face, red eyes. "So sorry to hear about your daughter. You poor, poor thing."

Her tone is honeyed but there's no kindness there. She peels off her coat and drops it over the back of a chair. She's wearing strappy high heels and one of her tight dresses. Her hair is stiff with product. There's something proprietorial in her movements as she crosses the salon toward me. My stomach heaves.

I say: "What're you doing here?"

"I'm taking over as emergency manager; didn't they tell you?" She comes closer, peering past me into the staff room. "Is that coffee? Any going spare?"

She's unashamedly gloating, loving it. I feel a sudden surge of rage stiffen my arms and have to ball my hands into fists at my sides to stop myself from hitting her. *How dare she?* My head pounds.

She sees my face and smiles. "No need to thank me. Happy to help."

I'm so angry, I don't trust myself to speak. She walks past me into the staff room and looks at the mess of half-opened post there.

"Did you come to drop off the master keys? I've only got the door spares," she says. Her hands riffle through the pile of leaflets and offers I'd just discarded. "Some of these might be worth trying, you know. Time for a change around here."

She picks up the envelopes from HR and hands them to me. "Better take these, though. There's a ton of paperwork. They're quite cross with you at HQ. Leaving them in a bit of a pickle, you know. I've been trying to smooth things over for you."

I snatch the envelopes and pick up my coat. "Don't get too settled. I'll be back before you know it."

She gives me an odd look. "Really? You think?"

I get as far as the street corner, then stop and lean up against the wall. My breath comes in short, shallow bursts and my head is exploding. Suddenly I feel a wave of nausea and turn into the wall to be sick, bringing up the biscuits and coffee and then nothing but bile.

Behind me, a thin traffic of pedestrians hurries past. No one stops.

A group of young men head up the hill toward the station. One says: "Take water with it, love" as they reach me and someone laughs.

I struggle back. The house is quiet now, the police dispersed, leaving the after-smell of chips. I make it up the stairs, hanging off the banisters, and crawl into bed.

Fran, her face strained with worry, follows me up with a glass of soda water and toast.

"You all right?"

Just the smell of the toast makes me feel sick again.

I lie on my back with my eyes closed and listen to the pain in my head.

Fran crouches somewhere nearby, on the carpet.

"They've got Angie." She sounds frightened.

I say: "Who has?" I just want her to go away, to leave me alone.

"The police. They took her off this afternoon. I thought it was just routine, you know? To answer questions. But it's all dark next door." She seems unsure if I'm listening. "She hasn't come back."

I try to think about this through the pounding in my brain.

Fran creeps closer to me and whispers. "That woman kept asking me all sorts about her. The one who bought me dinner."

The burgers. I try not to think about them right now. The greasiness. The stench.

"She's being investigated. That's what the police officer said. She wouldn't tell me anything else. She said it was"—she hesitates, reaching for the next word—"procedural."

She paws at the sheet near my head and her breathing gutters and breaks into ragged crying.

I reach for her hand and squeeze it.

CHAPTER FORTY-TWO

ANGIE

The police drop me home late in the evening. The copper waits outside in his car and watches as I go wearily up the path to the front door, as if he's been told to see me safely home. That's a laugh. The only threat in my life comes from them, that lot in uniform. If they'd only leave me alone, I'd be all right.

There's a queer deadness about the road. It's the cordon, blocking us off from the normal comings and goings. Marking us out as criminals. The TV van has gone this evening. No lights. No chatter. Just a solitary PC standing guard by the tape across the road, which lightly flutters in the night air. Yesterday, I thought his job was keeping people away. Now it feels more like keeping us in.

I go through to the sitting room, switch on the table lamp, and sit down in its light, a soft cone of life in a shadowy room. The curtains are open and headlights flash like searchlights across the carpet as the police driver turns the car around, points its nose in the right direction, and heads off again, back to the station. I sit in silence, still in my coat.

I've done my duty. I've come clean. I didn't have much to lose, in the end. I told them what I did, snooping in Teresa's bedroom, what I found under the floorboards. The life insurance papers. The funeral plan. It still breaks me up, just thinking about it. It's not much but I've done what I can.

There's a high-pitched buzz in my ears. I've been hearing it more and more recently, whistles and whines in my head, especially at night. My mum used to complain about noises. *I never know what it's like to be quiet*, she used to say. *At least when I'm in my grave, I'll get some peace.*

I didn't pay much attention at the time. I thought she was just being dramatic, but I hear it too now, the low-lying soundtrack, everywhere I go. It's the sound of my own body, of course, the pumping and pounding of blood and air through an old girl's tubes.

But it feels like more than that. It sounds like the voice of the past. The whispers and sighs and creaks of those who went before. People I've known, people who loved me, people I loved. All gone now. Their voices are just out of earshot, as if they were there in the next room, as if I could catch the words if I strained hard enough. I feel them with me now, stronger than ever. Calling me to come and join them, wherever they may be.

I close my eyes. I feel exhausted, not in my body but in my mind. All those questions. All the raking up of the past. It's lain buried now for so long that even I had started to believe my own lies. But they know everything, these sharp-eyed, merciless people. And so it is beginning, all over again.

I can't do it again. Up and change my name and start all over. I'm not strong enough this time round. I'm an old bird, getting creaky. I'm not tough enough to bear it, not this time.

I've only been out of the house a matter of hours but the room has a dead, chilled feeling. I can't summon the strength to stir myself, to get myself up the stairs and into bed. So I sit very still, my coat flaps wrapped around my thighs, listening to the voices in my head, and letting them call me back, to the past, to the dark days I've tried so hard to forget.

My mum always said I was a fool for love. She was right, of course, I see that now, but there are no shortcuts in this world. If there were, we'd all be geniuses in the school of life. But there's no telling a young girl. You have to learn your own lessons. You have to make your own mistakes.

I made a mess of my life, she used to say. *Don't make a mess of yours.*

As if she could stop me.

I never knew my father and I was sorry for it. For all my mother had to say about him being feckless, I liked the sound of him. An Irishman with the gift of the gab. Mum didn't talk about him often. She was ashamed. But, once in a while, when I pestered her with questions, she'd get a dreamy look in her eye and tell me a little.

I couldn't imagine Mum being young but I imagined him. A handsome man with dark curly hair and brown eyes. A great dancer, quick on his feet. A real charmer. Staying eternally young even as my poor mum thickened about the waist and grew wrinkles on her face and ruined her hands with hard work, earning enough to keep the two of us after he ran off.

If I played the fool or came home late when I was a girl, she'd say: *That's your father's blood in you.* It was meant as a warning, as a reprimand, but it didn't sound so bad to me.

So, given all the warnings, I didn't mean to tell her about Eddie at all but she guessed early on that something was up. I was on fire with happiness, with love. She smelled the flames on me when I went round to see her for my monthly Saturday visit.

"So, when am I going to meet him, this miracle on two legs? Why won't you bring him round to meet your old mum? Are you ashamed of me?" She was sharp-eyed, watching me. "Or is it him you're ashamed of?"

They never did meet. I didn't want her poking her nose into my business and spoiling my happiness, now that I'd finally found it. And I was happy. Living in digs with another girl, earning my

own money at last in a decent job as a live-out nanny to a posh
family. I was free. I was in love.

I trusted him. Eddie was older and more settled in himself
than the young lads who usually chased after me. He had his
own car and a steady job and he had a way about him, a calm
sense that he knew who he was and how to handle himself in
the world. He took me out to fancy places, smart restaurants and
riverside pubs outside London, and paid the bill without effort.

And he'd traveled, up and down this country and abroad
too, and he had such interesting things to talk about. I couldn't
believe my luck at first when he came to sit with us in the pub
and got chatting. I couldn't see why he'd show an interest in
me, a nanny, when he could have his pick.

I thought I knew best.

It was the oldest trick in the book and that only made me feel
more of a fool. When I realized I was expecting, I thought he'd
be thrilled. It was only later that I found out he was married all
along. That he had two children of his own. That there was a
good reason he drove me out to far-flung restaurants and never
invited me back to his place. And it wasn't, after all, because he
was such a gentleman.

I've never seen my mother so angry, before or since. But she
stood by me, in the end.

"I'm not getting rid of it." I stuck my chin out. I was afraid
she'd insist. "I'll manage."

She blew out her cheeks. When I looked up, her face was
white and shrunken and the anger was already collapsing into
sadness.

"I wanted more for you, Angie," she said at last. "I can't pretend I didn't."

Susie was a beautiful baby. I thought I loved Eddie but then
that little girl came along and my love for her was like an ocean

compared with a bucket of water. I can feel her in my arms now, all these years later. The warm, weightless, soap-scented bundle of her cuddled up against me, suckling. Her little face when her eyes rolled back in her head, milk-drunk, and she fell backward into sleep, her mouth half-open, snorting like an old man. Perfect with her snub nose and those tiny eyes and miniature fingers with soft, papery nails. I used to sit gazing at her while she slept, marveling at her. I didn't regret a thing. I was just sad for him, for Eddie, for missing out on such a gorgeous girl.

Mum loved Susie too, but it can't have been easy for her. Mrs. Matthews and the rest of the neighbors had a lot to say about it. From the day I moved in, she made me wear a wedding ring and call myself Mrs. Dodd. We worked out a whole story about a husband based overseas in oil—prices were sky-high at the time, it was never out of the news—and around the time of the birth, we quietly killed him off in an accident. I doubt we fooled anyone.

From the time Susie was about six months, I found work taking in other little ones for the day: working mums who lived locally and couldn't afford a lot but needed a regular minder. My old families gave good references and the fact they came on posh, cream notepaper from addresses in Kensington gave quite an impression. Susie was a sweet-natured girl, always good with other children and happy to share. There wasn't much cash left over at the end of the week, but we got by.

Later, around the time Susie started school, I managed to talk my way into a full-time job as a live-out nanny with a doctor and his wife. Dr. and Mrs. Braithwaite. They'd had trouble keeping help because their boys were such a handful but I didn't care; I loved kiddies. I never told them about Susie, just took off the wedding ring and told them I didn't want children of my own, I liked my freedom. What they didn't know wouldn't hurt them, that's what I thought.

For the first time since Susie came along, I finally felt as if I was back on my feet again, with decent money coming in. I moved out of Mum's house and shared a flat with another girl, a secretary who was out with boyfriends every night and wasn't bothered by a child around the place.

Susie was six when it happened. She was a happy girl but not a strong one, perhaps because of her poor start in life in my mum's drafty old place. She tended to catch whatever was going around. That night, she was up until the small hours, vomiting and crying and burning with fever. I dosed her up and got ready to take her to school, ill or not—I'd no choice, work was waiting—and she was sick again, right there in the hall, all over our shoes. Poor little thing.

"I'm sorry, Mummy." She started sobbing, standing there with her little uniform all spattered, her face pale. "I didn't mean to."

I'd never scold a child for being ill, she shouldn't have worried. But she was that sort of girl, never wanted to be a bother to anyone. I put my hand on her forehead. I was trying to ignore it, to push her into school whatever, but she was so hot, it was awful. I stripped off her clothes and put them in the laundry basket and tucked her back into the big bed we shared at the front of the flat and she just lay there, looking up at me with those huge, soulful eyes. Her skin was pale and so pure it was almost translucent. I didn't have time to sit and gaze at her but I remember that. The sight of her dark eyelashes and dark hair framing that white skin. It broke your heart.

I dashed down to the box on the corner and phoned Mrs. Matthews, trying to get a message to Mum. She didn't pick up. Nor did the other mums I knew who sometimes minded other people's children. It was already getting late and I was frantic. Mrs. Braithwaite didn't suffer fools and she needed her older boys taken to school and the little one, the toddler, taken off her hands. She was on all sorts of committees and in societies and Lord knows what; she was never around after nine.

By the time I got back to the flat, Susie was fast asleep in bed. It was the best place for her. She didn't even stir when I wiped a cool flannel across her forehead and kissed her cheek.

"Get some sleep," I whispered. Something like that. "Stay there. I won't be long."

I had an idea that I could get the older boys to school and bring the toddler round here, to the flat, to check on Susie and at least by then I might get hold of my mum or someone else who could keep an eye on her. Mrs. Braithwaite was a stickler about being reliable. She knew she was taking a chance on me. She just liked me, I think, and the fact the boys took to me from the first and I was a bit older than average by then. But we both knew there were plenty of other girls who were keen for work. And this was a job I couldn't afford to lose.

I so nearly got away with it. I can't tell you how often I think about that. It makes me weep all over again. If she hadn't been sick that extra time, just as we were heading out. If Mrs. Matthews had only been in and answered the phone. If Susie had only stayed asleep until I got back. How different life would have been.

I was only away a couple of hours. I came dashing around the corner, pushing the toddler in his buggy, and I saw the commotion at once. I didn't think it was outside our flat, not at first, I just thought: *Why are they making such a noise, they'll wake her up, poor love.*

There was an ambulance, right there in the street, and women standing around in cardigans, come out from nearby flats to see, not chatting but quiet. I thought as I hurried toward them that something had happened to the old lady across the road who lived alone and said she was ninety-two. I kept an eye on her curtains each morning to check that she was on her feet.

Faces turned toward me as I rushed up. I didn't stop to ask what was going on, I wanted to get up to Susie. But people parted strangely for me as I went through and their eyes lingered. And there was such pity in some and scorn in others—the beginning of the anger that came later. Someone nudged the ambulance men who were already closing up the back doors and getting ready to drive off and it struck me that there was no hurry in the way they moved and no siren blaring and whatever had happened, it was all over for some poor soul. I don't know if I really heard the words around me or if I imagined them. *That's her. The mum. That one.*

Oh, Susie, my sweet, gorgeous girl. My love. My life.

Afterward, when the police came, they took the toddler away, back to Mrs. Braithwaite. I never saw her or the boys again.

They wouldn't let me see Susie at first. *I wouldn't know her*, they said. Not after that fall. How could I not know my own daughter? Her smell, her skin, her hair.

And then the questions started. Hard eyes. Cold faces. *Did I know it was an offense? Leaving a six-year-old girl on her own. Did I know that was neglect?*

What did I care? They could prosecute me if they wanted, what difference did it make? Lock me up. My life was over anyway. I'd be in my own prison for the rest of my life. I knew it and I was right. There's no getting over losing a child. Not like that. Who's strong enough to bear the guilt? Not me.

I can't have made much sense. All I did was scream and sob. I scraped the skin off my face from tearing it with my nails. They gave me something, in the end, to calm me down.

They took me back to the flat with them and walked me around. I knew what she'd done, as soon as I went up there. The bed was still crumpled where she'd slept, the bedclothes kicked off. She must have woken in a sweat and tried to open the window to get air. Once before, I'd seen her climb up onto the dresser to reach the sill and told her not to. It was dangerous. What if the window broke? I said that but I hadn't really thought it possible. And the catch was old and stiff, she'd never wrench it open, not with her little hands.

But there was the window, unlatched and hanging open, blowing a breeze into the bedroom. I wanted to throw myself down after her, standing there, looking down at the railings and the hard, unforgiving pavement four floors below.

I believed in god until that day. Even through all the trouble with Eddie, I felt him looking down on me. That was the day I gave him up. No loving god could let that happen to an innocent little girl. She'd never done any harm to anyone in her short life. No god could be so cruel.

I tried to struggle on. *One day at a time.* That's what my mum said. One hour at a time, on bad days. They gave me a suspended sentence. I suppose I should have been grateful but I wasn't. I wanted them to punish me. To hang me if they could. I deserved it.

So then what? No working with children, not anymore.

That's when I moved back in with Mum. I don't remember too much about those days. They'd call it a breakdown nowadays. It was just called depression then. Everyone knew, of course. There was no hiding it. And the spite came bursting out. People were so cruel, so angry. Shit through the letter box. Hate mail. They fell over each other to think of worse names, to be more vicious. It seemed fair at the time. I deserved it. But I look back now and wonder about people. Had they no heart at all? Couldn't they see I'd suffered enough?

Then Mum got ill and died and the house became mine and I sort of stuck here. As new people moved into the street, I gradually made a fresh start. I couldn't pretend Susie never lived. I miss her too much. So I worked out a better life for her,

a happy life. I can almost see her, out there in Australia in all
that sunshine, with a good job, a job where she's helping people,
a lovely home and a family of her own. That's the way it might
have been, after all.

I've got by, finding work where I could. Shops and hotel
reception desks, at first. And in time, here and there when I saw
my chance, minding children again, as long as their mums and
dads weren't too particular about paperwork and background
checks. It's what I trained for. It's what I love, kiddies.

And now it's all raked up again, all out. I close my eyes and
feel myself tremble. The names. The anger. The shouts in the
street. The shit through the letter box. I can't take it again. I can't.
And I'm too old to sell up and try to move. What would I get for
this old wreck of a house anyway? I've nothing else.

I sit there, very still and chilled, and think about what I
can do, how I can escape this endless, painful mess. And then
it comes to me. Simply and quietly. A thought that makes
me giddy with relief. *Coward's way out,* my mum would say.
Wicked, to destroy what god made. But she isn't here to see, is she?
There's no one left to care what I do.

My eyes fall on the gas fire. What did that copper say?
Wouldn't want to poison the kids.

I close up the doors and stuff newspaper under them to seal
the room. Then I kneel down in the hearth and try to turn it
on. It's been years and the knob's so stiff, so encrusted with dirt,
that it takes me a few goes. The jet hisses when it comes out,
like air from a balloon. A tiny flame pops as it clicks alight and
steadies itself, before it leaps up and takes a proper hold. I bend
over and feel the heat hard on my face. *Better get used to it where
you're heading, my girl. No choirs of angels for you.*

It splutters and blows as it burns, and the moving flames set
the shadows dancing.

I pull myself upright and ease back into my chair and settle, ready for sleep, breathing in deeply, imagining poison flowing through my lungs.

In the quiet, the tangle of noises in my head expands into throbbing and buzzing. I sit very still and listen to the sounds. It reminds me of the old portable TV we had when I was little. We didn't get a full-sized telly for a long time; we couldn't afford a new one, but Mum liked to sit up in the evenings, right there, peering at the portable's tiny screen. Her hands were always busy, I remember that. Darning or knitting or sewing as she watched.

The memory mixes now with the whistles and splutters in my head until they too become fragments of hidden voices, just out of range. I can't quite make it out but I imagine my mum's voice in there somewhere, a little sharp at times but she never meant anything by it. She was always kind, always there for me, my mum, whatever happened. Always loved me.

And beyond that, buried deep in the crackles and static, there's a smaller, softer sound. High-pitched. A sweet voice, sobbing, saying: *I'm sorry, Mummy. I didn't mean to.*

And I want to say: *I know, my love. It's all right. I'm not cross.*

What did I say, that awful day when I last saw you in this world, when I tucked you in and kissed your hot forehead and left you all alone? Did I remember to say what I long to now?

I love you so much, darling girl, so much I can hardly bear it. Always have, always will.

CHAPTER FORTY-THREE

TERESA

I only sleep an hour or two and wake again, dragged back to the surface, to the world, wishing I could stay under. I reach for my phone and check it, my heart thumping. No messages. No missed calls. No news. I feel sick. The pounding in my head has eased but it's still fragile.

I lie still for a while, feeling the weight of my body on the mattress and listening to the dark quietness. I wonder where she is right now, my little girl. If she's awake. If she's frightened. If she's alive. I can so nearly hear her, smell her, feel her warm, compact body against mine. She must be alive. It's impossible to think anything else. I want to do something, to help, to look for her, but all they keep telling me is to stay here, to rest, to wait.

I'm torturing myself, lying here with my thoughts, and get up, stir myself, wash my face in cold water, and change my top. The house is silent. No sign of Craig. When I look up the stairs to Fran's room, the door is closed. I turn away from the darkness in Jessica's empty room.

The kitchen is silvery with shadows and I click on the light and pour myself a glass of water. I can't eat. The envelopes from HR sit there on the kitchen table and I shake them open and turn over the pages, restless, trying to distract myself.

One contains material from head office about training on offer for the year to come: glossy brochures about various courses and modules for managers and stylists and ways of applying for development funding. I push it all to one side.

The other contains the paperwork about Helena's transfer, the hard copies they promised to send me. It seems a long time ago now, that difficult phone call with head office. My hands clench. Helena looked so pleased with herself when we met in the salon. As if she'd won and was dancing on my grave. On Jessica's grave.

I sip my glass of water and look out at the shadows across the garden. It seems trivial now, her pettiness and point-scoring and silly games. So unimportant compared with what's happened to me now, to Jessica. But she still riles me.

I look over the papers. The whole application for transfer is supposed to come from the salon manager, from me. She's faked the lot. I think of the HR man's snooty tone as he suggested sending the papers over "to jog my memory." As if I wouldn't remember if I'd filed a submission like this.

It's almost funny. She clearly hasn't held back in ladling on praise for herself and they've fallen for it without calling me to cross-check. As the reason for transfer, she's put: "Helena is a talented and capable employee who deserves far more opportunity for growth than we can give her here."

At the end, in the summary, she's written a glowing testimonial for herself, pretending it's from me. It doesn't even sound like me.

It concludes: "Helena is an outstanding member of the team and an excellent stylist. She has great potential as a future manager. We'll be sorry to see her go."

And at the bottom, in her own bold handwriting: "With thanks and kind regards, Teresa Law."

I shake my head. I never say that. "Kind regards." I just don't. And I know my own handwriting. This is nothing like it.

I sit, looking at it, thinking. My head is thick and heavy but something bothers me. Something in the writing. That scrawl that slopes to the right. The confident loop round the capital "L" of "Law."

I push back my chair, seize the papers, and run back upstairs to our bedroom, open my bedside drawer and take out my ancient address book. The torn pieces of the love note, the one I ripped up in fury, are still tucked inside. I spread the pieces on the bed and examine the writing, compare it with the line of handwriting on the form.

It's her. I'm sure of it. The writing is too alike for it not to be the same hand.

I sit very still for a moment, my hands shaking. Slowly, I lift a piece of the ripped note to my face to smell it. Of course it seemed familiar. It wasn't perfume, that faint trace of chemical. It's the smell of the salon. Of ammonia. Hard to scrub away once it's on your hands and embedded under your nails.

My heart pounds as I think of Helena, in her stupid high heels, tripping down our path that lunchtime to push a love letter through our letter box. A letter guaranteed to upset me, if I got to it first. I swallow, try to keep calm, to think. Is she the woman Craig's been meeting, late at night? That brassy, manipulative...?

I think back to the times I complained to Craig about her over dinner. His noncommittal grunts and nods. I assumed he was only half listening because he was preoccupied, because there was only so much interest a man could have in the intrigues of a hairdressing salon. I flush, remembering. Was there another reason he stayed so vague and didn't rush to take my side?

I get to my feet and start to pace, up and down the length of the small room, trying to figure it out. How far had it gone? Just lunches and drinks after work? My skin prickles. Did he bring her here, into our bed, at lunchtime? Was that why she flounced out for so long and came back with fake apologies, with a stupid smile on her face? Was it possible that she left me to pick up work behind her while she lay here, in his arms?

I walk into the bathroom, frantic, and see my face in the mirror. The hurt, angry eyes and flushed cheeks. I can't bear to see myself. I can't bear to think about it. I stride back and pace again around the bed. It never loomed so large in the room.

She could have any man. This wasn't about lust. It wasn't about Craig. It was about me and getting her revenge. I could see that.

But if she did all that just to hurt me... I stopped dead, my legs trembling. My hands rose to my mouth.

What about Jessica? What about her? If Helena was driven by such destructive spite, what else might she do?

The family liaison officer sounds sleepy when I call. I hadn't thought she might be in bed.

I say: "I've found something. It might be important. It's about my husband. I think he's having an affair."

Her voice changes at once. Sharpens. She listens without comment as I blurt out my problems with Helena, why she has such a grudge against me, why I think she's chased after Craig, why she might be exactly the kind of person who'd try to scare me by abducting a small child.

The officer doesn't comment on any of it. All I hear at the other end of the line is the soft scrabble of a pen on paper.

Afterward, she says: "Would you be willing to cooperate now? If we wanted more access to the property?"

I blink. "What do you mean?"

She sighs. "We need evidence, Ms. Law. Leads. Your husband's made that very difficult for us. We're applying for a search warrant but it takes time. There has to be grounds."

I hesitate. "Is this . . . grounds?"

The noises change and I sense that she's moving now. I imagine her pacing around her bedroom with the phone pinched between her ear and her shoulder. Starting awkwardly to dress.

"We can call your employee in for questioning," she says. "But it might not take us much further. Do you see?"

I look around the room, imagining police officers rummaging through my clothes. I think about Craig and how resolute he was about blocking them, about the need for them to focus their resources in the right places.

"I don't know," I say. Whom do I trust, Craig or them? I'm not sure anymore. "Search her house, if you're going to search anywhere."

Her sigh is so loud down the phone that I can almost feel the air on my ear. "Ms. Law, with all due respect—"

I think about Craig. About the strange messages and calls. About Lorraine. So many secrets. Someone who knows what they're doing might be able to find out what's been going on. Find evidence.

"Maybe you could look at Craig's phone? And his computer?"

She says: "I can't just do that, Ms. Law. That's what I'm trying to say. They're personal possessions. He has to—"

"But they're in my name. All his work stuff is. We had to because he was declared bankrupt. His last company folded and there were debts and—"

She interrupts: "They're in your name? His phone account? And his laptop?"

I pause. "Yes."

"And you'd be willing to hand them over, to authorize us to search them?"

I hesitate. She sounds too pleased, too eager. I try to imagine Craig's reaction. All his work data are on that computer.

Everything. I feel my stomach clench. Maybe I should stall and talk to him first? Then I think about Helena. Of her smug face in the salon as she gloated about taking it over, about taking everything from me. Even Craig. Perhaps even Jessica.

I tighten my jaw. "Yes. I would."

"I'll be right there."

She arrives with the sharp-eyed detective and a uniformed officer and I feel betrayed, as if she shouldn't have told them without asking me. It all feels suddenly very official.

I stand in the doorway of Craig's study, my arms wrapped across my chest, hugging my body, and watch as they unplug the wires from the back of his computer. When they lift it, balls of gray, compacted fluff fly off. The computer leaves behind a square mark in the surface dust.

The detective says: "Is it password protected?"

I nod. "I don't know the password, though."

He shrugs. "Not a problem."

They're carrying it all downstairs when Craig walks in through the front door. He sees the computer in the constable's arms and starts. He looks past it to me, standing behind them at the top of the stairs.

"What're you doing? Have you got a warrant?"

The detective sounds stiff. "I understand this is your wife's property, Mr. Fox. She's given us permission to examine its contents."

"But it's mine! I mean, I'm the only one who uses it." He looks distraught. "It's confidential. Work stuff."

The detective nudges the constable back into motion, past Craig and out through the front door, then turns back and puts out his hand to Craig, palm up. He looks like a teacher demanding a confiscated toy.

"I'm afraid I need your mobile phone, Mr. Fox."

Craig's eyes widen. He looks dazed. "My phone? But I need it. It's got everything in it. All my contacts."

"We'll return it as soon as possible." The hand, waiting, doesn't move.

Craig turns and looks at me. He doesn't say a word but his eyes are beseeching. I look away.

A minute later, the detective pockets Craig's phone and they're gone, leaving us in silence.

Craig fumbles his way to the bottom stair and sits heavily. He sinks his face into his hands. "Why, Tess?"

I don't know what to say. "What does it matter?" I'm defensive. Inside, I'm sick with guilt. "I mean, if you've nothing to hide."

His shoulders are rounded and trembling and I realize he's crying. I move down and sit a few steps above him, keeping out of his reach.

"What?"

He doesn't answer.

I press on: "What is it you think they might find, anyway? Your love letters?"

He lifts his face and his eyes are red and his cheeks too, where his fingers have pressed against them. I expect him to look embarrassed or caught out. He doesn't. He just looks terribly hurt.

"Oh, Tess." He reaches a hand toward me, inviting me to go down to join him. I don't move and, after a moment, he lets it fall. "What have they said? Can't you see? They're lying. They're trying to turn us against each other."

I shake my head, trying to block him out. My head hurts. All I want now is to crawl back into bed, to sleep and then to wake and find Jessica, safe and unharmed, back in my arms.

He's still talking in that low, sad voice. "Why would you believe them? You know I'd never cheat on you. Never."

I snort, thinking about Helena.

"You're wasting your breath. I know what you've been up

to, Craig. While I was looking after our kids all evening and struggling to get my career back on track." I take a deep breath, watching his face. "I know about Helena."

"Helena?" He stares at me. He always was a good liar. He must have been to keep our affair secret from his wife for so long. "The one at work?"

"Oh, please."

He shifts his gaze and looks not at me but at the wall, as if he's seeing something there he never saw before. I look too. We chose that paint together. Citrus Surprise. We laughed about the name. "It's paint," Craig had said. "Not a pudding." I blink. It was already another life.

When he finally breaks the silence, his voice is little more than a murmur: "Oh, Tess. What have you done?"

CHAPTER FORTY-FOUR

ANGIE

A bird pecks at my face. Tap, tap. Sharp little beak. I want to bat it away but my arm is a dead weight and I can't lift my hand. Tap, tap. I groan and shift in my chair. My stomach heaves.

Bang. Bang.

Heavier now, the noise. Not a bird. I struggle to open my eyes. It's dark and hot and I'm tired, so tired and suddenly very sick. I want to shout: *Go away, leave me alone* but I can't; I can't open my mouth to speak.

Bang. Bang.

I manage to turn my head. There's a shadow in the moonlight, there on the far side of the kitchen. A short black figure at the back door. Someone's in the garden. I struggle to rouse myself and it all comes back. Susie and the police and the dodgy gas fire, quietly bleeding poison into the room. I try to feel my feet and move but I'm so tired, so heavy. In the end, I fall forward, out of the chair, onto the floor, and crawl on my hands and knees through the sitting room, out to the kitchen.

A face is pressed close against the glass panel in the door, peering in, framed by hands. The features are small and anxious.

"Fran?"

I get the door unlocked and she tugs it open and steps in. Cool, fresh air hits me like a wave of water. She's crying. Her face is blotchy and her eyes red.

"Angie!" She rushes at me and wraps her arms around my waist, pushes her face into my stomach. I pat at her back, stroke her hair.

We stand there for a few moments, each hanging on to the other. The air slaps me awake.

Finally, she pulls back and says: "Why's it so hot?"

I sit her down in the kitchen and go back into the sitting room, my hand to my mouth. I turn off the fire and open the sitting room windows so the fumes can disperse.

She is huddled against the table, her eyes wary.

"Just a problem with the fire," I lie as I lift milk from the fridge and pour us each a glass. "It leaks."

My fingers shake. The skin on the backs of my hands is sallow but my ears are clear, free from the noises, from the voices. I'm still here. I'm back. Back from the dead.

Fran's nose is running and I reach automatically into my pocket and hand her my handkerchief.

She points at the dislodged roll of newspaper by the open door. "What's that?"

"Nothing." I hesitate. "Just trying to keep warm." I sit quietly beside her at the kitchen table and sip the milk. Sickness rises again as it hits my stomach. *Much longer and it would have been curtains for you, Angie, my girl. This child brought you back to life.* I don't know why, but it must be for a reason.

"What were you doing out there?"

The night air still blows in through the open door and I'm glad of it, feeling it revive me. I start to shiver. Fran just has a jumper pulled on over pajamas and nothing but slippers on her feet. I think of her creeping downstairs from her bedroom and through the house, then climbing over the fence to my garden, out of sight, hidden from the police at the front.

Her face puckers and collapses again into tears. "Oh, Angie!"

I reach out and pull her toward me and we sway lightly back

and forth, hanging between our two chairs, balancing and warming each other.

"It's all right, sweetheart," I whisper. "You have a good cry."

Later, when she can, she tells me what's been going on next door. The police have been. First, they carried her father's computer away. Then they came back for him. Teresa is in a state again, sobbing her heart out, calling for Jessica. She's shut herself in her bedroom.

"Why've they taken Dad? And his stuff?" She can hardly speak for hiccupping. I wrap my arms around her and hold her tight.

"I don't know." I wonder what they've found.

"He'd never hurt Jessica. Never. They don't think that, do they?"

I tighten my arms around her and say again, helplessly: "Sweetheart, I just don't know."

"He didn't do it."

She pulls away from me and crawls under the table, crouches there with her arms around raised knees, and weeps. She looks like a much younger child, hiding away from the world.

"Do they know you're here?"

She doesn't answer. I tear a page from my shopping pad and scribble a few lines, telling them she's safe at my place for the night, then go out to push it through their letter box. The house next door is in darkness. I think of Teresa, all alone now in that big empty space with its glass and chrome and fresh paint and lift my hand to knock, then think better of it and creep back to my own front door. The police officer, standing guard at the cordon, sees it all.

The sitting room has cooled down again and I close up the windows. I go through to the kitchen and shut the back door, then coax Fran out. She's shivering. Her feet are blocks of ice.

I put my arm around her shoulders and draw her up the

stairs to my room and settle her in my bed, her head on my pillow, my old blankets tucked closely round her.

"There, now."

Her cheeks are pale. Her breathing is still ragged, after all that sobbing. I sit beside her and stroke her hair as if she were a little girl again.

"You let it all go, sweetheart. Set it down for a while. There's nothing that can't wait until morning."

She closes her eyes and I look at her young skin and lovely long eyelashes. She likes to think she's grown up but she's only a child. She must be worried sick about little Jessica. I've seen how close they are. And her mother so far away and now her father taken in for questioning.

I sigh. "Grown-ups are funny creatures." I keep my voice soft and comforting. Slowly her breathing eases and her shoulders fall as her muscles slacken. "They do strange things, sometimes. They're hard to understand. Even other grown-ups can't understand them, some of them."

When I'm sure she's asleep, I bed down in my old armchair with a spare blanket and try to get comfortable as I keep watch. Somewhere up above, the rats stir under the eaves, shifting and pattering and nosing for food. I sit for a long time, listening to the scrabble of their feet and, closer, Fran's soft, even breathing.

CHAPTER FORTY-FIVE

I don't know what I expected. I've lost sight of it. They'll ask me so many questions, I know they will. All I can do is stay silent. I just wanted to teach her a lesson, that was all. No one will believe me. It's gone too far and there's no way out.

I can't carry on like this. I know that. But I'm frightened of them finding out what I did. I'm frightened of what they'll do to me. They'll put me away. I think about that, whether I could bear it. Being locked up in a cell with a heavy door. Being at the mercy of cellmates and what they'd do to me. Being at the mercy of guards.

I keep thinking that there must still be a way of fixing it, of getting out of all this. I just can't see how. And with every passing hour, as the search grows, the pressure grows too. And so does my fear.

I never thought she'd suffer. They have to believe that of me, surely. I may be selfish and cowardly and even stupid, but I'm not cruel. I'm not sadistic. It just all went terribly wrong and I can't change what I did. I can't find my way back again, however much I wish I could.

CHAPTER FORTY-SIX

TERESA

I can't sleep. I spend the night wandering from room to room, through the house. Restless. Crying. Desperate for morning to come. Scenes play through my head from the night before. My body aches with the pain of it all, with the fear that everything that matters to me is lost and only darkness is left.

Craig and I both heard them come for him. Their boots down the path, the ominous pause, then the heavy bang of the knocker on the front door. Neither of us moved. Neither of us wanted to answer it.

They kept banging.

"Police. Open up."

Of course it was the police. Who else comes crashing on the front door so late? It was barely an hour since they'd left, since they took his computer away and his phone. We hadn't spoken, the two of us. We'd sat, estranged, both of us wretched and betrayed and too hurt by the other to speak. Whatever glue had held us together all this time, whatever love, seemed spent.

I went to the door, in the end. The detective came in and looked around with those cold eyes as if he expected to see evidence of something. Packed suitcases, perhaps, ready to flee.

I watched while Craig put on his coat and was led out to the police car. Nothing to say.

I managed to get myself up to the bedroom and lay there,

shaking. I thought I knew this man. I lay with him in this bed. I loved him. And I was the one who let him into our lives. If he'd hurt Jessica, if he'd done something to her, it was my fault.

I started to weep. How could he have hurt her? How was it possible? How could I go on, if he had? How could I live with myself? I sobbed into the pillow until my head ached.

Now, at six o'clock, the room is lightening and I drag myself under a hot shower and make a coffee downstairs. I'm still drinking it when I hear a car outside, and go to look. Since the cordon, engines mean only one thing. Police.

They see me looking as they open the gate and come down the path and they just stand there and wait, without bothering to knock. I pick up a note on the mat as I open the door. A bit of scribble from Angela next door to say Fran's gone to her.

In the back of the police car, I screw the note into a ball in my pocket. The detective sits in the front and tells me nothing. I watch the police officer lift the cordon to let us out. A passerby—I know him by sight, not to talk to—is walking his dog and stoops to peer into the back of the car, to see who's there.

A bulky camera appears from nowhere and a lens is held up at the window, running off multiple clicks as we move forward. I wonder what the story will be and if they already know what I don't. If a body has been found. If Craig's been charged.

At the police station, the detective shows me into an interview room. The family liaison officer is already there, looking shattered. I don't suppose any of us has had much sleep.

"Cup of tea?"

I'm shaking all over. "Have you found her?"

She narrows her eyes and gives me an odd look. "No, Ms. Law. We have not."

I sink into a chair and burst into tears and start to sob. I don't know anymore if that's suspicious or hysterical or even normal and I don't care, I can't take anymore; it's gone on and on and on and on and a new day is beginning and still my baby's gone and what chance is there now after all this time, hour after hour passing, of seeing her again, of taking her in my arms and holding her, of knowing she's alive?

After a while, when the sobbing subsides, the detective says: "Ms. Law, I know it's distressing but you'd help us if you try to stay calm."

A dry tissue is pushed into my hot, wet hands and I wipe my face, blow my nose.

The two of them, the detective and the liaison officer, sit next to each other, across the table from me. Their faces are stony.

"What's happened?" I sound hysterical. "Where is she?"

The detective lets out a long, steady breath as if he's blowing out a flame. He leans forward.

"Ms. Law. Please try to listen."

There's a beaker of insipid tea on the table. He pushes it toward me and I try to drink. My jaw shudders on the plastic. I nod and wipe my face a second time, trying to pull myself together so he'll tell me what he knows.

He says: "We've spoken to your colleague Helena Wright. She's admitted to writing that note. The one she pushed through your letter box."

I clench my jaw and my eyes slide away from him, thinking about her. My knuckles tighten around the tissue. I knew it.

He pauses, watching me. "She says it was just a nasty practical joke."

"A joke?"

He raises a hand. "I said nasty. The point is, she denies ever meeting Mr. Fox. It sounds like a malicious piece of nonsense designed to upset you. She wanted to make you suspicious of him, to distrust him. That's all."

I shook my head. She would say that, wouldn't she?

"Mr. Fox says much the same. He denies ever having met Miss Wright. And we've found no evidence to suggest they're not both telling the truth."

I think about Craig's late nights. "Someone must have seen them together."

He raises his eyebrows. "We've looked through Mr. Fox's messaging, dialing, and email history. If he and Miss Wright were meeting regularly in secret, I'd expect to find evidence of communications between them." He shakes his head. "We haven't."

I bite my lip. "Maybe they had different phones and used those?"

He gives me a strange look. "Maybe. Although given Mr. Fox's credit history, he might find it hard to pursue an application in his own name."

I sit very still. This isn't it. This isn't why they've come out to the house early in the morning and brought me in here. It's not just to tell me that they've failed to find evidence of an affair. There's something else. I straighten my back.

"So, what have you found?"

He blows out his cheeks. The family liaison officer stares fixedly at the tabletop.

"Mr. Fox has been in regular contact with another woman. By the name of Lorraine Williams." His eyes are on my face as I flinch. "You've heard of Miss Williams?"

I say: "I've heard of Lorraine. I didn't know her other name. She's phoned the house a few times, asking for him." I think of the messages I saw when I looked through his phone and the way I tracked him down. I flush. "I followed him one time. He went to meet her. I didn't get close enough to hear what they were talking about but I saw him sitting there, with a woman, with her. When I asked him about it afterward, he denied it. Said he'd been out late for a work meeting with another man."

They're both focused on me now. I turn my eyes down to my hands, feeling a fool. They must think I'm a basket case. Single parent. Missing daughter. Partner who cheats. My fingers twist inside each other in my lap. I stop abruptly, look up. They're quiet, too quiet.

"What do you know about her?" I sit forward. "Is it something to do with Jessica? Is it?"

The detective shakes his head. "Not exactly."

"What does that mean?" They know something. It's written all over their faces. What aren't they telling me?

The door opens and we all turn to look. Craig's there. An officer stands behind him, ushering him into the room. His face is so puffy that I hardly recognize him. He looks as if he's cried all night.

I jump up. "Craig? What's going on?"

The officer with Craig takes his arm and brings him over to a chair beside me. He helps him sit down. Already, Craig's weeping again, freely and miserably like a child. He buries his wet face in cupped hands. I want to reach out and take him by the shoulders and shake the truth out of him.

I turn to the detective. He's watching us both, a grim look on his face.

I say: "What is it? What's he done?"

The detective leans in. "I think it's better coming from you, Mr. Fox. Don't you think?"

Craig is crying so hard I can hardly make out what he's saying.

"I'm sorry, Tess. Really. I never meant to hurt you." When he lifts his head, his red eyes are streaming, his nose running. "I know you won't forgive me. I don't expect that. But try to understand, at least? Will you?"

He looks an empty shell of a man. Pathetic. Broken.

All I can say is: "For God's sake, what the hell have you done?"

CHAPTER FORTY-SEVEN
ANGIE

I didn't mean to fall asleep. I'm just so tired. I've woken abruptly and, for a while, I don't know where I am.

Susie was there, in my dream, calling me. I shake my head to clear away the small, desperate cry. "Mummy! Where are you? Mummy!"

I blink in the darkness and try to remember what happened before I dozed. Everything looks strange from this angle. My neck's stiff from sleeping upright in the chair and the bedroom's thick with shadows. I sit with the quiet for a moment and listen, trying to remember. Something woke me. Something else. Something outside my head.

Fran's still there in my bed. As my eyes get used to the dark, I make out the slight mound of her body under the covers, tightly tucked around. Her breathing is slow and heavy with sleep.

The poison from the gas fire must still be in my system, making me drowsy. My stomach heaves.

I push aside the blanket and cool air presses in. My feet find my slippers and I put my hands squarely on the arms of the chair to lever myself up.

I'm on the landing, on my way to the bathroom, when a noise comes. Indistinct and distant. A low moan. A scrape that sounds like a sudden movement above me, in the attic. I freeze and listen. A thin cry. I make it out more clearly, this time. My ears are so full of my own noises that I doubt them but it sounds like an animal. Too big to be rats. A trapped fox, perhaps.

I wrap my cardigan closer around me and knot the belt, then reach up for the rope that opens the trapdoor in the landing ceiling and pull. The square hole opens up and the rope brings down the bottom of the metal ladder for the attic. Chill air surges out at once and, with it, the dank, uninviting smell of the roof. I extend the ladder, secure it, and climb slowly up.

I stick my head up into the attic and peer around in the gloom. It's cold and dusty up here and I'm wary about going all the way inside, so I stay on the ladder. I don't like dark spaces. I only venture up here when I have to, to trawl through all the musty, dirty belongings stored up here over the years. So much of it belonged to Mum. She wouldn't want me sending it off to the dump.

There's one small window set high in the attic wall and low moonlight splashes in, breaking up the solid block of black. All those mysterious shapes. All the clutter from Mum's life and now mine, moldering here. Old suitcases with rusted buckles and broken sticks of Mum's furniture, draped with torn sheets and plastic. I shiver.

The moan sounds again. A low, animal sound. It seems to come from deep inside, from the far end, where the roof slopes low to reach the common wall between my house and next door. I imagine Teresa asleep there and think of the fancy bedrooms they carved out of their roof for the girls.

I never told Teresa about the rats. I didn't have occasion and, anyway, there's no point upsetting her. After all the building work they had done on their side, I don't think a rat would dare to show its whiskers there again. They must've cleaned out the old nests and skeletons and whatever other evidence of dead rodents Mrs. Matthews left behind when she died. I can't see Teresa putting up with rat droppings.

I take a look around, peering through the shadows and black outlines, and decide to retreat and climb down again. I'll give the council a call in the morning, if I hear anything else. I don't fancy tackling an angry fox on my own, even if I knew where to find it. They bite and they carry rabies and all sorts of nasties.

I'm just easing my hands lower on the dirty rungs of the ladder when I freeze. A different noise. A light scuffling and sighing. I strain to hear. It comes again.

I carry on quickly to the top of the ladder and step out onto the bare boards that make up the flooring. I thread my way with care, narrowing my eyes as I try to watch where I'm placing my feet, trying to avoid the treacherous open spaces between the sections of boards where there's just ceiling and I risk putting a foot through the plaster. Cobwebs hang everywhere. I keep one hand on the wooden beam that runs along the attic wall, steadying myself with it; the other hand stays in front of my face. I grimace as I brush away the trailing webs and the dead flies caught in them. The blackness is suffocating as it presses down on me and I struggle not to shake, to force my feet forward, farther into the shadows. Every step takes me farther from warmth and light and deeper into the dark unknown.

A cry. A human cry, muffled and quickly stifled. The hairs rise on my scalp. I sway and grasp again at the wooden beams to stop myself from stumbling. Silence. My legs shudder beneath me. I want to crouch but there's nowhere to perch, nowhere safe.

I close my eyes and try to get control of my breathing, of the banging in my chest, in my ears. My fingers grip the beam more tightly. The wood is gritty and rough with splinters against the soft pads of my palm.

A moment later, a gust blows through a crack in the roof and the air chills my face. I shake myself, open my eyes, and creep forward again, trying to work out exactly where the noise came from and follow its direction.

I reach the low slope of the far wall. It's the cleanest part of the attic, at least. This is where the council workers nailed up their boards to stop anything running through to my side, after they'd killed what they could with poison.

My fingers touch the smooth, cold surface of the plasterboard. I take a deep breath and lower myself to stoop and put my ear to the makeshift wall. The joists are hard and unforgiving under my slippers and I wobble a little and have to reach again to steady myself against the wood. My nose is filled with the earthy smell of mold and damp.

For a moment, I hear nothing. Then there's a sudden movement, so close, just on the other side of the board, that I start and pull back in alarm. A shuffling. Light, quick breathing.

I cling with one hand and lift the other. I rap sharply on the board with my knuckles. *One, two, three.*

Silence. Blood surges in my ears. I'm shaking with the tension of waiting, frightened of what I might disturb on the other side.

Then it comes. An answer. A clear *knock, knock, knock*, beating the same rhythm as my own. No animal sends a signal like that.

I stare, stunned. Then, with sudden hope, I lift my hand and knock again, with the same regular pulse. This time, the answer comes back at once. Rapid and clear.

I turn away, suddenly animated, pull sheets from the nearest boxes, and scrabble around inside them, searching. Clouds of dust swarm, choking me and making me cough. The motes spin in the low silver half-light as they rise. I pull out whatever I can find that might be useful. An old fence post with a jagged end. A length of copper pipe.

Eventually, near the bottom, I find a broken chair leg and use it to bang the fence post sideways into the thin crack between the freshly nailed board and the struts behind. I have to press my face against the old wood to see and it scrapes my cheek. I clamp my mouth closed, frightened of dislodging spiders. Hair falls in clumps across my face and I raise the top of my arm to brush it back.

There's crying in my ears now. A child's sobbing. Susie, I can hear Susie, calling to me from the bedroom, hot and parched and all alone. "Mummy!"

I'm coming, my love. Don't move. Mummy's coming.

I'm frantic now, tearing at the corner of the board with my bare hands. My fingers scratch and tear as I pull. The first nails, close to the corner, suddenly pop and jump away from damp, rotting timber. I push my fingers farther in, prizing it away. The side of the board tips and creaks in my hands, then groans and breaks suddenly away as a side pulls free.

I sit, panting, my hands raw, looking at the dark hole that has opened up behind. A tiny opening into the narrow, filthy rat-run, the crawlspace under the gutter that marks the boundary between our houses.

Nothing. I stick my head inside, shuddering. The stink there is filthy but fresh. A smell of ammonia. Of a child's wet bed. Of stale food. It's pitch-black. I push my shoulders inside now and start to crawl, shuffling forward, blinded by the darkness, seeing nothing but spilling threads of green and yellow, spangles that fly like fireworks through the emptiness. I grope, one hand reaching, reaching for Susie, for my long-lost little girl.

A touch. I pull back, startled. Stop. My heart thumps.

I whisper: "Susie?"

I lift my hand and reach again and touch warm, living flesh. A hand finds mine. The small, soft hand of a child. Its fingers latch on to mine as if I can save her, pull her up from the depths, up from the underworld and back to life, back into the light.

I'm babbling now, words spilling out of my mouth. Tears run down my cheeks and splash somewhere on the dirty wood under my knees.

"I've got you, sweetheart. You're safe now. Mummy's here. It's all right, my love. All right."

She creeps forward into my arms and clings to me, arms wrapped fast around my body as I hold her to me, grasp her, warm and compact, and ease us both backward out of the hole, back onto the open attic floor.

She curls up into my body and I take her properly into my arms and rock her, my own beautiful girl, safe at last, rescued, as I always dreamed she might be.

I croon to her as we rock: "It's all right, beautiful girl. It's all over. You're safe now. Mummy's here."

Later, I will carry little Jessica down the ladder and back into the warmth of the house. I will run a hot bath and wash the dirt from her streaked face and the cobwebs from her hair and wrap her in a warm, fluffy towel and gently rub her dry.

After I've dressed her in clean clothes, I'll carry her around with me in the shadowy kitchen, never letting her go, even as I warm her milk and butter her toast and feed it to her, piece by piece, in soldiers, snug on my lap.

She'll recover her own sweet smell. The fresh scent of shampoo and soap and the dampness in the folds of her young skin. And I'll kiss her all over her face, on her cheeks and eyes and the tip of her nose. I'll cuddle her so tightly she squirms.

After a while, feeling safe again, she'll sleep a little and I'll carry her upstairs, relishing the soft weight of her in my arms, and tuck her into my bed, next to Fran, and creep back, armed with a torch, up into the attic to look properly and try to understand.

I'll examine the hidden crawlspace, lined with blankets and toys and made into a den, with its half-eaten boxes of biscuits and cakes and an old foil carton of leftover moussaka and a dirty potty for a toilet. And there in the debris, in the strewn, soiled bedclothes, by the toy torch whose batteries are already spent, I'll recover Rabbit, left behind, and put her back in Jessica's arms, where she belongs.

And finally, when the day breaks and the outside world stirs and the time of make-believe is past, I'll do what I need to do and call the police and hand her back to them and to the mother who may now learn to deserve her. Questions will be asked and answers found and tears and reprimands and punishments will follow. There is a time for that.

But, for now, just now, while it's still dark and there's still magic, here in my own home, she is my Susie, come back from the dead, rescued by me, and I will lie beside her and hold her and kiss her as my own sweet girl, for the brief, precious moments we have left together, just as I always imagined.

CHAPTER FORTY-EIGHT

TERESA

When Craig starts talking, his words come tumbling out together as if a dam has burst and the story he needs to tell me will never stop. He seems unaware of the interview room with its solid black clock and battered table and chairs. He seems not to notice the detective and family liaison officer who sit, their eyes on his face, listening, or the constable who steps back and withdraws, standing by the closed door to bar our escape.

His eyes are wide and staring and focused just on me, and there's love and fear in them as he tells me what he did.

"It just all cost more than I thought. The building work and the loft conversion, especially with the problems they found with the rot, and you know the times we talked about the new kitchen and bathrooms and wasn't it worth doing it all properly, with decent materials, if we did it at all?"

I feel the struggle in him as he strains to let go and admit to me what a mess he's caused, and I bite my lip and hold his gaze and let him talk.

"It went on and on—the more problems they uncovered, the longer it took, and the bills kept rising but I thought, you know, we'd be OK. I'm a hard worker. I'm a good salesman. With the funeral thing, I could make it work. I had it all figured out. Every funeral plan I sold, I could cancel a grand of debt here or pay off a bill there. I could stall some of them too. People do. Right?"

I sit very still and listen, wondering where all this will lead.

"But it's been tough. Tougher than I thought. I never wanted to bother you with it; you've got enough on your plate with the kids and the salon, I know that. It's my job to provide. I promised you that." He shuddered, pulled out his handkerchief and blew his nose.

"So what happened?"

He stares at his hands. "Some of the guys, you know, the builders and the suppliers, they started to get nasty. They'd waited a while and they started to figure out I didn't have the cash, not right away. One of them even threatened me. Imagine. Saying I'd better look out for my kids, for you. Lowlife."

His forehead tightens. "I had to pay him off. That's why I was out so much, Tess. I was chasing down favors. Touching up mates for loans. Old business contacts. And trying all the time to sell bloody funerals to everyone I could. Anyone."

I think of Angie and the pressure he put on her to buy.

"Then I got to the stage where every time I did sell a plan, I needed some of the money for us."

He looks suddenly sheepish. His voice falls to a whisper.

"Sometimes, all of it."

I say: "You used other people's money?"

"Only short term. They were middle-aged, most of my clients. They weren't about to peg it anytime soon. I didn't think it would matter if I used the cash for their plans to pay our bills. As soon as I got back on my feet, I'd pay it back, see? With interest. I really would. It was just a stopgap thing, like a sort of bridging loan."

I shake my head. "And all this was on the computer?"

"Of course. I submitted one set of accounts to the company, with some of the plans cut back or even missing. But I kept my own accounts at home. Fair and square. Lists of everything I sold. Where the cash went. Everything I'd need to pay back, as soon as we could."

I look at him now, his eyes red, his face puffy. He looks so very tired. I think of him, out every night buttering up friends, asking for credit. Lying awake at night thinking about the hole he was digging for himself and seeing it grow steadily deeper.

"Oh, Craig."

He lifts his eyes and studies my face. I feel him reading me and deciding how much more to confess.

"There's something else." He looks like a desperate schoolboy.

"What?"

"That gold necklace I bought you. Your jade earrings. That time you missed takings from work…"

I stare, appalled. I hadn't even noticed the earrings had gone. They were my favorite. Set in eighteen-carat gold. "You stole from me?"

He winces. "Not stole, exactly. I just—"

I find myself on my feet. When my hand swings back, the constable is behind me in a heartbeat and seizes my wrist, stopping me from striking him.

"Calm down, Ms. Law." The detective's face is cold.

I sit down with a bump and rub my wrist. Tears well in my eyes.

"How could you?" I think about Angie and the way I'd suspected her. "Letting other people take the blame. That's despicable."

His face is wretched. He edges closer to me and tries to take my hand. I snatch it away and his eyes fill with tears again.

"It was all for you, Tess. You and the girls. I adore you. You must know that. I've just had bad luck, that's all."

Something occurs to me. "What about that woman? Lorraine?"

His face changes. I see him shrink into himself. "It's not what you think."

"Don't you dare lie to me." I jab a finger at him. "I saw you.

I saw you together. And when I asked where you'd been, you denied even seeing her."

He writhes. "It's nothing like that."

"Then what is it?"

He lets out a long sigh. "She's an investigator. An ex-cop. Brought in by the funeral people."

I shake my head. "Don't believe it. If that was it, you could have told me."

"It is true." His tone is begging. He turns to the detective, sitting in silence at the table. "You'll back me up, won't you?"

The family liaison officer lifts her eyes to catch mine and nods.

"Miss Williams deals with commercial fraud," she says. "We understand Mr. Fox was under investigation. For misappropriating funds."

I groan. "You should have *told* me. I could have done something. Got a loan in my name, maybe. Asked friends. Something."

He sinks his head in his hands again and his shoulders shake as he weeps. For a few moments, the only sounds are his sobs and the dull tick of the police clock.

The family liaison officer shuffles in her seat and addresses me directly.

"Mr. Fox told us that you'd already incurred a lot of debt because of him. He mentioned the mortgage on your current property. I believe that's in your name?"

I nod, miserably. We had to do it that way. Craig said he'd never be approved because he's been declared bankrupt.

She says quietly: "And although he sells through a company, technically he's self-employed. And that business is in your name, too, I understand, for the same reason?" She reads my face. "So, with additional debts and now possible fraud charges, well, legally, they could recover Mr. Fox's losses by seizing your assets." She pauses, letting this sink in.

I say at once: "What assets? I haven't got any." Then I stop and think and it hits me. "They could take the house."

She doesn't need to answer. Her eyes are just sad.

I sit very still. *Everything I've worked for.* I see our new home with its shiny fittings and freshly painted walls. We could lose it all. The house. And everything in it. Our furniture. Our clothes. Jessica's dream bedroom. Even her toys.

Jessica. My girl. I close my eyes, suddenly weary of it all. A week ago, the idea of bankruptcy, the prospect of losing everything, would have seemed the worst calamity I could imagine. Now I know better.

"It doesn't matter." I open my eyes. "It's only money."

There's a stillness in the room. Craig shudders and takes a deep breath and although his head stays bowed, he reaches out for me with a wet hand and it creeps hot and warm onto my knee. I put my hand over his and cover it.

I say: "All that matters is finding Jessica."

Craig and I sit together in the police waiting room. The seats are hard and bolted to the floor in rows. A sign hangs on the vending machine in the corner: "OUT OF ORDER." A long, narrow notice board runs along the opposite wall, pinned with promotional leaflets: *Don't be a victim of crime!* And *Car theft* and *Burglary* and *Street assaults.* Nothing, as far as I can see, about protecting your child from abduction.

I have one arm round Craig's shoulders, pulling him toward me. With my free hand, I stroke his hair. The clock says eight forty-three.

He used to be a proud man, proud of himself and proud of his family. Now he's humiliated. I feel it and I see it, even in the way he sits now, as if something inside him has collapsed. He's been a fool. A desperate one.

He even planned to kill himself, he says, in the car. Figuring out a way to make it look like an accident so I could collect on his life insurance. He had it all worked out. He forged one of his funeral plans too, naming all of us in the hope it looked less suspicious. Just so his company would step in, if anything happened to him, and take care of all the arrangements. And pay for it too.

It's all out now. The police say he'll be lucky to escape being prosecuted for fraud. But he does love me, I believe that now. He wanted to be my hero, to protect me and provide for me. He just made stupid mistakes. And now he needs me more than ever.

I lean over him and kiss the cold tip of his ear. "I love you."

He doesn't speak. I don't think he can. He presses my knee with his hand to show he heard, to say thank you.

For three days, time has been suspended. My heart stopped. My life stopped. Existence has been unbearable. There has been no way of going on.

Now, suddenly, time swings back into motion, and, more than that, into double time.

Everything happens at once.

There's a shout down the corridor. A woman's cry.

"What the...?" A glad, astonished cry. Then: "Sir! What happened?"

The door bursts open and the family liaison officer appears in the doorway, her face lit by a big smile. "She's OK! Jessica!" She stands there, glowing, already ahead of us. "She's here!"

Craig sits up straight and stares. I'm on my feet. My body shakes so hard I can't speak, can't move, can barely keep upright.

Craig says: "What do you mean? Where is she?"

The officer holds the door wide and beckons. "Come on. Come and see."

Her eyes are on my face and they're glistening and I know it's real, it's true.

I'm pushing and running now, past her and into the corridor and there she is. I don't know why or what happened but she's there, safe and alive, standing sheepishly beside Angie, pressing close to her side, her small hand clasping the larger one.

Fran stands on the other side, a larger child, hanging back, holding Angie's other hand just as tightly.

My Jessica. My own sweet girl.

I'm pounding down the corridor, running to her, then grasping her around the waist and lifting her high in my arms, squeezing her against me, smothering her.

"Where were you?" I'm sobbing. "What happened? Are you OK?"

Angie says: "She was under the eaves all the time. Hiding."

Craig, somewhere behind me, says: "Under the eaves?"

Angie nods.

"But...*how?*"

Angie shrugs. "Someone worked a panel loose. At the back of those new cupboards in the bedroom."

"Who did?"

Angie looks away. A tense silence. Finally, Fran bursts into tears. "I'm so sorry! I never meant to hurt her. I never thought it would go on so long and all the police came and I've been so frightened, I didn't know how to stop it."

"*Fran?* But why?"

Craig opens his arms and she flies into them and sobs there, her head on his chest.

"Will they send me to prison?" She pulls away from him and

her swollen face is terrified. "Will they?" She collapses again into tears.

Jessica, burrowing her nose in my neck, her hands grasping my shoulders, cries too. I tighten my arms around her body and feel the angular press of her bones, her small frame firm against mine. The weight of her. Her own smell, of freshly washed hair and clean skin.

"It was just a game, Mummy. She said if I kept very still, Lily the bear would come and fly me away." She breaks again into sobs. "But it was so cold. And so dark. And she never came."

"Shush, my love. It's all right." I rock her and cuddle her and hold her close. "You're safe now. I'll never let you go again."

Beside me, Craig is crying into his daughter's hair. "Why, Fran? How could you?"

The two of them cling to each other. I think how long it's been since I saw them like that.

"We've been so worried." Craig pulls his daughter away for a moment and tries to look her in the eye. "Don't you understand? We thought she'd been taken. Hurt. What were you thinking?"

Fran is barely intelligible between sobs. "I just wanted it like before. Before they came. With just Mummy and you and me, just our family."

"Oh, Fran!"

"She spoiled everything!" She's shouting now, her breath ragged with crying. A furious splotchy-faced child, cross with the world. "And she's always shouting and hitting people and you've been so miserable. She deserved it."

"No, Fran!" Craig wraps his arms more tightly around her and holds her close. "I know it's hard. I know you miss Mummy. But Teresa doesn't make me miserable. You must never think that. Never."

I leave them there, the family liaison officer hovering, and carry Jessica back to the waiting room. I sit down heavily with her in my arms.

"Let me look at you."

I run my hands over her face, sweep back her hair from her forehead, marvel at the sight of her, the curve of her cheek, her big beautiful eyes, the soft smoothness of her skin. I think of her lying in darkness for all that time, frightened and alone, trying to be strong, trying to believe.

She says: "They won't send her to prison, will they? It was just a game."

I shake my head. "Oh, Jessica. I missed you so much."

Her lip trembles. "I missed you too, Mummy."

I wrap my arms around her and hold her as close as I can and all I can think is: *I love you so much, gorgeous girl, so much it stops my heart. Thank god for a second chance.*

CHAPTER FORTY-NINE

ANGIE

The new family moves in at the start of December. Cutting it a bit close, I think, when there's so much to do. The run-up to Christmas is always a crazy time when you've got kiddies, even without moving house.

I stand at the window and watch through the gap between the thin cotton curtain and the frame. It was frosty overnight and the lorry takes its time backing into the space. They put those yellow council notices on the trees—parking suspended—to make sure there's room but, even so, there's always some idiot who doesn't read them or doesn't care and parks too close anyway and that's what's happened now.

The lorry goes out again and has another try. It's tight but he just squeezes in. Then he inches forward in the space until he's right up against the car in front, bumper to tail. I realize why when he and his mate jump out and go round to the back to lower the ramp. There's just about room.

They start carrying it all in. All sorts. And it all looks brandnew. It amazes me how much people buy from scratch nowadays. A great big dining table and eight chairs. A kitchen table and more chairs. Huge beds with iron bedsteads and mattresses, all done up in plastic. And so many boxes, I'm losing count.

I narrow my eyes for a better look as the men retreat farther inside the lorry and carry out more.

That's a kid's bed. It must be. And that one. And there's a rocking horse, wrapped round in plastic. I smile. A child would love that. And more boxes. It goes on all morning.

When the lorry finally closes up and leaves, I stand in the hall and listen. A door shuts and the floorboards creak faintly on the other side of the wall. Someone's in there.

I make a flask of tea and put a tray together with a plate of biscuits, those sweet ones with cream and jam in the middle, and add mugs and everything else we'll need.

A young woman answers the door. Short dark hair cut in a bob and not much makeup. I like the look of her. Friendly.

"I saw you moving in." I nod back toward my house, my hands tied up with the tray. "I'm next door. Angela Dodd. Everyone calls me Angie. Thought you might like a cup of tea."

She hesitates for a moment, surprised, then smiles and opens the door to let me in.

"That's kind. I'm Lynne." She ushers me through the hall to the kitchen. It looks a complete mess. Boxes are piled everywhere, stacked in corners and all down the wall. That kitchen table looks too big for the space. The legs and seats of the chairs are still wrapped up in plastic. The air's chill and dusty.

She points to a sturdy box and I set down the tray on top of it and pour us both tea.

"Thanks."

She takes the mug and turns away from me to set it on the floor. She kneels down beside it and goes back to unpacking kitchenware from an open crate. Every piece is individually wrapped in rough-grained, white paper, the kind they started using for fish and chips when they gave up on newspaper.

I say: "I could give you a hand, if you like." I look around at the cluttered surfaces. "I could unwrap and you could put away."

She smiles. "Well, if you're sure."

I pick up one of her parceled chairs and sit by the crate and start to lift things out, one by one. A pile of scrunched paper grows beside me on the floor. Kiddies could use that. For drawing or painting or just messing about. Pretend snowball fights.

I set the pieces on the counter. Glasses in all shapes and sizes. She fills the sink and starts rinsing things off.

I say: "Do you need a tea-towel?"

"That's OK, thanks." She points to a holdall in the corner. Washing-up liquid and a pan scrubber stick out. She must have tea towels ready too. Sensible.

I nod approval. "Well organized."

"You have to be, don't you?" She glances at the clock. "I haven't got long. If I can just get on top of the kitchen and the boys' room, we can just about function."

I think of the small beds. "How old are the boys?"

"Four. Sebbie and Alex. They're twins." Her eyes light up as she speaks of them and I think: *What a lovely mum. Children deserve that. To be loved and wanted and cared for.*

"Twins! Bet you've got your hands full, then!"

"Double trouble!" She says it lightly, as if it's something people always say but she doesn't really mean. "Mike's taken them to his mum's for the day. I got the easy option, believe me!"

"I've got a little girl. Susie. Well, she's grown up now." I unroll a wineglass, one of those modern ones with a huge bowl. I don't care for them, myself. They take a lot of filling. "She's out in Australia. She's a gynecologist."

She reaches for the wineglass and washes it.

I say: "I don't blame her. It sounds like a great life out there. And that's what it's all about, isn't it? Love 'em and let 'em go." I pause. "But I do miss her. You do, don't you, when you're a mum?"

We work on together in silence for a while, unpacking and scrunching up paper, rinsing and drying and finding spaces for glasses in one cupboard and crockery in another. All the bits and pieces that make up a home.

"Did you know the family who lived here before?"

I nod. "I used to look after the children sometimes. Jessica and Fran. Lovely girls. Especially little Jessica."

Lynne, at the sink, says: "Didn't she go missing? The estate agent said there was a big police hunt. And she was in the house the whole time."

I don't answer at once and she turns around to check my expression.

"Did I say the wrong thing? I'm sorry, I didn't mean to—"

I say: "No, you're right. They were worried sick. We all were."

She reaches for the tea-towel and wipes off the cereal bowls, then puts them away. She makes a separate place on the shelf for the boys' things. Small, brightly colored sets of plates and bowls covered with cartoon elephants.

I say, thinking about it: "It wasn't their fault. The parents. I mean, people blamed them afterward. They said some horrid things. People can be cruel, sometimes. But I was here. It wasn't like that."

She reaches for more dishes to dry, working quickly, only half listening.

I say: "That's not why they sold the house. In case you were wondering. They had money worries. They had to go into one of those debt programs where you pay a bit back each month." I hesitate. "But they'll do it. They'll get back on their feet. People do."

She's washed up our mugs too, and now she dries them and sets them back on my tray. I sense that she's ready for me to take it and leave and I feel a surge of sadness, of regret.

"Keep the biscuits." I lift off the plate and set it on the side. "The boys'll like those."

She hesitates and for a moment I think she may refuse and I

stiffen, more anxious about it than I've any reason to be. But she softens and says: "Thank you. They will."

"And if you need any help. You know, with the boys"—I push my arms back into my coat sleeves and button it—"I'm right here."

She leaves her work and escorts me out, wiping her hands on the tea-towel as we walk.

"Lovely to meet you, Angie. Really."

At home, I pour myself a glass of wine and take a chair over to the front window. Twin boys! I want to catch a first glimpse. What did she call them? Sebbie and something. Alex, that was it.

I stare out at the street, keeping watch. Four is a wonderful age. The magic's still in them, you see. They believe in everything. They'll be so excited at Christmas, about Father Christmas coming and Rudolph and all that.

And then I think of it. I could get to work on the make-believe room this afternoon, get it all set up again and ask them round. Get them out of their parents' hair while they're getting straight in the house. The boys'll love it. Little ones always do.

I get to my feet and stretch out my legs and think about making a start. *Come on, Angie, old girl. There's life in you yet.* I feel a surge of energy, of hope, as I head up the stairs, wineglass in hand, my knees creaking as much as the banister.

I bet they're lovely boys. They'll soon learn the rules. Maybe they'll even add a few of their own. I smile to myself, thinking about Jessica. I'll miss that little girl.

And, as I shake out the sheets and drapes and think where to hang them, as I open up the old puppet theater with its moldering puppets, as I tape up the window, plunging the real world at once into shadow, beneath it all, in everything I do, I think of Susie. My own sweet child. The most wonderful little girl that ever lived.

A LETTER FROM JILL

Are you a perfect mum? No? Neither am I.

Before I had children, I dreamed of being one of those amazing mothers with saintly patience. I had visions of smiling, happy faces as we did arts and crafts or made fairy cakes. And of course I'd still have a great career—and time for myself as well. Simple, right?

Then they came along for real—my wonderful, full-on, small people who rarely sleep through the night, are endlessly active, and frequently create mayhem. I adore them and I do my best but I'm painfully aware that it's a far from perfect performance.

After particularly frazzled days, I go to bed feeling wretched and promising myself I'll do better tomorrow.

So what must it be like for a mother under far greater pressures than I am? Someone so stressed, so overwhelmed by life that she feels she's failing as a mother, however desperately she loves her child? So much so, she's convinced that her daughter doesn't even like her? And what if the one person she relied on for help—the childminder keeping them afloat—wasn't what she seemed?

It was out of these thoughts that *Jessica's Promise* was born.

I hope you loved *Jessica's Promise*. If you did, I would be very grateful if you could write a review. I'd love to hear what you think and it makes such a difference in helping new readers discover my books for the first time.

I love hearing from my readers. You can get in touch on my Facebook page or on Twitter. Thank you!

All best wishes to you and yours,
Jill

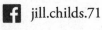 jill.childs.71

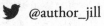 @author_jill

ACKNOWLEDGMENTS

Thank you to my wonderful editor, Kathryn Taussig, and all the team at Bookouture.

Thank you to my brilliant agent, Judith Murdoch, the best in the business.

Thank you to Ann, Dawn, and Glenys for encouragement and comments.

Thank you, as always, to Nick for all your love and support, and to Alice and Emily, just for being you.

And finally, thank you to my wonderful mother for wisdom, love, and always believing in me. This one's for you, pet.

READING GROUP GUIDE

When I chat with readers, one of the questions I'm most asked is: Where did the story come from? How did you make up the characters—are they based on people you know?

It's hard to explain. For me, at least, the story starts with a central idea, then it starts to develop around one or two characters, and finally, once I've "gotten to know" those central characters properly, it starts to develop into a plot—layer by layer—with secondary characters—husbands and parents and friends of the central characters—getting my attention last of all.

So what set me off on *Jessica's Promise*? Well, I think the very start came from an anecdote from a complete stranger a few years ago. My own children were still babies at the time and I was utterly sleep-deprived but also besotted by them. I was starting to look forward to going back to work (part-time, in my case) because I love my job but also worrying about leaving them. How could I be sure they'd be happy and safe without me?

Very unusually for me at that time, I went out one evening to meet some local women from our church—and ended up chatting to one about her childcare arrangements. She'd hired an older nanny, she said, a rather eccentric, motherly woman who was close to retirement age and had been a nanny all her life. To adults, this nanny could seem a bit awkward and formidable. I got the impression that the mother herself was a bit frightened of her, as if she might suddenly be told off—ordered to stop fidgeting or eat her greens.

But one day, she said, she'd come home from work unexpectedly in the middle of the afternoon to grab some papers—and when she opened the front door, she discovered Nanny singing lustily as she bounced down the stairs with an upturned colander on her head, one child riding on her back, arms waving, and the other lying helpless with laughter on the hall floor. In London, many nannies are twentysomethings who are having gap years doing childcare before they start their "real" career—and often seem glued to their mobile phones—so when I heard this story, I remember thinking: I LOVE this nanny! I want a nanny like THAT!

We did find a wonderful nanny—although she was a lot more conventional than the one in the story. But the vision of a rather odd, old-fashioned older nanny did stick. The more I thought about her, the more Angie started to appear.

Once I had a nanny, I also became fascinated by their profession and the role they play in our homes. In the past, here in the UK at least, only rich people had nannies. They conjure up an image of stiff uniforms and nurseries and of course Mary Poppins. But nowadays, with so many mothers working—and working long hours—and with the cost of day care centers so high here, lots of us "ordinary" families rely on childminders or nannies to keep us afloat.

But the relationship between nannies and the mothers who employ them is fascinating…emotional and very complicated. I've spent time getting to know other nannies on the days I'm at home with my own small children. We have joint playdates together and the nannies tip me off about good play centers and outings and fun activities.

I've been so grateful for their friendship—and I've learned so much from them. Again, it's a feature of modern city life, but I don't have sisters or parents or even childhood friends "just around the corner" to help out when one of my children falls ill or starts having tantrums or refuses to eat what I cook! My nanny friends have been an incredible source of cheerful support and encouragement and advice.

So it seemed strange to me that there is, in general, such a disconnect between mothers and nannies. Generally, mothers meet up with other mothers. Nannies meet up with other nannies. When my lovely nanny friends introduce me to other nannies, in the park, for example, those nannies seem uncomfortable, suddenly on their guard instead of just relaxing and being themselves. Maybe it's partly a holdover from those olden days when there was such a class divide between mistress of the house and staff (I live in Britain, after all, where class is a "thing").

But I actually began to feel there's something much more complicated, and more interesting, going on. One local mother friend said, with disarming honesty: "It would make sense for us to have a nanny but I don't want to. I'm frightened the kids will love her more than me."

That's the heart of it. In creating Teresa, I wanted to write a mother who's frazzling herself into toast by trying to do it all and barely managing. She's also gone from lover to wife, from romance to drudgery.

In writing her, I thought of my mother and her friends, sitting around the kitchen table when I was a child, drinking tea and darkly discussing other people's affairs when they thought I wasn't listening. I didn't always understand but the messages I took from the chat were warnings: Once a man strays, they seemed to say, he can never be trusted; he's likely to do it again. If a woman breaks up someone else's marriage, no good will come of it. That's not always true, of course, but it's enough of a guilty worry to Teresa to make her paranoid about Craig—and wonder if the man who once cheated on his wife might now do the same thing to her.

And of course she feels undermined by guilt. What mother really thinks she's doing a brilliant job—when she's pulled in so many different directions? Most of us are constantly exhausted, juggling the demands of running a home, feeding everyone, coping with laundry, working at least one "paid job," organizing presents for the children's friends' parties and costumes for plays and all the practical tasks that go into parenting—and then, oh yes, quality time…obviously, as every women's magazine and parenting book tells us (if we have time to read them) it is clear that calm, regular quality time with our children is essential. But when??

No wonder many of us feel inadequate. That nagging self-doubt creeps in: The nanny makes it look so effortless when we collect our children from her. What if they do like being with her more than they like being with their mother? It's an awful thought that could easily breed suspicion, even resentment toward the nanny…

After all, a nanny has access to your family, to your home, when you're not there. They take your place in every sense. They're supposed to. They see you in your underwear—both metaphorically and sometimes literally. Think of how many films and books tap into a mother's anxiety about that—stories about nannies who take over, who lure away husbands, who supplant the mothers utterly. What secrets might your nanny find if she went snooping around your drawers, rummaging in your dirty laundry—as Angie does?

All this helped me to imagine Teresa—anxious at work, stressed at home, and generally exhausted. Angie, the kindly nanny next door, appears such a godsend. Of course Teresa doesn't want to probe too deeply—the girls seem happy with her, she's affordable and right on her doorstep. Why spoil such a gift? And yet…the nagging voice won't go away. Do we, the reader, agree with Teresa? Can we trust Angie? Our doubts grow, too…

And from the nanny's side of all this? I mentioned Angie's real-life inspiration, the stout matronly nanny in a stranger's story. In reality, many nannies I know have a difficult, precarious job. They may stay with a family for a few years—sometimes less—but they always know their days are numbered. They know that as soon as the children become older, they'll be looking for a new family, a new job. I've seen wonderful nannies who clearly came to love the children they looked after and treated them as if they were their own—but once their contract ended, they were out of the family. That's really hard, especially if they haven't, for whatever reason, had children of their own.

And Angie's make-believe room? Well, it's an exaggeration of something I do with my own children. Partly in order to keep them safe when we walk to and from school, holding hands, I always tell them stories—making it up as we go along and ending with a hurried conclusion as we reach the gates. They're usually stories about a giant magic bear who takes them on amazing adventures. Into space. Up mountains. To visit dwarves and fairies or to meet their favorite storybook characters.

They still spend a lot of time doing pretend play. They're five now—a wonderful age. As Angie says, the magic hasn't died in them yet. It feels like our own secret world and I love the fact that, at their age, the boundary between real and imagined, what's rational and what's magical, is very fluid. We lose that, as adults. I wanted to show that with the scene at Angie's house when the police pull up the blinds and let the light in, ruining Angie's make-believe room and raising suspicions about her rules of play.

Of course, adults do pretend—but in the novel, their pretending is deception. I wanted to draw a contrast between Angie—whose make-believe with the children is benign—and the manipulative Helena, Teresa's backstabbing junior at work, who is also not what she seems—but in a more malevolent, ruthless way. And then there's Craig, Teresa's new partner—who is himself caught up in make-believe as he plays the fake part of a successful businessman. Perhaps the adult version of pretense is no less rare but a lot less innocent.

And what about the location? I live in suburban London. It's a community that's an eclectic mix. There are plenty of well-heeled newcomers who work in central London, have money, and, like Teresa and Craig, love to buy up dilapidated family properties and modernize them. The road is usually full of construction vehicles.

But right next door to these new professionals, there are families who were born and brought up in their houses. They may rent or they may have inherited the property—but they can't afford to modernize. Two different worlds, two different properties, side by side. Just like Teresa and Angie.

And of course the houses become symbols, too. Angie's worn, drafty house, stuffed with her mother's tatty furniture—she is poor but also stuck in the past, surrounded by it and burdened by it. Teresa? She's building a new family home from scratch—with a modern family without a shared history and two children, half-sisters, from different mothers. And appearances really matter to her.

There were several tragic cases in the news while I was writing this novel—involving the deaths of small children in accidents. In both cases, the child had been left unattended "just for a minute" by a mother who sounded overwhelmed. At once, columnists and the community chorus that is social media were quick to turn on the mother and blame her—as Angie's community turned on her.

Of course we all have a duty to keep our children safe. But I couldn't help feeling wretched for the mother. Imagine the guilt and grief she'll bear for the rest of her life—as Angie has. In Angie's case, her grief is so terrible that she needed to extend her make-believe to pretending her daughter is still alive and well and thriving far away—in order to protect her sanity.

I worried that readers would blame her, too, but so far the responses have showed compassion to both women, despite their mistakes and faults. Most of us who are lucky enough to be mothers know it's the best job in the world—but also the toughest to get right.

Discussion Questions

1. Teresa clearly struggles to be a kind, patient mother at times. Is she a good mother? Is the way she interacts with Jessica troubling? What makes a good mother?

2. Craig works hard to earn money for the family but Teresa seems in charge of the home and childcare. Is that an accurate portrayal of most modern couples? How fair is that?

3. Craig is a shadowy figure for much of the novel—and at times he seems to be the villain of the piece. Once his real secrets are revealed, does he emerge ultimately as a villain or a hero?

4. Angie has a secret tragedy in her past. Given what she did, should she be allowed to look after other people's children?

5. What part do the locations play in the story—for example, the common; Angie's shabby, old-fashioned house; and Teresa and Craig's newly modernized one?

6. Fran resents Teresa for, as she sees it, breaking up her parents' marriage. How much right, if any, does she have to be angry about what's happened?

7. Teresa feels terrible guilt when Jessica goes missing. She is also haunted by the fact that she slapped her. How will Jessica's disappearance change their relationship in the future?

8. Angie is constantly cooking and offering home-cooked food to people. What does food mean for her?

9. One of the dominant themes in the book is pretense or make-believe. Who pretends to be something or someone they are not? Why?

10. How important is the need to make things up—to tell stories—to all of us, from childhood onward? What purpose does it serve?

ABOUT THE AUTHOR

Jill Childs has always loved stories—real and imaginary. She's spent thirty years traveling the world as a journalist, living overseas and reporting wherever the news took her. She's now made her home in London with her husband and twin girls, who love stories as much as she does.

Although she's covered everything from earthquakes and floods to riots and wars, she's found some of the most extraordinary stories right here at home—in the secrets and lies she imagines behind closed doors on ordinary streets, just like yours.